The Madness of March

A Love Story

MARGUERITE NARDONE GRUEN

Kravitz & Sons

INNOVATORS IN PUBLISHING, MARKETING AND ADVERTISING

Kravitz and Sons LLC
204 E Arlington Blvd. Suite B
Greenville, NC 27858

Published by Kravitz and Sons LLC.

ISBN: 979-8-89639-624-6 (sc)
ISBN: 979-8-89639-623-9 (e)

Because of the dynamic nature of the Internet, any web addresses or links contained in this book may have changed since publication and may no longer be valid. he views expressed in this work are solely those of the author and do not necessarily reflect the views of the publisher, and the publisher hereby disclaims any responsibility for them.

A SPECIAL THANK YOU

A big THANK YOU to my Nephew and Godson Joseph Nardone who wrote the Prologue for me. He covers College Hoops for Forbes Magazine On Line and CBB Today.

Thank you to Angelo and Mark Genell for always letting me mention their names and restaurant in all my books.

Thanks to Brittany Bahner for taking the photo of me for my books.

Thanks to my 2 friends Molly and Judy who are Maggie's 2 best friends in the book. Although this story is fake—my friendship with them is very real.

Thanks to the University of Scranton Basketball Teams in the 70's and 80's for the memories of how exciting and wild those games became. Two National Championships and I got to see them both.

TABLE OF CONTENTS

University head coach Bob Barrow pulled a huge coup on the recruiting trail this week, landing the nation's top two point guards.

Despite playing the same position, Paul Tanner and Nicky Newman decided Barrow's system and vision was the right fit, committing to the program from nearly out of nowhere. Previous rumblings had both star guards projected to land at different blue-blood programs.

All reputable recruiting service outlets agree, Tanner and Newman are the country's best two point guard prospects. In fact, there's a considerable gap between the University's latest commits and those who fall directly behind them.

While grass root gurus are sometimes wrong, most believe this recruitment cycle has the strongest grouping of point guards in years, highlighting just how special both players project to be. The University, by landing both, now has a spoil of riches at the position.

Tanner, who is finishing up his high school career with St. Augustine's, is the school's all-time leader in total points, assists and steals. Furthermore, at the end of the season, the school plans to retire his number, preventing anyone else in the storied program's history from ever wearing it again.

As for Newman, he's played for a slightly less prolific basketball content mill. While nationally ranked since his freshman year, he's never transferred to a larger school, instead opting to play for his locally based public high school of River Forge. Led by Newman, the Catamounts have gone to three straight Class AAA State Championship games, winning two of those.

Outside observers do remain skeptical of the fit. While basketball at all levels is growing increasingly position-less, the idea of Barrow targeting two such highly thought of players who play the same position is scaring off some.

There are concerns over who will handle the ball the most, especially since each talented youngster is considered ball-dominant guards. Moreover, since each are a bit raw from a shooting standpoint, if two guys with similar skill sets will inevitably be a detriment to a school in desperate need for floor spacers. The University has been lacking in shooting from distance for several years, ranking outside the top 200 in 3-point shooting percentage.

At the end of the day, however, a college coach's job is to land the best talent available, regardless of positions played, as no sane basketball mind would consider it wiser for Barrow to have opted for only one of the two generational guards, then targeting a lower ranked small forward instead.

Time will tell if the chemistry between the two players inevitably wins out. Until then, it will be up to Bob Barrow to work out the rotations and style when Nicky Newman and Paul Tanner hit campus in the fall.

Nevertheless, since the news became public, a palpable buzz has hit campus. Season tickets are already sold out, boosters have been pouring in money and The University's recruitment exploits has been the opening segment for every national sports television show for the last four days.

No pressure on Paul Tanner or Nicky Newman to live up to those other- worldly expectations or anything. Except, you know, it is.

As reported by Bo Churney of The Daily Morning Sun

CHAPTER 1

Rock Bottom

It was a gorgeous day in September when the blinding morning sun crept through the window in the dorm and shown right on Paul's face while he slept. It was so bright; he opened one eye to see if maybe he left the lights on all night. He tried to focus but found it difficult... as he noticed a baggie that was empty alongside of the bed. His head was pounding so he lay still, trying to regroup and pull himself together. Then he opened the second eye, trying to see what was going on.

Who was he kidding? He was trying to see where he was . . . having not remembered anything from the night before.

He felt something heavy on his back and lifted up his head to see. He dropped it back on the pillow and moaned. A naked girl was draped across his back.

Next he felt something move on the other side of him, so he lifted his head again—another naked girl was sleeping away on the other side of him.

Now—he really moans when he looked down to see he was naked too and was disgusted with himself—for a brief moment only.

He tries to get up, carefully moving the one girl off of him as not to wake her. He didn't want to wake the other one either and once he was free of them both, he quickly dressed in his now wrinkled clothes he found lying on the floor and out the door he flew.

He looked around outside and didn't recognize the dorm he just came out of. He tried to get his bearings but couldn't get the cobwebs out of his head and the crisp morning air was not agreeing with him. Then his stomach flipped and he got physically sick. He leaned against the brick wall of the dorm with his hands to steady himself and gets sick behind some bushes.

Once he's done he quickly looks around to see if anyone saw him.

Luckily, it was still early and no one was up yet.

Paul staggered down many pathways trying to see where he was and then *finally* he recognized a landmark on the campus—St. Johns Center—the gym he played basketball and practiced at practically every day since coming to the University the previous year. He knew he never visited that part of the campus he just came from because it was new and his dorm was all the way across the campus on the other side.

He felt like crap! He was still drunk from the night before and just starting to come down off of the pill he took. He knew he was given 3 pills by his supplier the afternoon before-one for each day of the weekend and when he saw the baggie they were in—empty—he just figured he gave one each to the 2 girls he woke up with.

He finally made it across campus to his dorm and up the steps— into his room—where his best friend and roommate Nicky was there sleeping away in his bed. He hears Paul coming in and wakes. All he sees is Paul falling on his bed on the other side of the room and moaning. He let him go . . . knowing what probably happened to him last night. He took some pills and drank himself into oblivion. This seemed to be his pattern every weekend . . . but more and more frequently it seemed he kept continuing with his partying during some week nights too.

It was late in the afternoon before Paul woke up again. He was still in the clothes he had on the night before. He looked over at Nicky's bed and saw it was empty. Then he heard a knock on his door.

He drags himself out of bed and goes to answer it, just thinking Nicky forgot his keys. When he opened the door there were 2 girls standing there. He didn't recognize them, but they were just standing there gig-gling away.

He muttered out "Can I help you ladies with something?"

Well—both their faces dropped and then they looked at him and saw he was still in his same clothes as the night before. They knew he didn't even know them and felt horrible just then.

Finally, one started speaking with a shaking voice. "You partied in our room with us last night. You told us to come get you and we would party this afternoon. You said you could get more pills for us too!"

Paul suddenly got sick again. His head was spinning and when that happened he usually just took a pill which made him forget his headache and fly like he was on a cloud. But he was out because he gave them to the 2 girls standing in his doorway. He thought—*did I give them those pills or did they take them off of me?* He couldn't remember.

He ran to his bathroom and when he was done—he washed his mouth out with some water and remembered leaving 2 girls standing in his doorway.

In the meantime—Nicky arrives home and makes his way past the 2 girls to find Paul coming out of the bathroom looking like death warmed over. He never commented on Paul and his habits but now he couldn't let that go.

Nicky goes out to the girls and very rudely barked "Paul is in no condition to come out today. Please don't come here again!" Then he slammed the door—right in their faces!

He drags Paul back in the bathroom—turns on the cold water in the shower and threw him in it. Paul was screaming and yelling at Nicky and called him many names but Nicky held his ground and didn't let anything he said to him offend him. He knew he was coming down off of something and he was still drunk because he smelled it on him. Nicky was far from perfect too. He got home right before Paul did; spending the night with someone he just met. They connected with each other and drank the night away also, but he was not in the shape Paul was in, because Nicky stayed away from drugs. Sadly, he felt Paul was hitting rock bottom.

Once Paul came around he threw him a towel and said "We need to talk. Clean up—I'll be waiting for you."

Paul knew he was in for a big lecture from Nicky and prepared himself.

Once cleaned up, Paul had to admit he felt a little better. His curly blond hair fell just below his ears and his eyes were blue with a hint of bloodshot red. Paul was 6'2" and Nicky was 6'1" and both were in great shape with all the ball playing and practicing they did being the top point guards on the University's basketball team. Nicky's jet black hair was buzzed around the bottom and long and wavy on top. He was always neatly put together while Paul, looked a little disheveled all the time.

Paul took a deep breath and got ready to face Nicky, who as promised was out in their room waiting for him.

CHAPTER 2

You're My Brother

"*You know you're my brother right?*"

Paul immediately thought, *ok here we go . . . the you're my brother speech!*

He sits on his bed and just looks at him as if to say—*let's get this over with* and Nicky knew that is what he was thinking.

"Paul, you can't go on like you are! Do you know where you were last night? Do you know who you slept with? Did you know those 2 girls at the door before? Because if you could answer even *one* of those questions—I will shut up and let it go!"

Paul was stunned and realized he couldn't answer even one and lowered his head looking down at the floor.

"You came in drunk—and high on something. How long do you think you could keep that up? Not to mention—if you can't play ball— you'll lose your scholarship! Your education! Your life! Doesn't that scare you because it scares me? I'm scared for me and for you."

"I'm also thinking about those 2 girls in our doorway looking for you. Did you give them drugs? Did you actually turn them on to drugs? Have you gone insane doing that? Not to mention sleeping with BOTH of them? Do you know how you just hurt both their feelings? You used both of them!"

Nicky is now pacing back and forth trying to get through to Paul.

"We're the top 2 Division II point guards in the *nation! The nation!* Don't you remember how hard we worked at that? Practicing day in and day out. I know where you are on the court . . . you know exactly where I am. We barely made it through the end of last season. That's when you started partying like this."

"Your body is going to give out on you. Did you look at yourself in the mirror? Did you really look?"

"I don't want to go to your funeral. I buried one of my brothers already and I can't bury another one." Now Nicky is shook trying to reach Paul.

That last statement really affected Paul. He knew Nicky lost a brother to drugs. His brother David was his best friend and he loved him deeply. It took him a long time to get past his death and his friendship with Paul really helped him.

Nicky's parents divorced right after his brother died, each blaming the other for the reason. No one saw what trouble his brother was in or they just ignored it. They had money, so money was never an issue for Nicky. What Nicky wanted, was for them to come to some games to see him play. He wanted them to feel proud of him but neither one, did either. They thought they were doing their part by filling up his checkbook every month.

Paul on the other hand needed that basketball scholarship to get his education. His parents were a normal middle class income family. They afforded a nice lifestyle but nothing additional. No fancy cars or big house. They lived modestly and tried to give Paul whatever they could. He never complained about never having money. He learned to live on a shoestring . . . on the small salary his parents deposited into his checking account monthly.

Nicky had a full scholarship as well as Paul to the University and they both were highly recruited by the head basketball Coach Bob Barrows. Coach B for short. Everyone called him that and his wife Olivia, was Mrs. B. They were beloved by the whole community because he turned their little Division II basketball program into a first class outfit. Every year they got better and better with the recruiting Coach B did all during the off season.

Paul had his head down and couldn't look at Nicky just then. Half of him was trying to ignore him and the other half was telling him to pull himself together. The problem was—he didn't know which half to listen too. Now with what Nicky just said, pleading with him—he was leaning to the half that told him to grow up and shape up.

Nicky searched Paul's face to see he finally got to him.

CHAPTER 3

When Paul Met Maggie

Paul paces around their room thinking about what Nicky just said to him. Especially once he told him he was afraid he would die on him. That alone sobered Paul up. He also started thinking about the 2 girls he spent the night with. Paul rarely dated, simply because he didn't have the time or met anyone he was that interested in, but he never disrespected a girl before—he felt he did just that when Nicky brought it to his attention. He was disappointed in himself and sorry he upset so many people that day.

After every home basketball game, the Commons Center on the University Campus threw a party. They had beer, soda and snacks and usually a band. There was a minimal charge to get in to cover expenses. But the U allowed the party because it kept everyone safe and the crowd controlled. Maggie was at the party with her friends Jeanine, Judy and Molly after a game one Tuesday night. Molly and Judy knew Maggie had a crush on Paul Tanner, one of the point guards on the basketball team, which was one of the reasons they went to all the home games and even some away, that were still close enough to drive to. Jeanine went to school at the U and knew a lot of people. She went to some games but not many but this night she came out with them. Maggie asked Jeanine if she knew Paul Tanner and it turned out she did. "Will you introduce me to him?"

"Sure. I'll go get him." Maggie thought she was going to pass out, she got that nervous. She only ever saw him on the court. She looked at Molly and Judy and they both were laughing at her. Then they decided to let Jeanine only introduce *her* to him, so they went to get a drink, leaving her standing there by herself.

Jeanine comes right over with Paul. She said "Paul, I would like you to meet my friend Maggie Sardo."

"Maggie, this is Paul Tanner." Then she said "I'm going to get a drink and be right back", leaving her alone with him. She guessed Maggie had a crush on him too and let the 2 of them talk.

Maggie just smiled at her when she left and turned to look directly at Paul . . . standing less than 3 feet away from her and she was trying not to drool. He was much taller than her and had blond curly hair and beautiful blue eyes. When he smiled back at her his whole face lit up and felt so did hers.

"Nice to meet you Maggie. Do you go to the U here too?"

"No, I work down town at a gift shop. I have an Associate in Accounting and open and close the shop and balance the register. I price the items and things like that."

"Do you like it?"

"Yes and the people are so nice. I love working there, along with the owner being so nice."

"How about you? What are you studying for?"

"Advertising."

"Do you like it?"

"Yes, but I have been slacking off some lately. I know I have to get back to normal or . . ." Just then someone came over to talk to him and he looked away from her. He spent a few minutes talking to that person and then came back to their conversation.

"How stupid of me, I forgot to mention Paul. Congratulations on your win tonight. You had a really great game. Aren't you tired now, from all of that?" She asked laughing. Paul noticed her face just lit up when she smiled and laughed and he couldn't stop looking at her. She had beautiful blue eyes that sparkled when she smiled. Right then, another person came over to speak to him. Their conversation was always cut short with so many people interrupting them to congratulate him on the game or just to speak with him. Paul and Nicky were very popular because of their success on the court.

Well, all the time he spent standing with her—they just about said less than 10 sentences between them and when someone came to speak to him—they ignored her completely and only addressed him. Maggie's heart sank. Here she was, with her crush and couldn't get a word in edgewise.

Just then the lightbulb went on and once that last person left she turned to him "I have to go now. It was nice meeting you. I wish we could have really gotten to speak, but this isn't the place for a conversation."

"I wish we could have too Maggie. Do you really have to go?" And what happened? Someone else called him over to speak to him. Afterwards he turned to her again, to hear what she said.

"I have work tomorrow and should go now."

Paul shocks her, taking her hand in his and brought it up to his lips to kiss the top of it. Then he asks "are you coming to the game Saturday?"

"Yes, I'll be there."

"Will you meet me in the lobby after the game? We can hit a few parties and spend more time together."

Maggie just smiled and replied, "By Saturday you'll forget my name and I will be standing in that lobby by myself wondering what I'm doing there." She was laughing when she said it.

"Never Maggie. I won't forget. Meet me Saturday after the game."

Maggie nods her head yes which got a big smile out of Paul. Then he dropped her hand and turned to go. "Ok then. See you Saturday and I won't forget."

CHAPTER 4

I knew This Would Happen

Maggie was on cloud 9 all week. No one knew what was going on with her at the shop. They figured she met someone she liked but she didn't say anything. They just decided to wait and see.

Saturday couldn't have gotten over quick enough for Maggie. Molly and Judy were going to the game separately and Maggie was taking her own car because she was supposed to meet Paul afterwards. Maggie was skeptical about the whole deal and told Molly that. "I'm not getting my hopes up that he will even meet me tonight, so where will you be in case he forgets about me?"

"Maggie, why would you say that? He said he would meet you, so he will. Don't do that to yourself. Just go and enjoy the night. Even if he gets less than 10 words out to you. Make the most of it and have fun."

"Thanks Molly for saying that. You're right. I'll make the most of it and I will definitely have fun."

The game came and all throughout it, she just beamed. Paul was hers that night and she silently felt so proud of him when he was playing. Every point he scored—her arms flew in the air and secretly smiled to herself. He had a great game too, scoring 18 points and Nicky had 20. Once it was over, she sat in the bleachers and waited for the crowd to leave. She knew the players showered and it would take a while before he came out to meet her. Once the gym cleared out she went into the lobby and waited. Some of the player's girlfriends were there along with some assistant coaches. Paul came out and she gave him a big smile but he walked right past her and went to talk to some of his teammates. He walked right past her! They were making some plans, but she didn't quit hear about what.

Maggie knew this would happen, but she pulled herself together and walked right over to him and she didn't know where she got the nerve to do that, but she did.

She stands next to him and everyone looked at her as if to say—*get out. Who are you?* Paul noticed and walked her over to speak to her alone.

"Can you meet me in an hour back here?"

"Where am I going to go for an hour?"

"You could hang out at St. Theresa's Hall. They have a lobby and you could wait there. Or you could go to the Commons Center and wait there for an hour. Then meet me back here and we will go."

Maggie's heart sank. She was so disappointed and it must have shown on her face. Not to mention how angry she was at that moment. This was her worst fear.

"Ok, I will meet you here in an hour." She did not smile at him and he saw she was put off. So he just nodded his head he heard her and left with his friends, leaving her standing there.

Maggie walked to St Theresa's Hall and sat in the lobby, feeling like an idiot. She wanted to just go home and leave him there but thought—he could care less if she was there or not so it wouldn't make a difference to him either way. She knew something like this would happen and even though she expected to be disappointed—it upset her that she actually was.

After an hour she walked back to the gym and Paul was already there waiting for her. It surprised her and she smiled at him but had to force it. "Ok, let's go." he said to her.

"Where are we going?"

"We're going to a party at Louden House. It's right at the end of the campus. We could walk—it's really not that far."

"Ok." They walked down the campus and he didn't reach for her hand or say much to her on the way. Before they knew it they were there and the line to get into the party was down the street. It shocked her.

"Are all of your friends going to be here?" She asked trying to make conversation.

"Some people I know will be here." Finally they got to the door and there was a cover to get in but the person collecting the charge saw Paul and said "go right in" to him. Maggie at that moment grabbed Paul's hand and he told the guy "she's with me" and he nodded for Maggie to go in too. She was clinging onto his hand and he felt it and knew she was skeptical about going in.

Once they got in—immediately someone called him over. She pulled his hand and said "I'll go get us a beer. Did you want one?" Paul nodded and off she went to find where it was. There was a line for that too, but she got 2 and headed back to give him one. It turns out someone already gave him one but when he saw her coming with 2 beers he handed it off to someone standing with him and took the one Maggie got for him. The party was crowded and you could barely hear what people were talking about. The music was blasting with Peter Clapton singing Layla. Maggie looked at all of the people in that room and thought, *what am I doing here*. It was clear most of them were on something. This is the kind of party it was. She definitely needed more beer and downed the one she had. It took the edge off of her and relaxed her immediately. The second went down smoother than the first and then she was fine. She walked about the room or should I say squeezed her way around the room because it was so crowded, but did notice Paul watching her every move. She tried to strike up a conversation with some girls there and they were nice but she didn't know them and had even less to contribute to the conversations. She made her way to the bathroom and there was a line for that too. She just waited her turn and once in there—she heard someone say "Tanner brought his girlfriend here tonight. Did you see her?" She froze in the stall and just waited to see what they would say about her. "Yeah, I noticed. I also noticed this doesn't look like her style, being here. She looks like a fish out of water."

"What was he thinking, bringing her here? It's clear she doesn't belong. She looks too straight."

"You have to admit though, she *is* beautiful." Another girl said. "Did you think he wouldn't pick someone beautiful? I didn't even know he was dating someone. I saw them at the party Tuesday and now, here they are again."

Maggie just wanted those girls to leave. She was stuck in that stall with people waiting. Then they left and she came out.

Walking down the hall to get back to the party she met someone she knew. It was her cousin Mark. Mark pinned her against the wall and looked at her. "Hello Maggie. What are you doing here? You shouldn't be here! It's not a good party for you to be at" and Mark seemed mad she was there.

Mark knew Maggie didn't do drugs and that the people at this party were not for her. He was flying too and she could tell just by looking at him.

"I'm here with Paul Tanner." She said back to him.

"You came with Tanner? Are you nuts? Go home Maggie!" Almost yelling at her.

Maggie tried to free herself from Mark but he wouldn't let her go. His body was crushed up against hers and then he did the unthinkable. He brought his hand up and grabbed her boob. Right in front of everyone and to top it all off . . . he was her cousin.

Maggie was so fed up with the whole night. She grabbed his hand away from her body and struggled because he was strong and wouldn't move. Then she said "I'm going to take your advice and leave now. Please let me go!" pleading with him.

He released her and then realized he did that so she would leave. He was her cousin and knew she didn't belong there and wanted to get her safely away from those drug induced people.

She made her way over to Paul with Mark watching to make sure she left. Paul noticed and even noticed what just happened to her.

He bends his head down to hers to hear what she was saying, "I'm leaving now." That is all she said and turned to leave but he grabbed her by the arm. "It's early. Why are you leaving? Do you have work tomorrow?"

"No, I don't work on Sunday's. You are here with your friends. You won't miss me. I'm leaving."

He walks her over to a wall and is just looking at her. Then he sways a little.

"Whatever you took, just kicked in, didn't it?" She could see his eyes glazing over. He gives her one nod confirming what she thought.

"That is why I'm leaving." Then she lets him have it with his head still next to hers so he could hear her.

"Let's recap the night. I met you *reluctantly* after the game. You treated me like I was *forcing* you to meet me. You told me to wait *an hour* somewhere I had never been before and I did. I came back for you and we came to this party where you said less than 10 words to me in the two hours I'm here. People in the bathroom are calling me your girlfriend and said you shouldn't have brought me here. Are you with me so far?" Paul nods his head one time again.

"Someone pins me up against the wall, I saw you watching and you didn't even come over, especially once you saw him grab my boob! I had to have 3 beers just to adjust to being in this place. Did you look at me? Do you see me? Do you see I really *don't* belong here? No offense to anyone in this room but—don't you think I actually look like I DON'T belong here? Everyone else in this room can see it and knows it. How uncomfortable do you think it is for me?"

"I don't know what I thought about how this night would go—but I didn't think you would take me to a drug party. I don't know how it doesn't scare you. It scares me!" Now her head is lowered thinking about the night and disappointment is all over her face. This was the second time someone told him they were scared for him, Nicky being the first. Paul was struggling with what she was saying. He was struggling because everything she said was right. She didn't belong there and he shouldn't have taken her there. She wasn't that king of girl and that is what attracted him to her. He watched her the whole night and every minute he wanted to go to her but he was with his friends and he was starting to fly from what he had taken. He felt he couldn't because of what he was on.

Then he did something that stunned Maggie. He wrapped her in his arms and kissed her. She responded by lifting her hand and running it through his curly hair and wrapping her other arm around him. Once he felt her responding—he pulled her body in closer and they just stood there—making out. Then she broke away and Paul swayed again. She kissed him softly—closing her eyes, bringing her lips up to his. He loved it. She was an angel, and he just took her to a party with the devil.

Maggie released Paul and smiled at him. She was happy she kissed him and now felt she could leave. She also knew it was over. Even though nothing ever started between them—nothing could ever *be* between them. She just wasn't his type of people. She was better and for the first time in her life she did feel she was better.

She turned and released herself from his embrace, looked over at Mark, and left. She felt relieved she was out of there.

Paul stayed at the party for only another half hour. He was affected by Maggie, even being in the state he was in. The thrill of his high was over and he decided to leave and go back to his dorm. It was only 1 and he was done for the night. When he walked in his room—Nicky was there and was shocked he was home so early. He usually never came home until the next day sometime and felt maybe his speech affected him. Nicky had a girl with him in his bed. Paul just smiled at him and went to the next room and slept on the couch. Nicky came right over to him, "it's only 1 and you're back. Are you sick? Do you feel ok?"

"I feel fine, I just had enough tonight and wanted to get some rest. Nothing is wrong. I'm fine. I'm going to sleep off my buzz. You go back to what you were doing and I won't bother you", smiling at Nicky. Nicky was stunned and wondered what happened to make Paul come home so early. Someone or thing must have affected him. He had to wait until the next day to ask him, but he wasn't going to let it go.

CHAPTER 5

What Happened?

Maggie met Judy and Molly at the movies the next day and they couldn't wait to find out what happened. They were shocked at what she told them and couldn't believe he took her to a drug party. Not to mention he made her wait an hour somewhere before he came for her. They were stunned. They saw how disappointed she was and she told them "never did I ever think my night would turn out like it did." She even told them about her cousin Mark. Again they were shocked. They also noticed how bummed she still was about the night.

"How did you want the night to go Mag?" Judy asked. "Truthfully, I don't know how I wanted it to go. I guess I thought we would go to the Commons Center and everyone on the planet would pull him away from me but that would have been Ok because he was there with ME! His lifestyle was not mine. I could never fit in with his friends and somehow I felt everyone at that party knew it too. I did think it was funny when those girls called me his girlfriend. I barely spoke to him Tuesday night when I met him. It was odd how they picked up on that, seeing me there again with him last night."

"Do you still want to go to the games now that this happened?" Molly asked her.

"Yes, I really like going and it gets us out during the week and gives us something to do on the weekend. I don't really want to go to bars every night and then the week end too. I miss it, when the season ends."

Molly and Judy were both relieved because they really liked going to the games too and would feel bad if she didn't want to go anymore. Back on campus, Nicky and Paul went to the gym to throw some balls around and Paul asked Nicky, "are you going to tell me who your company was last night or do I have to beat it out of you?" laughing at Nicky. Nicky's face turned all red and he told him. "Her name is Elizabeth and I really like her. This was the second time we were together. I'm going to go find her later. She told me where her dorm was. I'm going to take a walk and start stalking her." Now Nicky was laughing saying that.

"You liked her that much?" Smiling at Paul he just nods his head yes. "Wow Nicky. I can't believe it. After all this time you finally found someone you like. All the girls who throw themselves at you and you finally found someone that turned your head. I'm shocked." Nicky was gorgeous and Paul was right when he said girls just threw themselves at him but he was never interested, which surprised Paul.

"Brother, it's me who is shocked. You coming in early last night and going right to bed. You better tell me what her name is so I can thank her."

Paul looks at Nicky confused. "Thank her for what?"

"Oh, so there *is* a girl involved! I knew it!"

Paul throws his ball at Nicky, "Nicky you just bated me and I didn't even see it coming." Nicky was laughing at Paul.

"Well, tell me all about her."

Paul has his head down and then decided to tell him the truth. "I did the worst possible thing to her."

"What could you have done? Was it illegal? Did you hurt her, physically?"

Paul just shakes his head, "no, but where I took her is just as bad and she let me have it too before she left."

Nicky stops dribbling and looks at Paul and could see he regrets something. "Tell me and we can talk it over. Let's see what happened."

Paul nods and goes to sit on the bleachers to talk to Nicky. "I met her Tuesday and she was so nice and her smile was so amazing.

I made a mistake and asked her to meet me after the game yesterday so we can talk more. It was a zoo Tuesday and every time I tried to talk to her—we kept getting interrupted and then she had to go because she had work the next day. I fully intended on meeting her but when I came out from the showers after the game and saw her there, looking so beautiful, I hoped she would just go away so I didn't have to be with her. I felt I would hurt her feelings and that is exactly what I did anyway."

"Tell me more. What happened?"

Paul recapped the evening with Maggie. Shocked – Nicky continued. "And brother, that is why I have to thank her. You found a straight girl, who you like, who is beautiful and now you are afraid because she will not want to be with you because of the way you live your life with your drug friends. That is why you sabotaged your night with her! But what is worse, is the fact that you *know* your life is going down the toilet and you like it that way! That is what I can't figure out about you. You are throwing your life away and for what? You are ruining your life and taking mine with you. We are the top 2 point guards in the nation. The nation! We worked so hard at that." Nicky stopped because he didn't want Paul to stop telling him the story about what happened last night. Paul's head was down knowing everything Nicky just said was so true.

"She was pissed or maybe so disappointed the way the night turned out. I took her to Louden House", Paul told Nicky reluctantly.

"There is something wrong with you Paul. You did that to that poor girl?"

"It gets worse!" Nicky was shocked Paul said that.

"I can't believe you. Who are you? I know you are my brother but this other guy pops out every week end. She must have been so disappointed, because I am", Nicky told Paul, stunned at what happened.

"I kissed her Nicky. It was the best kiss in the world. I just can't forget it. It made me want to come home early last night. Then she kissed me once more before she left and that was the sweetest kiss I have ever tasted."

"She kissed you back, after everything? You know what she did right?" Paul shook his head no. "She kissed you goodbye, so you are getting your wish. That poor girl will be running in the opposite direction when she sees you. She may never come to another game after this."

Paul dropped his head again and just let out a big sigh. He was upset and Nicky saw that. "You really like her don't you. Someone you just met—turned your head and you don't know what to do about it. She is everything you could ever hope for or dreamed about. Isn't she? Now you are stuck my brother. Once you find '*the one*', no one else will compare. You don't even date. You have one night stands and then you are so out of it, you don't even remember the girl or where you were. Maybe this is a blessing in disguise. Maybe someone besides me will get you to straighten your life out."

"Nicky, don't you see? She is out of my league. Not to mention how my life is going to hell right now. AND I'm only 20 and have 2 years of school left."

"Really? You're only 20, or is it you have more sororities to go through before you settle down to just one girl!" That was a low blow Nicky just gave Paul and Paul was shocked he even said that, but Nicky was mad.

"How could she be the one for me? How could I ask her to wait until I finish school before we can even make any future plans? I can't even afford to take her to dinner. I have nothing to offer her. Nothing!" Paul screamed at Nicky.

"*You* don't even see! You were already thinking about keeping her around by what you just said. You can't afford to take her to dinner? Pizza is dinner. So is just going for coffee. Going to parties together—the good ones, not the drug induced ones. There's hikes, movies that are cheap if you go early enough. There are long phone conversations, laying on the couch and sex. Who would turn all of that down? You have tons to offer her, so stop looking for excuses. If you really want her in your life, you will do everything you can to get her and keep her. So what if you are only 20. Sometimes you meet the person you are supposed to be with for the rest of your life—in grade school! There is no time limit on that. It happens—when it happens."

"You are in trouble my friend. She is already helping you and you don't even see it. She is exactly what you need. You have to win her back now. I don't know how you are going to do that after what you did to her. Did you get her phone # at least?"

"No, I never asked for it."

"That hole you dug yourself into, keeps getting deeper and deeper. I think you have a lot of thinking to do, but Paul, she isn't going to like your druggie friends. If you want her, you will have to give them up, along with taking them. Could you do that? Do you want to straighten out your life? I'm hoping you do for your sake, her sake and mine. I already buried one of my brothers from drugs and I don't think I can do it again Paul."

Paul listened to everything Nicky said to him. He was struggling with wanting to start up a relationship with Maggie and not wanting to, because he felt he was too young to get serious with someone. AND he didn't know if he wanted to give up his drug friends. Nicky would be pissed about that, but he was right. Paul knew Nicky never recovered from his brother dying from a drug overdose. Paul living his life that same way upset Nicky until he tried one last statement to get him to turn.

"Paul, I never said much to you before. I would never interfere in your life but I'm losing you to drugs and booze. It's killing me. If you continue on the path you're on—I will ask the housing department to move me. I can't sit back and watch you destroy your life. I cannot watch you die and I certainly don't want you dying in *my* room, next to *my* bed or in *my* arms. I won't be able to handle it."

Nicky is visibly upset and Paul sees it. Then he gets up and walks out of the gym, slamming the ball against the wall, leaving Paul there to contemplate everything he just said to him.

That was a knock-out punch of a line that Nicky needed to give Paul. Now he had to hope he heard him.

He thought he would do everything he could to make sure Paul changed his life around. Now there might be another person to help him try and help Paul, and he just learned, her name was Maggie.

CHAPTER 6

Try Again!

Tuesday came around and Maggie was so nervous going to the game that night. She wanted to get that first game 'after Paul' over with so she could start feeling more comfortable. Maggie felt Paul wouldn't even seek her out—so she wasn't worried about that. Her feelings were still hurt and she was trying to get over it and was still stunned she felt badly about it. It wasn't like they were dating—but she crushed on him for so long—it felt like they had broken up after all those months, along with how disappointed she was in him. She had this picture in her mind painted about him and when she found out he was like nothing she expected—it threw her.

The team is warming up and throwing some balls around and Nicky noticed Paul kept looking at the door. He knew he was looking for Maggie. He could say all he wanted about not wanting to start up a relationship with anyone, but Nicky knew—he was waiting for her.

Maggie and her friends finally get there and are walking in the gym, looking up at the bleachers to see where they could find seats together when Paul finally sees her.

He bounces his ball right at her—hitting her in her arm just then. She is stunned for a second and then turns to get the ball. Once she has it and gets ready to throw it back, she realizes Paul is the one who lost his ball. Did he lose it or did he throw it at her? She wondered especially since he was smiling coming over to her. There was a little boy standing next to her with his father all dressed in University gear and she bends over to him and says "would you like to throw this ball back to Paul for me?" Well the little boys face lit right up like he just won a basket full of candy while he nods his head excitingly at her. She hands him the ball and Paul is beaming too when he saw the boy and heard what Maggie asked him. As he goes over to him, he lays his hand on Maggie's back and bends down to talk to him.

"How about I teach you how to dunk a ball in the basket? Would you like that?"

Now that poor kid looked like he was just told he was going to Disney Land he was so excited and just nodded his head so much he looked like a bobble head. Paul and Maggie looked at his father who also was so happy about it. So Paul picks him up and puts him on his shoulders and Nicky saw what he was doing as well as the other players. They all stopped throwing their balls in the hoop and just watched. Nicky ran over like he was throwing the ball to him and put it right in his hands while Paul walked over to the basket and told him "ok now, throw it in" and unbelievably—it went right in. The whole room was watching the play and it erupted with cheers when the kid made the basket. Nicky took him down from Paul's shoulders and they both fist pumped his hand and turned him around to go back to his father following him. His father was so happy about what happened telling them, "Thank you for doing that. I think he will want to play basketball, now that he made that basket." They all laughed. Maggie was still standing there with the boy's father and Paul did something that almost made her fall over. Before he went back to practice he kisses the side of her head and said "see you later Mags".

Maggie was in shock. She was stunned. Everyone including Molly and Judy saw what he did and now *everyone* was going to think she was his girlfriend. She went to sit with them and Molly just said "what the heck was that about? I think he threw his ball at you on purpose. He must have been waiting for you."

"Molly, I have no idea what that was about. I thought I made it clear— his friends couldn't be mine and can't believe what just happened. I don't know what to think. Do you really think he threw his ball at me to get my attention?"

Molly and Judy just gave her the biggest smile and said together "yep!"

"Did he say anything to you?"

"Yah, he said 'see you later Mags'. Can you believe it? He called me Mags!"

"Well—see what happens next. It will be fun to watch."

"Fun for you and Molly but not me Judy. I have no idea what he is thinking about us."

Now the 3 laughed about it and sat enjoying the game. Every time Paul made a basket someone turned around to look at her or say something to her. The person in front said "nice basket" to her and the guy behind said "Paul is on fire tonight—isn't he?" Maggie would smile and nod to everyone who spoke to her about the game, then shoot Judy and Molly a look as if to say "I am **not** his girlfriend!" They both laughed at her the whole night.

After the game they went to the Commons Center for a drink or two but they usually left by 11:30 on a work night. None of them wanted to feel like crap the next day at work and they realized that from many lessons learned in the past.

Again, people came over to her and said 'nice game' to her and her friends would turn their heads not wanting to laugh right at them. Maggie would smile and nod and she was smiling and nodding all night to people.

She headed to the bathroom and once again she learned a lot in the ladies room. Some girls were talking and they said "you know, that's not his girlfriend, right? That's his sister. That's why he kissed her on the head; otherwise he would have kissed her differently."

"Get over it Marie! That's his girlfriend!" Another one said.

She just laughed to herself and waited for them to leave but when she walked out—Paul was there waiting for her. She smiled at him thinking about what she just heard while walking towards him.

He pinned her against the wall with his 2 arms caging her there and holding her captive. She laughed and he asked "why are you laughing?"

Well, then she couldn't stop and her face was all red and tears were running down her cheeks she was laughing so hard.

"Tell me. Do I have all my clothes on or did I put them on inside out?" as he is looking down at himself.

She tells him what she heard. "It seems you can get firsthand information about us in the ladies room. This is the second time I heard something about me and it just makes me laugh. I'm going to have to start hanging out in bathrooms more to see what is going on with us." Now Paul is laughing too and it relaxed them both. Paul didn't know how she would be towards him after the other night and he was happy and relieved she was still smiling at him.

"Well, are you going to keep me in suspense? What's the word on us? Tell me—what's out there now."

"You are not going to believe this but NOW I'm your sister, NOT your girlfriend. Last week, I was your girlfriend and today I'm your sister." Maggie is now laughing again and Paul starts up too. Now he knows why she is reacting the way she was.

Paul took that opportunity to put all rumors away about who Maggie was. How did he do it? He planted the softest kiss on her lips just then and knew everyone was watching.

Maggie smiled back at him and he took it as a good sign. "Do you think they will still say you are my sister now?"

"I don't know—maybe if you do it again, they will really get the message."

Paul thought he was hearing things and bent his head down again while Maggie lifted hers to meet his lips. The kisses were soft and full of emotions. They both could feel them at the same time. Maggie loved how Paul kissed her and Paul felt the same as he stole one kiss after another. Finally, she broke away and flashed him the warmest smile and wrapped her arms around him which stunned him. He felt her body next to his as he did the same—engulfing her within the circle of his arms, laying his head down on hers, closing his eyes and enjoying the moment between them.

She looks up at him and says "that was really nice, what you did for that little boy earlier. Did you see the look on his face? It's like you told him he was going to Disney he was so happy."

"You gave me the idea Mags. When you gave him the ball to throw back to me, that's when I thought of it, seeing how happy he was to just throw the ball back."

"Well you did a good thing. That kid will never sleep tonight." They were both smiling from ear to ear at each other when she leaned in again and laid her head on his chest. Paul did not want to let her go. He held her and they talked some more and just then the band played a slow song. She grabbed Paul's hand and dragged him on the dance floor where he tried to protest because he didn't like to dance and didn't want his teammates to tease the hell out of him at practice the next day. But he did realize he would be holding Maggie in his arms on that floor and as soon as everyone saw her do that—it turned out all his teammate's girlfriends dragged *them* on the floor too, for that song. Then Paul felt a little better about it. No one can say anything to him the next day. Truthfully—he didn't care if they busted his chops. He was loving every minute of that song with Maggie wrapped in his arms. He also knew—she was now definitely tagged as his girlfriend. Now, not only would no one else make a play for her, but everyone would know she was his girlfriend and NOT his sister which brought a smile to his face when he thought that.

The song was over and she said "Come meet my best friends before I have to leave."

"It's only 11:00. Why are you leaving so soon?"

"I have work tomorrow and we always get home by midnight on a work night so we don't feel like crap the next day. It works out well for the 3 of us."

"Ok, now I understand. Let's meet your friends. I want you to meet my best friend too before you go."

He takes her hand and they walk over to Molly and Judy who were all smiles when they saw them both coming over.

"Paul—these are my best friends, Molly and Judy. Molly, Judy this is Paul." Now looking between them.

Paul reached out to shake both their hands and told them it was nice to meet them.

Then he sees Nicky and motions to him to come over. It turns out Nicky was watching Paul all night. He saw that he made up with Maggie and now couldn't wait to meet her.

"Maggie, this is my best friend and a brother to me, Nicky." Maggie held out her hand to shake it but Nicky did something unexpected. He took her hand but pulled her into a hug. Paul was just beaming away. Then she turns and introduced Molly and Judy and they were thrilled to meet Nicky.

Judy said "you guys looked great tonight. It's like you always know where you both are on the court. It always amazed us on the chemistry you both have when you're playing."

"You could see that?" Nicky asked.

"As clear as day" Maggie continued. "We always talk about it. The way you know where Paul is on the court all the time and he knows where you will be all the time. It's amazing to watch and fun for us spectators." Smiling at them both.

Nicky and Paul were all smiles and just looked at each other. They both patted each other on the back and Paul said "Don't hug me Nicky. Everyone will think *you* are my girlfriend now."

Only Paul and Maggie got that joke and everyone saw it, so they had to explain. Once they did, they all laughed about it.

After a while it was time for her to go and she had to say goodbye. It killed her because that night, was the exact opposite of the previous night they were together.

She turns to Nicky "it was so nice meeting you Nicky."

"Maggie the pleasure was all mine" and he hugged her again. He also hugged Molly and Judy and for some reason felt they all would be good friends now.

Paul hugged Molly and Judy too—again shocking them and turned towards Maggie. "Can I see you Saturday?"

"I won't be at the game Saturday. My cousin is getting married and I'm her maid of honor."

Paul tried to hide the look of disappointment on his face when he heard that. "Ok then, when can we meet up? You never gave me your

#." They quickly pulled out their phones and exchanged #'s making Nicky smile.

Then he kissed her ever so softly and watched as she left with her friends. He watched her every step out of that building with Nicky just smiling away at him. He sees the look on Nicky's face and punched him in the arm. "Why did you do that?"

"Don't bust my chops Nicky or I won't tell you anything about what happened tonight!"

"Let's go home. I'm done for tonight." Paul told him. Nicky again smiled and thought—*I am going to love that girl for saving my brother.*

To change the subject Paul asked "where is your girlfriend tonight.

I thought I would get to meet her. Couldn't she make it?"

Nicky was upset and Paul could see it. "What's wrong? Did she dump you? Did you dump her already?"

"No, I can't find her. I went to her dorm and no one even knew her. They didn't even recognize that name. It's like she disappeared. I'm upset about it because we really hit it off and I thought she might actually be the one. There was just something about her."

"That's so strange. Are you sure she was a student here and not somewhere else?"

"At this point I really don't know. I don't know where else to look?"

"Do you know her last name?"

"No, just her first and where I thought she told me where her dorm was."

"Maybe you just got the dorm wrong. Go to the admin's office and see if you can find her there. They might not give you her information but it could be a start."

"Ok, good idea. I really want to find her. I liked her a lot."

CHAPTER 7

The Wedding

Maggie and Paul texted and talked all week. Everyone at the shop knew those texts were from her boyfriend because her face would just light up.

On some days he would even surprise her if he had time between classes and bring her lunch, which meals were part of his scholarship at the U. He would call and say "it's hamburger day today in the caf. I will bring us lunch—I have time before my next class and I want to see you." Maggie would be thrilled and then her whole shop got to meet him. That first time he showed up with lunch she was in the middle of something so she ushered him in the back to her office to wait for her. She said she'd only be a few more minutes. "Sit here and don't touch anything" she told him. Everyone kept walking by, gawking at him and he would just smile and say hi. Then he would catch them all looking at each other. Maggie had a boyfriend! They were so happy for her and they saw how happy she was. She was the youngest one in the shop and everyone loved her, especially Sarah the owner. She was a substitute mom to Maggie and confided everything to her.

Sarah knew he was coming because Maggie told her and also asked if it was Ok for him to be there having lunch with her. Sarah did not have an issue with it and couldn't wait to meet Paul. She sees him sitting in Maggie's office and goes right over to him. "Hi, I'm Sarah Walker—I own the shop." Paul stood and extended his hand to shake hers replying "I'm

Paul Tanner. I brought Maggie lunch and she told me to sit here and not touch anything." That made Sarah laugh. Sarah knew who he was because she followed the U's basketball team in the paper and because Maggie told her but she acted like she didn't know. "Paul Tanner from the U's basketball team?" Paul just laughed and said "Yes, in person!" Then Maggie came back and saw them talking as she walks in smiling to Sarah.

"Well, I will let you 2 have lunch before it gets cold. Maggie, close your door so you can have some privacy otherwise you will never get to take a bite of your lunch. Paul can meet everyone later."

"Thanks Sarah." Smiling at her so much.

Maggie closed the door and gave Paul a hug and sweet kiss once they were alone. "Let's eat. I'm starving. How are the hamburgers? Are they good?"

"Yah, it's one of the things that are decent in the cafeteria. Nicky and I never miss hamburger day!" They both laughed when he said that. Once they were done—Maggie took him around and introduced him to everyone in the shop and they were all smiles.

When Saturday rolled around—she texted Paul and told him to have a good game. "I want to hear good news about the game when it's over." She told him.

"I hope to give you only good news Mags. Enjoy your wedding today. I will miss you more than I can say tonight. TTYL." Maggie smiled to herself when Paul confessed he would miss her.

Maggie did enjoy the whole day of the wedding. She would be with family and she loved her family. She had 2 brothers Frank and Joseph. They both worked for her father whose name was Frank also, at his appliance center he owned. She adored her brothers and they felt the same way about her. Her father on the other hand, was a monster. He never smiled and treated them all like they were nothing but burdens to him. He yelled a lot too. They all were afraid of him, even at their age. Frank was 27, Joseph was 25 and Maggie was 22. Maggie's mom died when she was just 16. It was her cousin on her mother's side of the family that was getting married. Everyone knew how mean Frank Sr was and they could never understand how her mother put up with him for so long. They came to the conclusion—she must have really loved him. So they all put up with him. They had to talk him into going to the wedding. He was going to refuse the invitation but Maggie embarrassed him into going, so she got his suit cleaned and pressed a beautiful white shirt and tie for him. When he walked into his room after work that day, she had it all laid out for him and he smiled to himself, pleased with how she took care of him. He knew he was rotten, but that is just the way he was.

Maggie spent the whole day at her cousins' house helping the bride get ready. Everyone always loved her because she was so sweet but never dated. They always wondered if Frank forbade her to date. They thought he would never allow her to even leave the house and was surprised she had a job and went out with friends. It was that bad at her house with her father.

The day went smoothly and the reception was exceptional. She always felt being the only girl in the family—*her wedding* would be exceptional too. They ate and danced all night. She danced with her brothers and then she pulled her father on the dance floor. He was so pissed and everyone watched to make sure he wouldn't hurt her.

She is holding onto his hand during the slow song and had her head resting on his chest. The cameras were clicking away because it was totally out of character for Frank. She looked up at him and said, "Thanks for dancing with my dad. We have to practice more, so you will be able to dance with *me* at *my* wedding."

Just then it was like a tidal wave hit. His face got so red and he whispered in a nasty voice saying "you are never getting married. You will never leave my house and I am going to forbid you to go to work if you keep up that kind of talk. Who would want to marry you anyway? You aren't even pretty."

Maggie froze and stopped dancing. They saw something happened and guessed he said something pretty nasty to her—if for any reason but just to ruin the mood and the night. Her brother Joseph rushed over and tapped his dad on his shoulder to cut in and he dropped his hands off of Maggie. She was so white they thought she was going to faint. Joseph grabbed her and wrapped his arms around her and then Frank came in and did the same. The 3 of them were swaying but slowly to the rest of the song, arms all wrapped around each other. Everyone in the room knew Frank Sr just hurt his daughter's feelings and felt so badly for her. Maggie finally calmed down but she was shaking. They took her out to the hall and sat on a bench with her. Frank had both arms wrapped around her and she laid her legs across Joseph's lap. She was spent, because after having such a great time, her bubble was burst and she just let the tears flow.

In the meantime, Paul knew where the wedding reception was being held. After his game he thought, I just have to see her. He wasn't going to tell her he was there but he just wanted to see her. He is walking up the steps at the hotel and stops because he heard her talking and being upset. He looks up and sees her on the bench with her legs across someone and another person holding her. It shook him for a minute. Who where they and why was she so friendly with them? Then he hears her crying and those 2 people trying to talk to her.

"What did he say to you Maggie?" Someone asked.

She started crying harder and he could see how upset she was. "Maggie, please try and clam down. I'm taking you home with me tonight. You don't need to go home and be with that monster tonight." Someone else said.

"Ok, thanks Frank. I don't think I could face him right now after what he just did to me."

Paul is in a panic. Who did what to her?

"Please tell us what he said." He heard one of them say to her. "Everything was fine and I thought he even liked dancing with his daughter and then I ruined it. I said—Dad, we have to practice more so you can dance with *me* at *my* wedding. That is when he flipped. He told me I am never allowed to get married or leave his house. If I didn't stop talking like that, he would forbid me to go to work or out with my friends. Then he said 'who would want me anyway. I wasn't even pretty. Can you imagine saying that to your own daughter?"

She looks at Frank and Joseph and asks "Do you think I'm ugly too? Am I ugly like he said?"

Frank and Joseph were shocked and so stunned. Frank said "Maggie— your problem is you believe everything he tells you and he tells you stuff just to upset and hurt you. You are so beautiful and never seem to know it. How guys aren't knocking down your door amazes us. We talk about it all the time between the 2 of us."

Paul was still listening on the steps. He couldn't believe Maggie thought she was ugly. When he looked at her, he only saw the most beautiful person on the planet to him. He felt so badly for her and wanted to run to her and hold her to get her to feel better. Then he guessed those 2 guys were her brothers she talked about. Someone takes a picture of the 3 of them sitting there and Paul turned and ran back down the stairs. He waited around the corner to see if she is coming out and he does see her. Frank is carrying her because she is fast asleep and Joseph went to get the car.

"Give her to me. I will hold her." One of them said.

"No, I got her. She weighs about 5 lbs. I think this dress is heavier than her. You drive and I will hold her. She's coming with me anyway."

"I can't think of how we can get her out of there. We would both be fired if we tried taking her in. I just don't see what we could do. I don't know if she could afford an apartment on her own. She is in hell and we can't even help her."

After hearing her brothers talking—Paul felt so much for her just then. It upset him as he walked up the hill back to the U.

He passed Louden House and some of his friends along with his dealer were there and saw him walking. "Paul you're here! Come on in! We have some pretty good shit tonight. You look like you need something too. Everything alright?" His dealer asked him.

"Yes fine, but I really have to go. I can't stop tonight. Some other time."

"Come on. Only for a few minutes to see everyone."

Paul was tempted but held his ground. "Not tonight guys. I have to go now. See you soon."

Then his dealer hugged him and slipped something in his pocket. "This is on me Paul. Have a good time with it."

Paul nodded but kept walking back to his dorm. He took what was in his pocket and looked at it once he got to his room. Nicky was out so he decided to pop the pill someone gave him. He was upset and thought this would help him. All of a sudden his emotions were heightened and he was sweating and anxious. Whatever he took—was powerful and he didn't like the way he felt. He texted Nicky to come home and he doesn't even know if it *was* Nicky that he texted or what he even wrote. But Nicky did get it and it was all gibberish but he knew something was wrong. He called Paul's cell and he managed to answer, slurring his words. Nicky couldn't make out what he was saying and just kept asking "where are you". Finally, Paul got out "home". Nicky said "I'm on my way" and flew out of the Commons Center and down to their dorm where he found Paul crawling on the floor.

Nicky was scared seeing his brother like that and goes right to him but very slowing as not to startle him.

"I'm here Paul. Can you tell me what you took? Show me. Do you have more?" Paul shook his head no.

"Do we need to go to the hospital? Let's go. Maybe they could help." Paul got more anxious and Nicky saw that, so he just said "let's go throw up. Maybe we can get that pill out of your system. It won't be fun but we have to." Paul crawled to the bathroom on all fours. It was breaking Nicky's heart but he was dammed if he'd lose another brother to drugs. "Give me your hand Paul" He took his fingers and shoved them down his throat causing him to gag. Paul screamed and moaned but Nicky was adamant. He would not back down and after a third try—he finally threw up the pill.

Thank God Nicky thought. Most of it was still there and intact. If the little that dissolved in Pauls' stomach did that much to him, the whole pill might have killed him. Thank GOD, again Nicky thought, falling back on the bathroom floor, that Paul had enough of his senses still alert, to call him for help. If he didn't, he would have found him incoherent or dead in their room.

Nicky grabbed Paul and carried him to his bed. He pulled up a chair and sat with him. Paul moaned and the room was spinning but they just had to wait for that drug to make its way out of his system. He kept giving him water to try and flush it out and after 6 hours, Paul was finally coming around. It was 5 in the morning and Nicky was up all night with Paul. When he opened his eyes he saw him sitting next to the bed in a chair and then moaned again. Nicky jumped up immediately and asked him how he was.

Paul was trying to pull himself together—there were so many cobwebs in his head right then. Nicky got him some water and asked if he needed anything. Paul shook his head no. Then he broke down and lost it. Nicky got emotional too as he went to hug him.

"I'm so happy you are still alive. I can't even yell at you right now." He said to Paul.

"I'm so sorry Nicky. I'm so sorry. I will never do that again. I'm so sorry."

"Do you know what you took? Where did you get it? If someone else got this drug too, there must have been massive OD's last night. If you couldn't handle it—I'm sure others couldn't too. Thank God you threw up most of that pill or you wouldn't be alive right now. I am not kidding Paul! You were in bad shape. The worst I've ever seen you and the whole pill hadn't even dissolved in your stomach. I am so happy you called me when you did. Were you with Maggie? Where was she tonight?"

"Maggie had a wedding. I didn't see her tonight. I went to the Hilton to see her—I wasn't going to tell her I was there. I just had to see her Nicky. I thought I would feel better just seeing her face. But I got upset because she was upset at the wedding."

"What happened at the wedding?"

"From what I gathered, her father is a monster and all 3 of his children are afraid of him. He said terrible things to Maggie and her brothers didn't know what to do to help her."

I left when I saw her going home with one of them and then passed Louden House and my friends tried to talk me into staying but I told them not this time. I really didn't want to be there with those people. But one hugged me and slipped a pill in my pocket. When I got home I just thought I would take it to take the edge off of me tonight. I had no idea it would have done that to me. You were right Nicky. Thank God I got that call thru to you. I would be dead if you didn't come and save me. Thank you Nicky. I am swearing it to you right now. I will never go to Louden House again. I am doing it for you, me and for Maggie."

Nicky was so relieved and happy Paul said he would never go to Louden House again. He had been so scared for him ever since he started hanging out there and absolutely hated his friends he had there.

"Are you going to tell her what happened and about seeing her?"

"Yes, I don't want to keep secrets from her."

"My head is pounding. Let's get some sleep. Thank you Nicky. I will never stop thanking you for saving my life" as he goes to Nicky and hugs him.

CHAPTER 8

Telling Maggie

Paul and Nicky slept to about noon. Nicky heard Paul moaning and it woke him immediately. They had practice at 3 so they had to get up and try and pull themselves together. "Paul, how are you feeling? What do you need? Let's go to the caf and get something to eat. Maybe it will make you feel better. We have to eat before practice or our asses will be dragging."

Paul nodded to Nicky and they pulled themselves together and walked to the cafeteria. But while Nicky was in the shower getting ready to go he called Maggie. She didn't answer on the first ring and it concerned Paul. Then she picked up. "Maggie, how was the wedding? I want to hear all about it and I want to see pictures. I can only imagine how beautiful you looked."

Maggie let out a small sigh and then he heard her sniffling. "Maggie—I have practice at 3 but I had to hear your voice. Will you say something to me?"

Finally, after silence on the line "How many points did you have last night? I hope you won the game . . ."

Paul smiled from ear to ear and said "20 last night. You missed a good game but we won in the end. I missed you last night Maggie. I just had to tell you that." Now she was crying and Paul knew why. He wanted to go get her and hold her to help her and he needed her to hold him to help him.

"What are you doing this afternoon or for supper? Let's get a pizza and come back to my dorm. We have a living room so we won't be eating on my bed. We have a small kitchen too. Will you come here to see me? I need to see you so badly and will tell you all about it later. I have practice at 3 and it should be done by 5."

Maggie sniffed some more and said "yes, that would be great."

"Maggie I hear you are upset and I want you to tell me all about it. Promise me you will and not hold anything back."

"I promise, I will tell you all about yesterday. I want to."

"I want to tell you too. I have a lot to tell you about. But I promise you too, I won't hold anything back. I don't want any secrets between us. OK?"

"Ok. Thank you Paul for calling. I needed to hear your voice as well. I can't wait to see you later."

Nicky was right before, but even though they ate, their asses were still dragging. Coach was mad at them both and thought they partied a little too hardy last night and made them pay for it. Paul threw up 2 times during practice and Coach just thought he was hung over. He could never know he almost died last night. When he saw he couldn't get much out of his 2 point guards he called the practice short at 4:30 which thrilled everyone but you could see the steam coming out of Coach's ears he was so mad.

Bobby from the team said to everyone getting cleaned up in the locker room "did you hear about the ruckus at Louden House last night?"

Everyone including Paul said no, so he continued the story. "Well, someone was giving out a drug that was so toxic, they took 12 people to the hospital to get their stomach's pumped out. I heard someone is still there. He didn't come to yet."

"Paul, you go there. Did you see what was happening?" Another player Jimmy asked.

"I wasn't there last night. I walked past it but didn't go in. I just didn't want to be there and now see it's a good thing. I can't get involved in that or I'll lose my scholarship." Jimmy just nodded to him. Everyone knew Paul frequented that place along with some other players and wondered if this would make him want to stop. Little did they know he already decided he *was* going to stop. He couldn't do that to himself again.

Paul texted Maggie to say he was done early and she offered to pick up the pizza which he was ok with. She went home to shower and change and tried to avoid her father but he was there, right in her face. "Where are you going? What am I having for supper?"

"Whatever you find in the frig or choose to go get. I won't be home for supper. I'm eating out with my friend." She didn't look at him and walked right past him. He knew she was pissed and didn't say a word after that, which was unusual for him. Once she got out of that driveway and on the road, she breathed a sigh of relief. Her mood changed drastically and was now happy she was on her way to see Paul. She was so happy he called her and said he just wanted to hear her voice. It stunned her he admitted that.

Pizza in hand she arrives at Paul's dorm and he is waiting for her in the lobby with Nicky. Once he sees her he takes the pizza and gives it to Nicky who says' "I'll see you both upstairs" and turns to leave. She looks at Paul who pulls her into a hug and feeling his arms around her made her so emotional right then. She hugged him back so tightly—hanging on him and he stayed in her embrace, needing that hug from her as well.

Let's eat and I have so much to tell you. Just then her cousin texted a picture of her sitting with her brothers on a bench in the hall at the hotel. She smiled when she got it because she fell asleep in her brother Frank's arms and she remembered why they were sitting out in the hall. Paul said he wanted to see pictures and this was a funny one to send. She would just tell him "See, I was the life of the party" with her sleeping the night away.

Nicky stayed and ate some pizza with them but left to go see some friends. He wanted to leave them alone and when he left, he hugged Paul which Maggie thought was nice, but also thought something must be wrong. He said he wanted to tell her something and now she panicked a little.

She decided to pull up the picture again to show him and she blew it up so he could see and her face dropped. Behind her and her brothers was someone standing on the steps at the hotel that looked just like Paul. Paul saw her face drop and couldn't imagine what she was looking at.

"What's wrong? You look like you saw a ghost. What are you looking at?"

"She hands him the picture and he saw it as plain as day—he was in the picture."

"Were you at the hotel and if that is you—why were you there?"

"This all ties into what I want to tell you about. I don't want there to be any secrets between us. Something terrible happened to me last night. I almost died, and if it weren't for Nicky—I would have."

Maggie doubles over like the wind was knocked out of her just then. He goes to her on the couch and said 'Please, will you listen to my whole story and then you can tell me yours. Please Mags!" But she had to hug him first after just hearing he almost died. She grabbed him and held him tightly and he returned the hug—resting his head on her shoulder. Her heart was pounding away and was breaking, hearing what happened to him last night.

She nods her head yes as he gets up to start, while pacing back and forth in front of her. "I am never going to Louden House again Maggie. I am making that promise to you right now."

Maggie is relieved and so happy about that promise and is carefully listening to his story with wide eyes and trying to keep it in order.

Maggie was stunned and when he was finished—she started crying. He went right to her and held her in his arms—rocking her back and forth. She wasn't saying anything and it worried him.

"I had to see you last night. That is what you do to me. I had to at least just see you and then I was going to be fine. Then I heard you being so upset about your father—talking to your brothers and it upset me. Maggie, I heard you say your father told you you were ugly. You fell asleep but I heard your brothers say, you are so beautiful. They didn't know why guys weren't knocking down your door."

Maggie cried even harder when she found out what her brothers thought of her. "My dad always told me I wasn't pretty, my whole life, so I kind of believed it. My brothers think I'm beautiful?"

"Your brothers and me and a lot of other guys including Nicky. I think you are the most beautiful girl on the planet. I would never just say that. When I kissed you in front of everyone Tuesday at the Commons Center, I did it for 2 reasons. One was, I wanted to kiss you so badly and the second was so everyone would know—you were mine and stay away from you." Paul smiled at her when he said that. "I wanted to tag you as mine."

Maggie smiled and looked at Paul wiping away her tears and she leaned in to kiss him. He was so happy she still wanted to kiss him and was worried how she would take the story he told her.

"You took that pill because you were upset over me?"

"Yes, I can't lie to you. I didn't want to like you so much. You were too nice and good. I hung around with a drug crowd. I knew you wouldn't like my friends and didn't think I wanted to let them go. But right after I took you to that party at Louden House—I knew you didn't belong there. I knew you wouldn't belong. I hoped you wouldn't want to see me again but after you let me have it—things started getting clearer and clearer. I went home right after you left and Nicky thought I was sick coming home so early. But—I wanted to be a better person, for you Mags. I wanted to deserve having you in my life. You are the type of girl every guy wants. The one they take home to meet their parents. The one they truly love and want a life with. That is what I want with you. I want to deserve you. I want a life with you. You are the one for me. I had this conversation with Nicky the night I came home from our first date. You couldn't even call it a date. I treated you so badly the whole night and I want you to know that Nicky let me have it too. He read me the riot act, but finally—I heard him. It was then I decided to change my life around and I was so nervous and scared."

"Scared you wouldn't be able to pull yourself together?"

"No, scared you would never speak to me again. Nicky said I met 'the one'. The one for me and I threw it away. He said I will never find another person to compare to you. I didn't know if you would even look at me but when I threw that ball at you in the gym and you smiled at me—I thought there might be a chance. Then at the Commons you were laughing at what you heard again in the bathroom and it relaxed me immediately. Once you kissed me—I melted and then knew you forgave me. I can never apologize to you enough for that night. I am so sorry and will always be. I will even tell our kids how bad our first date went."

Maggie laughed when he said 'our kids' and smiled at him taking her hand and bringing it to his cheek to touch.

"Why? Why didn't you want a girlfriend?"

"I thought, I was only 20 and had 2 years left of school. I have nothing to offer you. I can't even afford to take you out to dinner, but Nicky said, pizza is dinner. We could go for coffee or for hikes or early movies. We could go to parties—the non-drug kind. As long as we are together. I never really thought of it like that."

Maggie is smiling and leans in for another kiss. "You really want *me*?"

Paul shakes his head back and forth because he knows she doesn't believe she is so beautiful and that someone would want her.

"I want you and only you. I will promise myself to you and you alone. Will you have me too? Will you promise yourself to me and me alone? I will be so upset if you don't want this relationship."

Maggie's water works started up again. She managed to get out a "yes. I will promise myself to you and only you. I will want you and only you and a relationship for us."

Paul got emotional too and kissed Maggie passionately. She started pulling his t-shirt off of him and he quickly helped her undress too. He picked her up and saw what Frank was talking about. He thought *my basketball weights more than her* as he lays her down in his bed. He continues to undress all the while keeping his eyes on hers and watches as she removed what was left of her clothing. He saw how beautiful she really *was* looking down at her body. She was gorgeous and he was going to constantly tell her and remind her. Paul lays next to her and kisses her slowly. He wanted to make this first time for them special and he wanted to make it last. She ran her fingers through his hair and he moaned when she did that. He caressed her body, gently running his fingers over her nipples and listened to the soft sighs she was whisper-ing. He sucked them and nipped at them and then went back for more kisses. She stroked him up and down and felt he was more than ready for her. Just then he stopped, "I have to get something" and she held him down shaking her head then whispered, "I'm on the pill. I will tell you why later", not wanting to disrupt the moment. His kisses traced her whole body until she couldn't wait another minute—pulling him on top of her. She lifted herself and helped him find where he needed to be and once he entered her he stopped as to not hurt her. He gently and slowing moved his hips until he filled her up completely and then felt she was ready for him. They moved together moaning and groaning—trying to take in every emotion between them they were feeling and when they exploded together it shocked them both. Paul looked at Maggie placing his hands on the side of her face while laying his body down on hers and whispered "I love you Maggie." Maggie wrapped her arms around him and said "Please stay like this. Don't move. I want to hold you. I like this." Paul rested his head on her shoulder and stayed right where she wanted him. "Paul . . ." She whispers, "I love you too!" You couldn't wipe that smile off of Paul's face or Maggie's at that moment.

Paul picked her up and rested her body on top of his chest— wrapping his arms and legs around her—engulfing her like a cocoon. She was tiny compared to him and he loved holding her. He felt like he was protecting her. Just then he heard Nicky come in and pulled the sheet over them both. Maggie fell asleep almost immediately—once she felt safe and warm in Paul's arms.

Nicky comes in their room, not knowing if Paul was there or not and once he saw Paul with Maggie wrapped up in his arms—he just flashed him the biggest smile and was so happy for them. He whispers, "I'll take the couch tonight." Paul said—"Maggie has to be home by 11:30. She has work tomorrow." Nicky nodded "Ok, I'll be out here until she leaves."

Paul could not take his eyes off of Maggie. He couldn't believe she committed herself to him. He couldn't believe he committed himself to her but knew- he couldn't be without her. No one ever turned his head like she did. No one ever made him feel the way she did. She was everything to him and at that moment he realized and truly believed, she actually *was* the one for him. Nicky was right. If he let her slip away—no one would ever compare to her in his whole lifetime. She starts to stir and looks up at Paul and smiles. "Am I really here? Did we really commit ourselves to each-other? Was I dreaming? It isn't a terrible joke, is it?"

Paul pulls her up so he could speak to her face to face. "This would never be a joke Mags. I would never joke about committing myself to you but could see why you would think that after how badly I acted when we first met. I will never disappoint you again. You are mine and I am yours forever." He kissed her lips softly and she sighed happily.

"You're on the pill?"

"Yes, and not because I sleep around. In fact I haven't felt close enough to anyone to want to have sex with them. I always wanted to find someone I was in love with. Now you are really thinking—what have I gotten myself into!" She smiled at him.

Paul was shocked hearing Maggie say she didn't sleep around and asked "You never had sex before?"

"Just once when I thought I loved someone but it was a disaster. The whole experience was uncomfortable. He was odd and the whole situation was awkward. That's probably why I decided I wasn't going to do it again until my heart overflowed with feelings for someone."

Paul smiled at Maggie knowing her heart was overflowing with feelings for *him* and once again felt he didn't deserve her.

"Maggie I have to tell you the truth. Sometimes when I was in the state I was in—I would wake up with girls in my or *a* bed, not knowing where I was or even who I was with. I don't want that life anymore.

I don't know what I was thinking at the time. I wasn't all there and I know that is no excuse but the only one I have."

"I appreciate you telling me, so I'm not blind-sided if anyone wants to hurt me telling me that or hurt us or our relationship. You said you didn't want secrets between us and let's promise that. No secrets and no steps backwards. If you are upset about something, find me. I will be your pill. I will be what you need to help you. What do you think about that?"

"I like that idea Mags. I will find you if I ever feel I'm taking steps backwards. I promise you."

"This might be a good time to tell *you* something too."

"What do you need to tell me?

"I had a big crush on you when I met you. When I kissed you before I left your drug induced body that night (she lets out a small laugh) I was really saying good bye to you. But, I crushed on you for so long—it felt like we finally broke up after a year, when I really had just met you. I know it sounds crazy but—that is how I felt. After waiting forever to meet you and having a mental picture of how you were—it wasn't like anything I imagined it would be and I felt hurt that we were finally over after all that time. Wondering about you. Imagining if you were nice or full of yourself! Smiling as she told him. I don't want anyone coming to you saying, she was after you for so long. It wasn't like that."

"It's a good thing I didn't meet you until now. I was stupid for so long and now I finally see what I was doing to my life. We might not have even liked each other back then."

Now he looks at her to tell her, "Mags, I think I make a wise choice not letting you get away from me and feel peaceful now that you are in my life."

She responds with a kiss and replies "Good. Would you like to feel peaceful once more before I have to go?" She asks laughing at him.

"I will never refuse you that Mags . . . Never! As he flips her on her back hovering over her—planting kiss after kiss on her whole body where she is giggling away.

Nicky hearing them, is smiling too and knows, his brother will be fine now that he has Maggie *and* him.

CHAPTER 9

Lois and Mike Tanner

Paul wants to tell his parents about Maggie. It's been a while since he spoke to them. They lived 2 hours away and used to come to every home game to see Paul and support him, but once Paul started doing drugs—he kept telling them not to come see him. It got too hard for him to see his parents stressing over the way he was living his life and saw their hearts breaking over and over again, over him.

He told Nicky, "I'm going to call my parents to see if they will come to the next home game."

Nicky was shocked. Nicky's parents never came to one game and it really bothered him. He was now their only son ever since his brother died and thought they would want to support him. The only way they wanted to support Nicky was to fill up his checkbook every month. His parents were in the middle of divorcing and it hurt Nicky that was happening to them. Each blamed the other for his brother's death which took a fatal toll on their marriage.

"Do you want them to meet Maggie?"

"Yes. I can't wait for her to meet them. I think they will love her and she will love them right back."

"It's been a while since you called them Paul. They will be shocked."

"I know and I have to remedy that. Now that I'm clean—I want them to be a part of my life and Maggie's. I never really realized how much I missed them until I cleaned up my act. I will always regret what I did to myself and to them."

"You are their son Paul and they will forgive you and take you back with open arms. I know they will."

"I have a lot to apologize for and better start now before it's too late. Can you stay here with me while I call them?"

"Of course. I won't leave until you're done."

"Thank you Nicky."

"Hi Mom."

"Paul, is everything alright? We haven't heard from you in months."

"Yes. It's better than alright. I wanted to know if you and Dad would like to come to the next home game I have."

"Really? Let me get your father on the line too." Lois was shocked he wanted them to come to a game.

"Mike, Paul is on the line and wants to talk to us." Paul heard her yelling for his dad and then hears the phone click and his father now on the call too.

"Hi Dad."

"Son, how are you doing? You don't call, so we don't know anything about you."

"I'm sorry dad and I want to make it up to you and Mom. Can you come in for the next home game? I would really like to see you and talk to you both. It has been a while and I have lots to tell you. Please don't worry. I'm fine—I just want my parents to come see me if you can spare the time."

"Spare the time? Of course we can. All you had to do was ask and we can be there whenever you want us to. We love you son and always will."

"Thank you both. The next game is Friday. Can you make it?"

"Of course we can. We will be there."

"Would you like to take us for dinner before the game?"

"You and Nicky?"

"Yes, and my girlfriend, I really want you to meet. I think you will love her. Mom—you especially."

Mike and Lois froze just then on the line. The first thought they had was he got someone pregnant and was trying to prepare them ahead of meeting her.

"I hate to ask you this son, but are you in trouble? With the girl I mean."

"No dad—we are not pregnant if that is what you mean. I found someone who helped me straighten out my life and I want you to meet her. She is the one for me mom. You know I never dated anyone seriously but when you meet her—you will see what I mean. She is an angel. That is the only way I can describe her to you, so you know how special she is to me."

There was a silence on the line and Paul just looked at Nicky— waiting for someone to say something.

"We'll be there Friday and stay overnight so we are not driving home so late. We'll make the reservation now."

Paul gave a sigh of relief and continued "thank you both. I have a lot of explaining to do and when we are done—you will see what I mean. I think you will be happy about my life for a change. I actually can't wait to see you both. I love you mom and dad. It's been too long since I told you that."

Paul's mom Lois and his dad Mike were surprised with the conversation they just had with their son. Now they couldn't wait to come in to see what was going on and who his girlfriend was. Lois was crying when they hung up the call—hearing Paul say he loved them. They were both stunned about what was happening and kind of just stared at each other trying to process all he said.

CHAPTER 10

Meeting Maggie

As it turnsout, Lois and Mike frequented the restaurant right across the street from Maggie's shop where she worked. Lois always admired the way the windows were decorated but never got a chance to go in to see what they had. They were always in a hurry to get back on the road to go home and it had been a while since they had dinner there, having not visited Paul in months.

The night before they came in, Maggie made Paul and Nicky clean their dorm apartment. "Your parents are coming so let's clean this place up a little." It wasn't that bad but the refrigerator had pizza in it from 2 weeks ago and needed to be cleaned out and the milk was definitely spoiled. It smelled up the frig. They reluctantly dusted and vacuumed and cleaned the bathroom. It looked great when they were all done and they had to admit they liked it all cleaned up too.

Paul was waiting in the lobby for his parents, just pacing back and forth with Nicky there. They kind of adopted Nicky and knew his parents never bothered with him. They also knew it bothered Nicky so they tried to always include him in things when they came in to see Paul. Nicky was so nice and they loved him and felt badly for him, not having anyone.

Paul saw them coming and flashed the biggest smile at them. He went to his mom first and wrapped his arms around her telling her "I'm so happy to see you. I'm so happy you came today." It made Lois almost cry she was so thrilled with her son. Then he went to his dad and did the same, engulfing him in a big bear hug and patting him on the back. He told him too "I'm so happy you are here dad. I'm so sorry it's been so long and promise it will never be like that again." Mike also got emotional when he told him that and grabbed him into a hug again not wanting Paul to see him tear up.

Nicky lightened the mood, standing there with his arms open "Mom/ Dad, where's my hug?" They all laughed as they went to Nicky next and called him son too . . . "We couldn't wait to see you too son", Mike said and Nicky was smiling from ear to ear.

They walked up to the second floor to their rooms and when Lois and Mike got in, they were shocked. The place was so clean and no clothes were lying around and they even had a candle lit to make it smell nice. "OMG, what happened here?" Lois asked laughing.

"Maggie made us clean yesterday because you were coming." Paul told them smiling. "But it looks so good, Nicky and I think we are going to try and keep it this way." Nicky is just nodding his head agreeing, "But after today the candle goes!" Again Nicky made them laugh.

They sat and Paul gave them something to drink. He was nervous telling his parents about how badly his life was turning out. He told them about Louden House and about how he met Maggie and how badly he treated her on their first date. He told them if it weren't for her and Nicky—he might not even be alive today. That really shook Mike and Lois and Mike just lowered his head while Lois cried. Paul went right to her to comfort her and it helped as she hugged her son with Mike putting his arm around them both. Then he told them all about Maggie and how much he loved her. "I know I love her mom. I had never felt this way about anyone I have ever dated before. That is why I never had a girlfriend before. I never felt for anyone the way I feel about Maggie. She is everything I could ever want in a girlfriend or a wife." Lois was shocked he said wife and knew at that moment—he was that serious about her. It shocked both parents. He continued "I know I'm only 20 but I can't be without her. She makes my heart beat mom. I don't know how I was alive before I met her. Maybe that is why I chose the path I was going down. I was looking for something that was missing. I had you both and Nicky but something was not right and that something was Maggie. I know that now."

When they finally really looked at their son—they saw how good he actually did look. His eyes were clear, his complexion wasn't clammy and he was so calm.

Paul told him all about Maggie's family. He especially told them about her dad. They could not believe he treated her and his sons like that. They also could not believe how afraid of him his 3 children were. Mike had to ask, "Son, you are not latching onto her because you feel sorry for her situation at home are you? Or is she after you for that reason too? To get her out of a bad deal at home?"

Paul was so shocked his dad said that and so was Nicky but they both knew he had to ask.

"No dad! Not at all! She handles her situation at home. She's been handling it for her whole life. It's not like that at all." Nicky chimed in as well, "I can't wait for you to meet her. She is a keeper and if Paul didn't claim her—I would have."

"Dad—*I* went after *her*! She did not want to date me and for good reason. How terrible I treated her. Thank God she gave me a second chance."

Mike felt relieved about Paul's response to his concern and now couldn't wait, so they all headed downtown and got there early so they could go to Maggie's shop and meet her. Maggie had a feeling they would do that and also told Sarah they would be in. Everyone was waiting and could see Maggie was nervous about it. When they walked in the shop Lois didn't know where to look. The things were beautiful and the shop was exquisite. Sarah saw Paul and immediately went to him and hugged him. It shocked his parents they were that friendly. She introduced herself to Lois and Mike and brought them back to meet Maggie who was on a call about an order being placed. She hangs up and walks out of her office smiling at Paul who is just beaming when he sees her and she looked beautiful in her sweater dress that hugged her body and she had suede boots on too. Her light brown hair was pulled off of her face and fell down her back in soft curls. Her blue eyes sparkled especially when she looked at Paul. She looked like a doll because she was so petite and Lois and Mike both noticed his face just light up when he saw her and Mike nodded to Nicky almost saying—*I see it now Nicky*. Sarah was beaming too feeling like Maggie was her daughter and was so proud of her.

Paul goes right to her and kisses her softly and starts the introductions. "Are you ready?" he asks her and she nodded her head. "Maggie, I would like you to meet my parents." Maggie flashed the biggest smile at them both as she extended her hand to shake but Lois grabbed her and drew her into a hug and Mike followed suit. She looked at Nicky and went to hug him too, and Nicky was smiling away too. Paul joked and said "That's enough Nicky. Let her go!" and they all laughed.

Lois turned to Sarah, "Paul told us you are Maggie's adoptive mother so we'd like to invite you to dinner also. Can you please join us?" Paul and Maggie were thrilled and so was Sarah who happily accepted. Everything was going well so far. It was too early to walk across the street for dinner and Sarah felt Lois wanted to speak to her about Maggie so she said, "Maggie has a few more things to do before we go, so come and sit with me in my office Lois. We can get to know each other better" as she slipped her arm through Lois' to walk her to her office. The men went for a walk outside and across the street to make a reservation while the women stayed at the shop getting to know one another. Maggie introduced everyone who came in the back to Lois and they all gushed over Paul and how nice he was, making Lois feel so proud of how he was straightening out his life.

"I know you want to talk to me about Maggie. I will tell you the truth about anything you ask me. I love Maggie like a daughter—that much is true, but I won't lie about anything you ask me about her."

"I don't know where to start. I was leary about her relationship with Paul until I saw how his face lit up when he saw her."

Sarah is nodding her head agreeing. "They are like that all the time. He brings her lunch from his cafeteria when he has time in between his classes. I have never seen her this happy."

"Sarah, do you think they are too young to be this serious?"

"How old were you when you met Mike and knew he was the one?"

Lois smiled and said 18.

"I was 17 when I met my husband. He passed away 5 years ago. There isn't a day that goes by that I don't tell him how much I still love him. We had no children by choice, but now with him gone—I wish I had a few. Just so I could see his face in theirs or his mannerisms on them. It would have been comforting for me. That is probably why I love Maggie so much. She fills that void and it keeps me going. You know she is 22—right? I know Paul is 20."

"Yes, he told us she was older. She is beautiful too."

"She is, and never seems to know it. She could put on a burlap bag and look stunning." Now they both smiled at each other.

"I was worried about her latching onto Paul because of her home life. Paul told us all about her father."

"Don't even worry about that. She would never do that in the first place. She could afford to move out and it would be tough, but she loves her brothers. She feels if she moved, her father would forbid them to speak to her again. That is why she stays. She has been juggling him her whole life and knows just how to survive living there. I too cannot believe the things he says to her and wish she *would* move out. I worry about her all the time. I would take her in—in a minute but she would never let me. She would not want to burden me or anyone." Lois finally felt relieved hearing what Sarah said about Maggie's home situation.

"Lois, I know you think your son is too young to tie up with someone, but just be happy it is with someone like Maggie. She said he turned his life around for the better and take that as a sign they are right for each other. No one could predict how life is going to turn out for people. They found each other and are so good for each other. I am so happy for her. She so deserves to have that smile on her face. Paul so deserves to be happy too. She will only make his life wonderful. Trust me. She will only make his life wonderful. She is exactly what you see. Kind, happy, hard working. She wears her heart out on her sleeve. Everyone who meets her—just loves her. You should too."

That is what Lois was hoping to find out about Maggie. She was happy now—after talking to Sarah and could tell Mike she was starting to love Maggie already. It was time to go and the 3 women walked across the street to the restaurant where their men were waiting for them. Paul immediately held his hand out for Maggie and she took it still being a little nervous. Lois and Mike both saw that and smiled at each other. For some reason Paul was right. She was the one for him and they now saw it as plain as day.

The Game

After dinner, Sarah and Maggie headed back to the shop. She had to balance the register and close up and then change into more comfortable clothes for the game. "We'll save you a seat Maggie", Lois told her. "Can you save 3 seats? I want you to meet my 2 best friends. They are meeting us at the game too." Lois was thrilled she would be meeting some of Maggie's friends. She could see who she hangs around with. "Of course. I'll save 3 seats then."

"I will get there as quickly as I can. They are meeting me in the lobby so we'll find you."

Everyone headed off in different directions. Maggie went and hugged Nicky. "Nicky, have a good game tonight." Nicky returned the hug and said "Thank you Maggie! See you later."

She walks over to Paul who was beaming again and he bends his head to kiss her goodbye. "Mr. Tanner, I hope you have an awesome game tonight, for your parents!" He smiles and kisses her again and then hugs her.

He watched her every step crossing the street—until she got inside the shop. Then turns and sees the 3 of them just smiling at him. "What! Why are you looking at me like that?" Nicky just put his arm around him, walking him to the car—laughing at him.

Once again Paul was watching the door until she got there with her friends. Once again he throws his ball at her. She turns and knows this time he *did* do it on purpose but what they didn't see was the line of little boys waiting to catch that ball for her. She looks and one had the ball in his hand as Paul and Nicky come over to him. He says, "Did you want to try and dunk the ball tonight?" With the boys dad standing behind him. He said "He has been standing here all night waiting. He saw his friend make the basket Tuesday and he wants to now. Will you let him?"

Paul and Nicky just laughed and now knew this was going to be a tradition before every game. The rest of the team thought that too and stopped drippling and shooting as Paul lifted the boy onto his shoulders and walked over to the basket where Nicky took a pass from Bobby(Now everyone wanted to get involved) dribbling it up to Paul where he put the ball in the boys hands. Paul said standing under the basket "ok your turn. Dunk it!" And again it went right in and the whole gym clapped and screamed for the boy. Nicky took him off of Paul's shoulders and he ran back to his dad yelling, "I made it. Did you see Dad? I made the basket!" They had a lot of explaining to do to coach who was just looking at what was happening, *again*! He let it go the first time!

Lois and Mike were shocked too at what happened. They thought it was so sweet with what they did for that boy and knew the kid was so happy afterwards. They motioned to Maggie where they were sitting and she went right over to them. Molly, Judy this is Paul's parents, Mr. and Mrs. Tanner. Mr. and Mrs. Tanner, these are my best friends Molly and Judy. Lois and Mike got to talk after they dropped off Paul and Nicky at the gym and decided they were going to support Paul and Maggie however they needed them to. They were so happy the way things were turning out and they felt so much for her already. She really was nice and so lovely for being so young. They saw their sons face light up just mentioning her name and were thankful to her for helping him straighten out his life. As the 3 sat down in their seats, Lois takes Maggie's hand and said "Please call us mom and dad. I don't think it's a secret, you now belong to our family." Maggie's eyes teared up and she put her head down while Lois leaned into her, squeezing her hand. The game was phenomenal and Paul and Nicky shined with his parents and Maggie being there. They were amazing on the floor together. They even caught coach smiling with some plays they pulled off. Especially the one were Nicky throws the ball half way down the court—off center of the basket where Paul is waiting and catches it—feet off the ground—in the air and dunks it. That play was their signature play and the whole gym usually erupted when they did it. The night was amazing.

In the lobby waiting for Paul and Nicky, some of his Louden House friends come right up to him when he came out of the locker room. "Paul are you coming over tonight?" His dealer asks.

In front of all of his players he just said "No, I can't make it anymore. I'm sorry. See you around campus!" The person looked shocked he refused and knew if Paul was not going—they would lose a lot of business. "Are you sure you can't make it?"

"Positive. Sorry, it's not for me anymore. Please don't seek me out." The guy just stood there, kind of with his mouth hung open. He didn't know what to say so Paul just walked by him and right over to Maggie and his parents. Nicky passed by that guy and couldn't wait to say "You heard him! Stay away from him or I will turn you in myself!" He was still so mad about the pill they gave him, that could have killed him.

Lois and Mike hugged and kissed the whole bunch of them waiting in the lobby. Even Molly and Judy. They liked them a lot. Then they decided to meet for breakfast the next morning at 8, right around the corner where Maggie worked, that way she could join them. Molly and Judy even said they would meet them too. Everyone was so happy with the way things were turning out.

At the Commons Center, Maggie said to Paul, "I'm going to the ladies room to see what is going on with us." Laughing all the while. Paul smiled and let go of her hand so she could go. Once again, there was chatter about them. "Did you hear his girlfriend was pregnant? That is why his parents came in to see them. He had to tell them this weekend." That did it. Maggie flew out of the stall and the girls turned white seeing she was there. "Hi, I'm Maggie. I am not pregnant. Please spread the word for me. OK?" What could they say except they were so sorry and left before she said more.

Paul sees Maggie coming out and she was not smiling. He goes right to her. "What happened?"

"Well, it seems I'm pregnant. That's the word. But I straightened them out before they left. I told them I was not pregnant and that is not why your parents were in."

Paul just smiled and bent down to kiss her. "Let's go practice so when we want to get pregnant, we will know what to do." Maggie burst out laughing and nodded her head, "Let's go!"

Paul all but dragged her out of there as she waved bye to her friends and Paul waved to Nicky too. They ran back to his dorm and started undressing as soon as they closed the door. They left a note for Nicky, wake us at 1:30 if you are home in time. Maggie has to get home."

Nicky got in at almost 2 and found them sleeping away with arms and legs wrapped around each other. He smiles and shook Paul who woke immediately. It's almost 2. I just got your note. Paul nodded and Nicky left to hit the couch so Maggie could get up and dressed. Paul kissed her softly and she stirred in his arms. She looks up at him and he told her what time it was. She nodded and got up slowly to dress and leave to go back home. "I will see you in a few hours which is the only way I think I can leave you now." That thought made them both relax. Paul watched as she got in her car safely and drove off.

"Everything went well with your parents tonight. They seemed to like Maggie a lot."

Paul's head was down. "What is it? Is something wrong?" Nicky asked.

"I hate seeing her leave. I don't want her to. I have to change that. I have to talk to my parents about it. She has to live with me. I can't take being away from her Nicky. Do you think I'm crazy? It hasn't been that long but I can't let her go. I have to marry her Nicky!"

Nicky wasn't shocked. He knew Paul and knew he was having a hard time being without her during the week. That is why he brought her lunch so many times. He had to see her and be with her.

"I'm not surprised. I see how much you need her. I think she needs you just as much. I also think you 2 do belong together. Talk to your parents and see what they say."

"We won't be roommates anymore if she agrees to marry me."

"But we will still be brothers and that is all that matters and you let me stay with you once in a while when I don't want to go back to my dorm alone."

"Nicky, you will always be my brother and you can stay with us as many nights as you like. Nothing will ever come between us."

"Thank you for saying that. Then—I give you my blessing. You can ask Maggie to marry you." He flashes a big smile at him.

CHAPTER 12

She's the One

Everyone met for breakfast the next morning as planned. They all enjoyed being together and Mike and Lois loved being with their son and his friends. Molly laughingly asked while they were all sitting having their coffee before their order arrived, "Maggie, what was the news in the ladies room last night? Did you find out anything new about what you and Paul are up to?"

Without missing a beat they both said at the same time "We're pregnant!"

Judy and Nicky nearly spit out their coffee and just looked at Paul and Maggie and everyone turned white just then. Mike and Lois didn't know what to think because Paul told them she wasn't pregnant when he called home.

Paul continued "Maggie heard in the ladies room—everyone was saying we were pregnant and that is why my parents came in this weekend. So we could tell them."

Then they all let out a sigh of relief and got what was going on. The color came back in Mike and Lois's faces too after that. They explained more; about every time Maggie went to the ladies room there was a new rumor about them. First she was his girlfriend and then his sister and now she was pregnant.

"Don't worry. I straightened those girls out once I heard what they were saying. I told them to spread the word I was NOT pregnant and that is *not* why Paul's parents were in this weekend."

Everyone laughed and relaxed once they knew what was going on. Then she teased everyone more saying—"I can't wait for those sweet cream pancakes—I was *craving* them all night knowing we were coming here for breakfast!" Even Paul got a laugh out of that as he leaned over to kiss her.

Molly and Judy had to go so they got up and hugged Nicky and Paul's parents. "Thank you for the invite to breakfast. It was so nice meeting you." Judy said and Molly followed it up with "Hope to see you soon."

Maggie had to get to work and got up to leave also. She went to Lois first and kissed her. "Mom, have a safe trip home. I hope to see you more." Then she kissed Mike and said "You too dad!" Paul was smiling at everyone and took Maggie's hand and told his parents "I'll be right back. I'm going to walk Maggie down the street."

"Ok, we'll still be here" Mike told him.

"I think it went well with my parents Mags. What do you think?"

"I think so too. They told me to call them mom and dad. I almost cried when your mom told me that. I love them already Paul."

"I will call you later. What are we doing tonight? We didn't talk about it."

"What do you feel like?"

"I feel like staying in, watching a movie, holding and kissing you all night."

Maggie's face turned all red. "I think that . . . is a good plan. Let's go with it."

Paul smiled and kissed her goodbye and watched her unlock the shop and go in. Then he turned and went back to meet up with his parents and Nicky.

"Mom/Dad, can you wait a few minutes? I'd like to talk to you some more."

"Absolutely son. We will leave when we are done here." Nicky stayed put, knowing Paul would want him to stay too.

"Dad, I don't want you to think I'm crazy but—I want to marry Maggie and soon."

Mike and Lois expected this. They saw them together and knew they needed each other but they listened to what he was going to say.

"I love her. I cannot be without her. I cannot be away from her. I can't breathe when I'm not with her. I changed my whole life around since the day I met her and I know she is the one for me. I told you that on the phone. I'm begging you to support me. I have to marry her and make her a Tanner. She has to be mine. I don't know how else to explain it."

Nicky chimed in. "I believe he can't breathe without her. I see it every day. Every time she has to go home or can't make a game, he is lost. She is the one for him and I know it isn't a mistake."

Lois spoke next. "Nicky, if he gets married, you will lose him as a roommate and possibly a friend. Won't that upset you?"

"He is my brother and we already discussed it. We will always have each other and I will support him and Maggie however I could. He promised I could sleep on his couch as many times as I want. We will always be family. After he promised me that, I gave him my blessing." Smiling now at Paul who was nodding his head at Nicky.

Lois drifted off remembering her conversation with Sarah the previous day. Maggie felt if she moved out, her father would forbid her brothers to speak to her ever again.

"Mom, what is it?" Paul asked.

"Something Sarah said to me yesterday. I know you think Maggie's home life is bad, but Sarah said she could move out if she wanted to. She could afford it, but if she did move out, her father would forbid her brothers to ever speak to her again. That is something she couldn't do. She loves her brothers and that is why she stays."

"I know that mom. We talked about it. I didn't ask her to marry me yet. I want to make sure we have your blessing. We will hope her father doesn't ban them from speaking to her but it will be Maggie's choice to move out and marry me."

"What if she chooses her brothers over you? You will be crushed Paul, and we couldn't take seeing anything happen to you again. You look so good and healthy. We haven't seen you look this good in months." Lois continued.

"I know you are worried for me. Maggie will choose me. I am positive she will."

Mike and Lois nodded as well as Nicky. "We hope she does for your sake son. We will support you however you need us to."

Paul went to both parents along with Nicky into a big group hug. They kissed them both and walked them to their car. "Thank you for everything this weekend. I will call you soon."

"Let us know how you make out. Let us know immediately. Don't wait, especially if you need us. Good luck Paul. We really do love Maggie. We can see she is the one for you. We want you to know that." Lois told him.

CHAPTER 13

Will You Marry Me

Paul couldn't wait for Maggie to get out of work. He had his parents blessing to ask her to marry him and he wanted to do it that night. He didn't want to wait another minute.

Maggie drove to his dorm where he was waiting in the lobby for her. She flashed him a big smile and he returned it holding his arms out for her to walk into. He held her tightly and she looked up at him with a questioned look. "What is it? Is everything alright?"

"Better than I could ever have imagined. I love you Maggie and wanted to tell you."

"I love you too Paul."

"Come on—I got us supper." He took her hand and up they went to his room.

The snack bar was set with dishes and silverware and he had a candle lit. He fussed and she loved it.

She smiled and asked "It's not my birthday, so what is all this?"

"I'm terrible in the kitchen so I got us some Chinese. Is that ok?"

"Perfect. Can I change into something more comfortable? I have been dressed up all day and just want to get more comfortable."

"Yes you can, and I will get everything ready here, while you go change."

Once she does she comes out, the food is ready and on the snack bar. They sit and eat and he asks her about her day and she was a chatter box that day. She asks him and he has lots to tell her about practice and studying. They move their conversation to the couch and she thought they were going to watch a movie but he surprised her. He kissed her softly and kept looking at her smiling.

"What do you want to say? I know you have something on your mind so you should just say it."

"Maggie, I love you more than my own life. I want you to know that. Do you believe me?"

"Yes, I do believe you but you are worrying me Paul."

"Don't be worried. I want to know if you will marry me and soon."

Maggie's face dropped and she was trying to process what he just said. "You want to marry me?"

"Yes, I cannot live without you and every time you leave to go home, it just kills me. I have to marry you Maggie. I have to be with you every day or I can't breathe. That much I know. I told my parents I was going to ask you and they said they would support us however they could. They weren't even shocked. They saw how much we meant to each other. Nicky even approved and asked if he could sleep on our couch when we get married. He is my brother and I told him he could stay as many times as he wanted. I hope you don't mind me telling him that."

"No, not at all. Now, back to—you want to marry me? I can't seem to wrap my head around you wanting me."

"Maggie, I want you, I need you and I love you and cannot go another day without you. Trust me. I can't breathe without you. I want you and only you. Please—please say you will marry me. We can work out the logistics later but right now, will you marry me?"

Maggie starts crying and says "Yes, of course I will marry you. I can't be without you either. I love you Paul and I want a life with you. So yes, yes yes."

Paul picks her up and swings her around being so happy she accepted. He was in heaven and knew he would be the rest of his life. He carries her to his room and lays her down smothering her in deep passionate kisses. She said yes and he was flying high—this time naturally.

CHAPTER 14

The Promises

While lying in Paul's arms he confesses to her, "I was thinking of what I had to offer you and realized I have nothing but these few things I will promise you. I will never go back on any of them." For some reason when Paul said he was going to do something, he did.

Maggie braces herself and can't imagine what he could possibly promise her but saw how serious he was just then.

He begins with:

"I will never let you down."

"I will always be there for you."

"I will take our marriage seriously."

"I will respect you and take care of you the best I could."

"I will love you until the end of time."

Maggie is listening to all he is promising her. She felt he was being sincere in his promises. She sees he is anxious now, being so stressed about what he was promising her.

Trying to ease his mind she tells him "I want you to know . . . I believe all of those promises you made to me. I know and somehow feel you are sincere about them and really mean it. It means a lot that you would worry about me."

"I know you are probably worried about how and where we would live, but I can tell you a few things now and answer any questions about what I just promised you. You know I have a full scholarship to the University for 4 years—so I went to my advisor Jimmy and told him I was getting married and asked him what my scholarship would cover. Right now it covers room and food. He told me it would cover an apartment if I was married and he would be the one finding one for us. We would have to pay utilities except for heating. So having a place to live is covered."

"I get an allowance from my parents monthly. They make a deposit in my account for $500 a month. I rarely touch that and have some money built up in it. We could use it for whatever we need. Dishes and stuff like that."

Maggie was so pleased he was thinking about their lives together so she chimes right in. "Well, I work and make $35,000 a year which is average for this area. But I really love my job and prefer to keep it. Do you think that will be enough to support the both of us? Between food, phones, cable and electricity? I take home $437 a week. We could see what our monthly bills will be and budget for it. In the past my father took most of my money. I will happily tell him I can't do that anymore. I will be needing it now."

"He took your money?"

"Yes—I bought a car and I pay him monthly for it. He paid for it and I pay him back. I could have just bought it outright but it was his way or no way."

Paul just nodded his head that he understood.

"OK, so we know where we are going to live and how much money we will have. Now, let's talk about us." Paul got nervous saying that.

"Paul, you made some really beautiful promises to me. Can we talk about them again?"

"Yes. Are you bothered about any of them?"

"No—not at all but I want to talk them all out. I want to tell you the truth and what I would expect from you. I don't want you to say down the line—we never discussed things."

"Maggie—are you worried?"

"Yes." And now she has her head down and couldn't look at him. "Ok. Let's talk about them all." As he tightens his grip on her—making her feel more comfortable with what she wants to tell him.

She nods her head and starts.

"You said you will never let me down. I will never let you down either. I will help you however I can. We will talk out all issues that come up!

"Agreed?"

"Agreed!" he says smiling at her.

"You said you will always be there for me. I will always be there for you too. Whatever you need from me. I will try and keep you as calm as I can. But I will need support from you too!"

"Agreed?"

"Agreed!"

"You will take our marriage seriously. You really have to promise me this one Paul. Say it out loud, so I could see if you mean it!"

Squeezing her he says "I am promising you right now—I will take our marriage very seriously. Always Mags . . . always!"

"I think what you're really asking, is if I would cheat on you because of my past. I'm telling you I will never do that. I will promise myself to you and only you!"

She smiles widely at him once he reassures her about that promise. "You said you will respect me and take care of me the best that you could."

She just sighs . . . "I will be the one working and making money. I don't want you to take me for granted. You will be going to school and playing ball. I want to keep your life stress free so you could do this and I want you to respect me for it—not be beholding to me for doing it. There is a difference."

"I do know there is a difference Mags. I understand everything I am asking you to do and I do and will appreciate what you have to do for me. I will take care of you Mags. I promise you!"

"Thank you Maggie for being so straight with me. Right now looking at all I've done with my life the past 6 months—I feel I really do not deserve you. Maybe what I'm asking from you is too much!"

"I just want to talk things out first, so we know what we are getting into. I know I love you Paul with everything in me and I know you feel the same. I know we can work everything else out." He smiles when she makes that statement.

CHAPTER 15

Telling everyone

Paul immediately called Nicky who was out, leaving him and Maggie to sort things out. "I never officially asked you but, will you be my best man? You are my brother and I need you Nicky."

"Yes, of course I will. Thank you for asking. I would be honored."

"Maggie is asking her 2 best friends Molly and Judy if they will be her bridesmaids. We can't afford a big wedding so there will only be a few people at it. We want to keep it small."

"Sounds good to me Paul. Whatever you two decide, I know will turn out great."

Maggie called Sarah first to tell her about Paul proposing. Sarah was so happy for her and not surprised. She knew those two belonged together and supported them. She also knew they were so young but did see how much they needed each other. The wheels started turning the minute she told her and Sarah was already thinking about holding a shower at the shop. She would call Lois about it once they set a date.

"When are you thinking of getting Married? She asked Maggie. "In the next 2 weeks. Paul is going to ask Fr. Neilson his spiritual advisor at the U if he would marry us. I love the chapel on campus and would like to get married there. We are calling his parents as soon as I hang up with you."

"Ok, just let me know if you decide anything else. Did you think about how you were going to break the news to your father yet?"

"Yes, I am going to meet with my brothers first and tell them. Then I will tell my dad with them there."

"You know what he will do right? I'm not trying to upset you Maggie. I just want you to be prepared. That might be the last time you speak to your brothers. You should expect the worst because it truly will be."

"I know Sarah but there is always hope. I know what I'm up against and I'm expecting the worst. That is why I will speak to my brothers alone. We will come up with something. Whatever happens—happens. I can't be without Paul. He is my life now. My future is with him. I've made my decision and will not go back on it no matter what my father says or does to me. I know he will want to make my life miserable."

"Well Maggie, I will be here for whatever you need. I love you and will help you however I can."

"Sarah, I love you too and thank you so much for all your support. You know I will need you until the end of time. You're the only mother I have now. I hope you know I feel that way towards you."

Sarah cried when Maggie told her that. "I do know Maggie. Call me if you need me and call me immediately once you tell your dad."

Paul called his parents next and it seems they were waiting for the call. "Mom/Dad, I asked Maggie to marry me and she said yes. I want you to know how happy I am too and so is Maggie. We don't want to wait and we are going to ask how soon Fr Neilson can marry us. Maggie has Tuesdays off so we would like to get married on a Monday."

Lois was crying and Mike was happy too for them. "Let us know when, so we could make plans son. We will come in for as long as you need us to."

"Thanks Dad. I appreciate it and will let you know. Maggie is meeting with her brothers to tell them first and then will go over to tell her father. She won't let me come with her. She said that part was nonnegotiable. I feel badly letting her do this alone but her two brothers will be there once she tells him."

Maggie wants to talk to them so Paul hands her the phone. "Mom, once we set the date will you come in to help me find a dress? I could use your help and advice." Again Lois was so happy and cried. "Yes, I would be honored to help you find your wedding dress. Thank you for including me. I love you already Maggie. Just seeing how happy my son is because of you, makes me love you so much." Thank you for saying that. It means the world to me." Maggie replied.

"Good bye son. Call us when you have more information and good luck to Maggie telling her family."

They hang up and Maggie told Paul. I don't want to prolong this. I want to go tell them now. I will call Frank and Joseph and ask them to meet me at Franks so I could talk to them, then go over to my dad's and tell him. I will have them meet me there too—I know he will forbid them to speak to me but we will work out something. I know we will." Paul nods his head and walks over to Maggie with his arms out and gave her the biggest hug. "I know how hard this is going to be and wish you would reconsider and let me come with you."

"There is no way on this earth you could ever come with me. It would be too dangerous for you. Trust me. I will call you as soon as I tell him and let you know how it goes."

"I don't like this Maggie. I don't like this at all. I won't be able to stop worrying until you call me."

"No steps backwards. Promise me! No steps backwards Paul. Just wait for my call. I will be fine."

"Right Mags. No steps backwards. I don't like this—but will promise you—no steps backwards."

"It seems you have a lot to do. Find a priest to marry us and see if the chapel is available.

Maggie once again walked into Paul's arms so happy that he was already making plans. She knew he loved her and wanted to marry her but now she knew he wanted to be married to her yesterday and it pleased her.

"Kiss me. I have to go and this is going to go from being the best night of my life to the worst night of my life."

CHAPTER 16

Frank and Joseph

Frank and Joseph paced back and forth waiting for Maggie to come over. They couldn't imagine what she wanted to tell them.

"Do you think she is going to finally move out on her own?"

"Frank, I don't know what to think and here she is now, so the agony over what she wants to talk to us about will be over."

Maggie immediately went to them both and hugged them and wouldn't let them go making them even more nervous than they already were.

"Maggie, we are going crazy wondering what you want to talk to us about. Is everything alright?" Joseph asked not wanting to wait.

"I came to tell you how happy I am. I met someone and he asked me to marry him and I accepted."

Both of her brothers' faces just dropped. "What do you mean? You never said a word to us. How long have you been dating him?"

"Not long but we both can't breathe without each other. His parents love me and I love them. Sarah even approves. So does Molly and Judy. Please believe me. We love each other and don't want to wait. We are going to pick out a date as soon as we can get the Chapel on the U campus and find a priest to marry us. You will be invited to the wedding once we have the date."

Now Frank chimed in. "Maggie, we are so happy for you but you know dad is not going to let you get married. He will never let you leave the house once you tell him and the worst will be he will never let us speak to you again. What can we do about that? We work for him and he will throw us out if we try to keep in touch with you."

"Frank, I know you both are happy for me and this is what I am doing. I know he won't allow you to speak to me again but I have a way for us to keep in contact. I know you can't see me but we could always talk."

"How do you think that is going to happen? Joseph asked.

"I am going to give you Paul's cell # and when it comes in—save it as Mark. That way when I call you—Mark will come up as the caller. I will be able to speak to you and I will never call you during the day. I will only call at night when you two are home or not with dad."

Joseph and Frank just looked at each other. It sounded like a good plan. It might actually work.

Frank continued, "That might work Maggie but you have to only call us at night and we will only call you at night. We have to agree on that."

Joseph and Maggie looked at Frank and both nodded their heads.

They had a plan that might actually work.

"Do you think you will be able to stay at home with dad wanting to kill you?"

"I have been handling him for my whole life. I can do it and I know it will be so difficult but it is something I want to do. I want to start living my life the way I want it. You know the pressure we all are under just being his kids. I don't know why he is like the way he is, but dodging his bullets are not my way of life anymore. I am looking forward to living a peaceful life with my husband."

"Well, who is he? Do we know him?" Frank couldn't wait to ask. "You never met him. His name is Paul Tanner."

"Paul Tanner from the U's basketball team?" Joseph asked.

"Yes, he is only a sophomore but we don't want to wait. He has a full scholarship and it will cover an apartment for us. His advisor is looking for one for us now."

"Maggie, you will be starting off in a hole! He can't even support you. How are you going to live? Have you thought this through?"

"Yes, we discussed it in length and talked about our finances and what we would need to start up a household. We are fully aware of what is needed. Please, believe me. We both know what we are getting into. I love him and he loves me. I know what I will be up against. I will be the breadwinner and he will go to school and play ball. Please trust me. Trust us. We know and understand."

They did believe her and trust her. She was smart and level headed and if she thought she knew what she was doing—then they knew she did. I am going home now. Meet me there. Give me a 10 minute start.

Both brothers nodded and off she went.

Get Ready

Maggie arrived home and her dad is in the kitchen cleaning up from making himself something to eat. Maggie had stopped cooking for him since he hurt her so badly at the wedding.

Joseph and Frank arrive and Frank Sr knew something was going on. "What's going on? Are you here to stick up for your sister?"

"No dad!" Maggie barked at him. "I asked them to come here because I have something to tell you all."

She took a deep breath and continued "I met someone and we are getting married. I wanted to tell you all at once."

Maggie's father's face was beet red and he looked like he was ready to explode and he did.

"No, you are not! All because of what I said at the wedding and now you are going to test me? I told you, you are never getting married. End of story and now you are never going to work—ever again."

"I finally don't care what you say or want dad. I am getting married and I still have a job. End of *my* story, so get over it. What you chose to do to me next will be on you. I'm ready!"

"Really? You're ready? Well then, let's not prolong this any longer;" as he looks at Frank and Joseph, "you do not have a sister any more. You will never talk to her again or you will be out of a job." He just about stamps his feet when walking to the garage to leave and slammed the door so hard they thought it would come off the hinges.

Even though Maggie was prepared, it still shocked her and she turned all white. Joseph goes right to her and hugs her. Then he handed her an envelope. "We have a plan. Let's stick to it. It will work, I know it. I love you and always will." Then he turned to leave.

Frank went to her next. "I wish you all the happiness in the world. We will keep in touch. I have the # and will call every chance I get. I love you Maggie." Then he hands her an envelope too. She took both and went to her room and locked the door. She didn't want to speak to her father and certainly didn't want him coming into her room to torture her some more.

She calls Paul who is pacing, waiting and he answers on the first ring. "Maggie, please tell me if you are alright? I have been going crazy here just waiting."

Maggie started crying once she heard his voice. "Please Maggie, I will come get you."

"No, don't come here. I'm fine and he did what we thought. He forbids my brothers to speak to me. But I told them our plan and they put your # in their phones and changed the name to Mark. So no one but us will know it's me calling or them calling you."

"Great Maggie! I'm glad they liked that plan, so you really are not losing them. You will just not be able to see them and maybe after a while your father will give in. I know you are shaking your head no right now, but let's just wait. You never know what could happen."

"Ok, you're right. It was a miracle we found each other and maybe there are some more out there with our names on them."

"That's my girl Mags. Always think positively."

"I have some news that will make you feel better."

"Good news is what I need right now. What kind of news?"

"Jimmy my advisor found us an apartment to look at tomorrow. Can you be there at 12:30? It's right up from the gym in that big green house with the big deck. 901 Quincy."

"Paul, I know that house and always loved it. I didn't know it was apartments for students."

"Yes, on the second floor and that big deck will be ours Mags. I can't wait to see it now and I can't wait to see you. I am waiting for Fr Neilson to call me back so I can ask him to marry us too. I am doing everything you asked me to and want to be married to you tomorrow. Would that be too soon for you?" Now he is laughing and Maggie is smiling away. "Never Paul. Tomorrow would never be soon enough."

"My brothers gave me 2 envelops before they left. I'm going to open them now. I'll put you on speaker."

"OK Mags, go ahead."

She opens the first from Frank and then decides to pick up the phone. "OMG Paul! There is money in this envelope. Let me count it. Holy cow, $2500! There is a note too. 'Maggie, I am so happy for you and Paul. I don't want you to start out in the hole so please accept this as a wedding gift. I love you Maggie'."

Maggie is stunned. "Maggie, that was so nice of him to do that. I hope I get to meet him one day." That made Maggie cry when Paul told her that. She wished he could meet him now, not someday.

"OK, here goes with the second one from Joseph. Paul—$2500 again! His note says 'I love you Maggie and wish you and Paul a very happy life." Now he hears her crying.

"Maggie do you want to call off the wedding? I can't bear to see you this upset over me."

"No, I will never call it off and can't wait to marry you Paul." That made him so happy.

"There is that peaceful feeling I get when I'm near you or just talking to you. If you were here, I wouldn't let you out of my bed."

"Soon you won't have to and it will be *our* bed Paul. It can't come soon enough. I love you."

"I love you too Mags. Get some rest and I will call you first thing in the morning. Call me if you need me tonight, if your dad tries to bother you."

"Ok, I will. Goodnight Paul."

CHAPTER 18

Shady Business

Lois had been in contact with Paul's advisor Jimmy about an apartment for her son and new daughter. She told him whatever he finds—she and Maggie's mom would like to view it first—before Paul and Maggie. Jimmy was confused but Lois insisted, so, she was driving in first thing in the morning and planned to call Sarah to see if she wanted to meet them at the apartment. She also told Jimmy, Maggie and Paul could never know. He agreed to that too.

"Sarah, this is Lois." Sarah wasn't surprised to hear from her and knew they would be great friends somehow. They both liked each other and had the same common denominator. Their son and daughter.

Lois explained to Sarah what she did and Sarah was pleased. "I would love to meet you there. I will see you at 10. I know exactly where that house is too."

Off she headed to meet Jimmy, Lois and the landlord. Once she walked in that apartment she was shocked and saw the same look on Lois' face. It was filthy.

The landlord spoke first, "you can go take a look around and see if you like it."

Lois was afraid to even step on the rugs, they were so dirty and ratty looking.

They saw the bathroom in the hall and thought it only needed to be cleaned from head to toe and it would be acceptable. They walked in the bedroom and saw the room was large and had a lot of closet space. Then they looked at the mattress and it was a mess. There were so many stains on it; there was no way they were letting their kids sleep on that. Next was a big bathroom with double sinks and a huge shower. Again, it would be acceptable if it were scrubbed down from top to bottom. They walked back out to the kitchen and there was a dining area right next to the kitchen with a French door leading right out to a beautiful deck. The kitchen was in good shape and they both thought the previous renters probably didn't cook much because the dining area was in good shape too.

"Well, what do you think? It comes fully furnished." Lois spoke first. "Sir, do you have children?"

It threw the landlord when she asked that. "Yes, a son and daughter."

"Would you let you son or daughter and their wife or husband walk on these rugs?" Lois was not smiling when she asked him that. Her face was red and steam was coming out of her ears. The landlord could see it. He stuttered and said "Um, well . . . I guess I could have them steamed cleaned." But by the look on Lois and Sarah's faces he continued. "Um . . . I guess I could replace them." He whispered. He really didn't want to, but they weren't done with him yet.

Sarah took right over. "Here is what needs to be done and it needs to be done yesterday. You will replace the rugs, paint the walls and replace the mattress. There is no way you would ever let any of your children sleep on that mattress or walk on these rugs. When you get done with that, and remember—it has to be done yesterday . . . you will hire a professional service to come and clean bathrooms, the kitchen and dining area. Are we clear now on what needs to be done here?"

Jimmy and the landlord just looked at them. Then they addressed Jimmy. Lois said, "Jimmy, how much can you spend for Paul with his scholarship on rent. Write it down if you don't want this landlord to know." Jimmy wrote down $700 a month—heat included.

She takes the note and shows Sarah. "OK Jimmy, you will pay this man $700 a month for the length of Paul's tenure here at the U and that will include heat."

The landlord could not believe they were going to pay that much because the students before them only paid $450. Then he felt better about changing the rugs and painting and even replacing the mattress. "I think that should cover everything. Sarah could you think of anything else?"

"I saw a washer and dryer hook up and we both know where to go for that." Smiling at her.

"OK, it's almost 11 and we should go. We don't want Paul or Maggie to see us. Are we all in agreement on what needs to happen and when?"

The landlord and Jimmy both replied together and just said "Yesterday."

Lois and Sarah turned and left and they both started laughing as they walked to their cars. "Lois, do you think you have time to go pick out a washer and dryer?" She just smiled and said "I can't wait. Let's go pay him a visit. We are on a roll."

Off they went and were determined to confront Maggie's father and were not going to be bullied by him.

They got to the store and Lois said, "I'm not even nervous. I think two are better than one and that is why. We did good back there, so let's hope it continues."

They walked in and Maggie's father was doing something on the showroom floor. He didn't know either one. They told him they needed a washer and dryer for their son and daughter getting married and gave him the dimensions. He showed them two and Lois asked, "Which ones would you choose if it were for your daughter or son?"

He pointed to the two and Sarah said "Ok, we will take those. Here is where you can deliver them and they have to be delivered tomorrow any time during the day. They are changing the rugs and painting tomorrow."

"OK, no problem. How did you want to be pay for this?" They both just looked at him as Lois spoke, "Sir, *you* will be paying for them! They are for your daughter and my son. Don't even think of arguing with me. Just deliver them!" Frank Sr's face just dropped. He was pissed but before he could even say a word, they turned around and left. They left him with his mouth hanging open. Frank thought he was going to drop right then. They tricked him and he didn't see it coming. It really upset him.

All day after they left, Frank Sr was not himself. He was shook and even went home early. While he was sleeping that night he had a dream. He called out "Maggie, is that you?"

"No my darling husband. It's me, your loving wife. How did I love you for so many years? How come some of me, didn't rub off on you? Why do you continue to torture your sons and our daughter? Do you have a reason for me so I can finally rest my love?" Frank tossed and turned but kept dreaming. "Well? Why did you do that to her? She has taken care of you and our home all of this while. She deserves to have her own life with her own children. Why Frank? Tell me why?"

Frank mumbled in his sleep, "because she looks just like you and I can't let her go. You left me and now, so has she. I can't, I can't!"

"I had no choice, I had to go and you forgot what I told you that last night we were together. I told you I would do it all again Frank, if it meant marrying you. I still mean it. Maggie is not my replacement. She is your daughter. Part of you. Do the right thing! Release her and you will feel peace too. Do it for me Frank, so I may rest in peace too!" Just then Frank woke up in a cold sweat and he was gasping for air. Once he got to work, both sons saw there was something wrong with him. He loaded up a washer and dryer and headed out first thing. He stopped and got a card too and was all set. He didn't want to be haunted by his wife again. He heard her speaking to him and she still looked so beautiful. She is the only one that was ever able to reason with him. But seeing her in his dream also made him long for her even more and he wept openly on his way to his daughter's apartment.

As fast as his heart melted seeing his wife again, is how fast it turned back to stone once he delivered them and hooked them up. He placed the card inside the dryer, walked around the apartment to see where she would be living and off he went.

CHAPTER 19

Looking at the Apartment

Paul and Maggie headed out on her lunch hour to go look at the apartment and both were so excited about it.

The owner who met them there told them the next day the whole place would be painted and the carpets replaced. The couple who rented before them made a mess out of the rugs and they were destroyed. He asked what color they would want on the walls and showed them the rug he was replacing the old one with. It would go in the living room— down the hall and in the bedroom. They actually loved it too.

"Maggie—what color do you want for the walls?" Paul asked her. The owner stepped right in and said "I won't paint it any wild color. I would like to keep it in neutral colors."

Maggie nodded her head and agreed. "I don't like dark colors so it would be great if you could paint the walls in different shades of beige. Nothing dark please if you wouldn't mind. I don't need to see the colors. Whatever you choose will be fine with us." Looking at Paul for approval. "That sounds good to me too."

The owner was thrilled with the both of them. They seemed grateful for the rugs being changed and walls painted. He also knew who Paul was, but also because he had secretly just met both mothers.

"I am getting the bathrooms, kitchen and dining area professionally cleaned for you too. As you can see the rooms are big and it should be enough if you are having a family." He didn't want to come right out and ask if she was pregnant.

They both just laughed and looked at each other. Maggie took that one "Sir, we are in no position to afford a family at this time but thank you for your concern about us." Paul thought she did a good job responding to that and knew everyone would think the same thing, getting married so young.

So they happily told the owner and Jimmy they would like to take the apartment. They both could see how happy they were. "Can I walk around some more? I want to see what I would need to get in order to move in."

"No, go right ahead. Take the keys—it's yours now."

Paul shook the man's hand and so did Maggie and thanked him quit a few times. Then he turned to Jimmy who told Paul he was so happy they liked this place. He felt it was more of a home for a married couple than a dorm apartment even though they were nice. The fact that he found it so close to the gym for him was like icing on the cake. Paul signed the papers for the lease and his advisor told him he would send their rent payment monthly to the owner, not to worry about it. He said he had to go and left them both there, to go over what they would need.

Still Seething

Frank Sr was still seething about the washer and dryer. Not as much about giving them to Maggie as the way he was tricked into it. The more he thought about it, the more his temper flared up. Finally, he couldn't take it anymore and was ready to explode, so he went into Maggie's room on Friday when she went to work and trashed it. He opened the window in her bedroom and threw out all of her clothes. He went through every closet and every drawer and threw everything in the driveway. His neighbors saw what he was doing and just barricaded themselves in their houses. They knew all about Frank and knew he was mad at his daughter for something, but they didn't know what. They all felt so sorry for her.

When Maggie got home from work that night, she found all of her things lying in the driveway and was devastated. She called Molly, Judy and Paul who was with his parents who came in to help with the wedding and shower and Nicky. They rushed right over to get her out of there thinking her father would physically harm her. Paul was a mess and thought—*look what I did to her. Because of me she is in hell with her father.*

Lois immediately went to her and held her in her arms trying to calm her down. "Maggie, there is something wrong with him. Everyone knows it. I know you feel badly about everything, but it's time you started thinking of yourself. What do you want to do? Do you want to marry my son? Do you want your own life? Or, do you want to live with that monster for the rest of your life? I know he is your father, but does he act like it? Does he keep you from harm? Does he hug or kiss you. Does he tell you he loves you? Does he tell you how beautiful you really are? Because there is a guy standing right over there—stressed out to the max—thinking *he* did all of this to you. We both know the answer to that. Don't we?"

Maggie turned her head and looked for Paul. His mother was right. He was stressed to the max and she could see it on his face and the way he was pacing and running his hands through his hair almost ripping it out. She nodded to Lois, turned and ran to Paul who opened his arms for her. She jumped right into them and he held her tightly. "I'm so so sorry. I did this to you. I don't know if I can bear seeing you so upset over me." She gripped him even tighter once he admitted that to her and shook her head. "Don't even think that. I came alive the moment I met you and will never go back to the way it was before. As long as you love me Paul, I will be forever grateful to you for saving me and giving me a life. I can't imagine anyone loving you the way I do. Please tell me you feel the same, or all of this won't be worth it."

Paul pulls away from Maggie so he could look right at her to tell her "it is worth it already. All you have done for me has already changed my life around for the better. I never imagined loving someone the way I love you Maggie. I can't be without you for even a few hours. I know that much. Please believe me Mags. I love you more and more every day and will make up for any heartbreak I may have caused you. Now, let's get you out of here before something else happens." Paul takes her hand and they get in her car after they told everyone "see you at our apartment." Everyone nodded and said ok. Nicky went with Molly and Judy and Mike and Lois even had some of her things in *their* car as they all headed to Paul and Maggie's new home.

They unloaded the cars and put everything in the bedroom where Maggie made piles of things that could be hung up and things that had to be washed. She was still upset and Paul wrapped her in his arms trying to calm her down when she just started crying and crying. "Why can't he just love me the way father's do? I just don't understand. I have been waiting my whole life for him to just hug me once and tell me he loves me. I know it will never happen now and I'm going to accept it and know—I don't have a father. That is the way I will look at it from this moment on."

Mike told everyone "Ok, enough drama for tonight. Let's go to Arcaro and Genell's for dinner. We have many plans to make, so we might as well do it during dinner."

Nicky chimed right in and told everyone "you know, many big deals are made over dinner, so let's go." Everyone laughed at Nicky and leave it up to him to lighten the mood right then. Even Paul and Maggie laughed at him, relieving them from the stress of the night.

CHAPTER 21

Planning the Wedding

Over dinner they talked about the wedding. Maggie and Paul told them how much her brothers gave them and then asked Paul to go to the bank to make a deposit and put his name on her checking account. It turned out that Paul was not a big spender and had close to

$5000 in his account too. His parents deposited $500 a month in that account for his expenses but he knew they couldn't afford more than that and always was careful with his money. "I will transfer that balance over to our checkbook."

"Ok, great, now we can pay for our wedding. Mom, are you still going to arrange the dinner for us?"

"Yes, of course. Sarah and I already spoke about it and are meeting with Angelo and Mark tomorrow here at 10. We will take care of everything."

"Thank you and I will thank Sarah too. But we are paying for it. Just so you know. We have about 35 people counting Paul's team and some coaches. Coach B and his wife can't make it. They are away for the week."

"Maggie stop stressing. We will take care of everything."

"Rings!" Paul blurted out. "We didn't get rings!"

Just then Lois pulled out a beautiful blue velvet pouch from her purse handing it to Paul. "I don't know if you will like these or not but they are your Tanner grandparents wedding rings. If you like them—you could use them. We won't be offended if you want your own, but take a look at them. They are quite beautiful."

Maggie and Paul were shocked and so touched. Paul loved his grandparents and couldn't believe he would be able to honor and remember them in this way.

Maggie opened the pouch and gasped! The bands were gorgeous! They were platinum and hers had a row of tiny diamonds going down the center around the whole band. Around the edges there was an etching that complemented the style of the band. Paul's would have the etching but no diamonds but the band was beautiful and he loved it. Lois could see by the look on their faces they loved them. Maggie looked at Paul and whispered "It would be an honor to wear your grandmother's wedding band. I love it Paul. Are you Ok with it?" Paul nodded he agreed and both looked at Lois and Mike and told them they loved them and wanted to wear them, making them so happy.

Nicky chimed right in and said—"Give me those. I'm the best man and only one here that won't lose them." Everyone knew Nicky was so happy he was his brothers' best man as he took the rings right off of Paul laughing.

Later when everyone was about to leave, Mike and Lois pulled Maggie and Paul aside to tell them something. "We wanted to tell you that we will still deposit the $500 a month into your now joint checking account for as long as Paul is in school. We know Maggie, it will be hard on you being the only one working while Paul is in school and we want to help. We are not asking for your permission to do that. We are telling you we are." Maggie and Paul's faces dropped and so did their heads. Then they went to both parents and hugged them—thanking them for being so generous to them. They didn't know how they ever got so lucky and at that moment Paul was so happy he pulled his life together for his parents, Maggie and himself and thought—*I would have missed so much if I didn't straighten out.*

CHAPTER 22

Our Home

Maggie would be homeless if they didn't already have their apartment ready for them to move in so quickly. Paul was staying with her so she wouldn't have to be alone that first night since her father threw her out.

When they got back home—they walked around to see all the landlord had done to it. Yes, they were in it earlier but they were so shook—they hardly noticed anything.

"I love these rugs—it makes the place look like brand new."

"I love them too Paul and I love the colors they choose for the walls. It would be colors I would have chosen if it were my home."

"Maggie, it *is* our home."

She just smiled and nodded "right, it *is* our home. We just said *our* Paul." Now tears are rolling down her cheeks.

He goes to her but she just said "I'm so happy right now. I miss my mother so much and you just gave me one, not to mention a dad. They are both so nice. I love them already."

Paul is smiling so widely and so happy also.

"I can't wait to get this over with Maggie. I want to be married now, so we can start our lives." He didn't know how else to tell her he wanted to be married and settled so he just blurted that out. He knew it would only be two more days until that would happen but he was being impatient. He just wanted to start a new chapter in his life. A positive one!

She takes his hand "let's go see what else was done for us."

They walk around and saw the landlord had a new mattress on the bed frame because it still had the wrapping on it. They laid down on it and saw it was nice and firm and turned to look at each other and smiled.

Walking to the end of the hall where there was a washer and dryer hook up they saw a brand new washer and dryer. They hadn't noticed them before.

"OMG . . . how did we get these? Do you think the landlord had them installed?" Shocked while opening and closing the doors to them.

"Maggie, here is an envelope in this one."

"Who did this for us?" So surprised as she opened the envelope and it was signed "We will always love you Maggie." She dropped the card and started weeping in buckets.

Paul picked up the card and thought it was from her brothers Joseph and Frank. How they slipped by their dad delivering them—she didn't know.

"I feel so much better now Paul. I don't know why. Maybe because I know they will keep watching me from afar. It doesn't feel like I lost my two brothers now and it makes me so happy."

Paul puts his arms around her and he too feels she just got her brothers back and was so happy about that. "I think you are right. I think they did this to let you know they will always be watching you. I am so happy now for you Mags and we can still communicate with them. We have a plan and I know it will work."

She tightens her grip around his embrace and just said "Let's see if we could find a blanket. I imagine tomorrow at the shower I will be getting sheets and a comforter for the bed. I will make it then. We can take the couch tonight."

She found a blanket and Paul positioned himself and she got comfortable lying in between his legs where she rested her head on his chest. She covered them and both took a deep sigh.

"I'm so tired from all the drama today" she told him.

He leans down and kisses her head while rubbing her back to sooth her and she goes right out like a light.

Paul didn't fall right to sleep. He loved how comfortable she felt in his arms. He kept looking down at her, finding it hard to believe all that happened in his life. He found it hard to believe he was so happy. Once he did realize it—he smiled to himself, closed his eyes and fell asleep.

CHAPTER 23

The Dress

Maggie, Lois and Sarah headed out to find her a wedding dress that Saturday afternoon. The bridal salon was right around the corner from her shop and Sarah called in advance to make an appointment for Maggie to find her gown. Molly and Judy were there and picked out something they wanted to wear. They settled on navy gowns and Maggie was going to order yellow roses with navy and yellow streamers for them to carry. They were all set.

Maggie tried on a few gowns but none were hitting her until she saw an all lace off the shoulder dress. It was exquisite. She had to try it on. Sarah and Lois were a little disappointed she did not want a gown but they saw her face light up when she saw it. She didn't have that reaction when she saw the other gowns she tried on, so they encouraged her to try it on. When she came out in it she was crying and they all knew, that was the dress for her. It fit her to a T and hugged her body like it was made for her. They all gasped when she came out in it. She pulled her hair up in a loose bun and it looked beautiful. Sarah spoke first wiping the tears from her eyes telling her "Maggie we all see this is the one for you. You didn't have that reaction with any other gown you tried on and it fits so well like it was supposed to be yours."

Just then the owner comes over and says "I have an idea for this dress. I'll be right back." She comes out with a long chiffon skirt with a wide satin waistband that tied into the most beautiful bow in the back falling to the ground and along the train. She wrapped it around Maggie and tied the bow and then everyone including Maggie couldn't stop the tears from falling. Maggie was smiling and her face was all red as she turned to face everyone to see and by the reaction she saw on all of them she excitedly told them "This is it. It's perfect. I could take the skirt off for dinner but wear it for the ceremony at the chapel." They all agreed happily.

Sarah went and got her simple drop pearl earrings to wear and she found shoes at the salon also, so she was all set. She got a good price for everything because she bought the sample. While she was changing, Sarah called Lois over to show her something. "Paul should buy her this as a wedding gift. Maggie will love it and she will have it forever and remember he gave it to her every time she wears it."

"Good idea Sarah. I will send him over to look at it before the shower. He will be happy too!"

CHAPTER 24

Maggie's Bouquet

Before the shower Mike and Paul went to the florist to pick out a wedding bouquet for Maggie. Mike picked out Lois' when they got married and told Paul it was customary for the groom to buy his bride her bouquet. Paul was shocked he knew that. Off they went to Mary's Flower Shop down town. Mary the owner greeted them and they introduced themselves. "You aren't Paul Tanner from the U's basketball team are you?" Paul smiled and said "yes that's me" and held his hand out to shake hers. "I hear everything here and didn't hear you were getting married."

"Yes in two days. I'm sorry we are so late ordering this. We wanted to get married yesterday but Monday is the best we can do." He saw Mary looking at him and continued "No, we are not pregnant! Everyone wants to know, but we just want to be married and now." Mary started laughing and said "Well in my defense, that is what everyone would think."

"I know but if you see my soon to be wife, you will see there is no way she is pregnant!"

"OK then, let's get down to business. Do you know what you want to order?"

"No, not really. Can you help us out?"

"Absolutely, tell me about your fiancé? Is she tall like you?"

"No, she is short, as in petite."

"Ok, is she classy and elegant or does she play ball like yourself? Or is she plain and doesn't like fancy?"

"She is elegant. That is what I think of, every time I see her. She is so natural and sweet and wears her heart out on her sleeve. She is kind and gentle."

"Great! That is exactly what I needed to know."

"One more thing. I bought her a pearl double strand bracelet for a wedding gift. I think she will love it."

"Now you got me Paul! I know exactly what to do. Come in the back and I will show you." They both followed Mary in the back and saw buckets and buckets of flowers—all colors, shapes and sizes but Mary went in a cooler and came out with the most beautiful small little flowers, white with only about 4 or 5 petals on each one. Then she went to get some greens and something else he couldn't make out.

She calls them over to her work table. "Smell these" she said to Paul and held them up to his nose. They were the sweetest flower he had ever smelled. "Here is my thought. I am going to make a loose bouquet with these little flowers. In between I will use these greens for a filler and in between that I will use these pearls to match her jewelry that day. What do you think? It will be exquisite."

Paul was thrilled and said to Mary, "That is exactly what I think every time I look at her. That's the word I couldn't think of. I think she is exquisite. Thank you so much Mary. I appreciate all you are doing for us." Mary was also doing the flower arrangements for the tables at the reception and now had an idea about those too. Mike was beaming at Paul just then and so happy for him.

CHAPTER 25

Shower Time

At the shower Saturday night, Maggie got so many gifts from so few people. She was overwhelmed with everyone's generosity and so was Paul. They let him, Nicky and Mike stay and they were happy because all of the food looked so good and they wanted to eat. Of course all of the ladies from the shop dotted over them and they loved it. Halfway through opening the gifts—she got Paul to come over and help her. Every time he opened one up, his face would light up, like he just was given a new basketball. Nicky laughed at him all night. Then it came down to a very special gift. Antoinette, who was their friend Bobby from the team's girlfriend, was invited to the shower at the request of Paul. Bobby was a close friend to Nicky and Paul and he asked if she would invite Antoinette to the shower. Maggie was thrilled because she knew her from the games and Commons parties. She even sat with Maggie at most games.

"This is a special gift for *you* Paul!" She was all smiles and when Paul looked at Nicky he saw the biggest grin on his face too.

Paul's face got red immediately as he opened the card. All it said was "Congratulations on your wedding, from your boys! We hope you enjoy this!" Paul was afraid to open the gift and looked at Maggie who was shaking her head and saying "I have no idea what it is."

He unwrapped it and it was a box from Victoria Secrets! Maggie turned 10 shades of red and so did Paul. "Maybe you shouldn't open it here" Maggie told him and everyone was yelling—no way—open that now—we want to see. So, he was forced to open it. He pulls back the paper and sees a beautiful white nightgown for his soon to be bride. He put the lid on it immediately and said "Ok, thank you, next gift" and everyone howled it was so funny. The color of his face was even funnier. Finally Sarah said "We are not moving an inch until you show us what is in the box." He looks over at Maggie who was hiding her face behind some tissue paper being so embarrassed. Then he says "Sorry Mags. I have to show them." She nodded her head.

Again he opens the box and pulls out a beautiful floor length sheer nightgown with an umpire waistline trimmed in lace. The small straps were also made of lace and it was both beautiful and sexy. Everyone clapped as Nicky and Antoinette both snapped many pictures. Before she left for the shower, Bobby told her, "make sure you get a picture of him opening the gift. We all can't wait to see his face." Well she snapped many and even got how red his face was. Nicky said "hold it up in front of Maggie so we can see if it will fit."

"Shut up Nicky! You are never going to picture MY WIFE in it. So keep dreaming." Everyone got a big kick out of that too. Maggie was just looking at Paul as if to say "Keep it up and *you* might never get to picture your wife in that." They both just laughed and went in for a kiss. Everyone went AWWWWW . . .

They cleaned up in no time and loaded up their cars and took it all to their apartment. Everyone helped put stuff away and made the bed with her new comforter she just got and the bedroom looked so beautiful. Maggie kept staring at it. It looked like it came out of a picture. Paul came in and saw it and went right to her, "this looks great. I can tell you love it by the smile on your face." She just nods her head yes and went right to him for a hug. He wrapped his arms around her and just said, "one more night Maggie and you will be all mine. I wish it were right now, not in one more night." She tightened her grip on him once he confessed that to her.

Everyone left and Maggie panicked. "You are not leaving too are you?"

He saw she was getting upset and settled that right then, "No Maggie I will be here tonight. Tomorrow Molly and Judy will stay with you and after that, I will never leave you." She calmed right down.

"Paul, I don't want you to think I'm crazy but I don't want to sleep in our bed until Monday night. I want to wait until we are married."

"So . . . sex tonight, is off the table?" Maggie laughed at him "Tonight and tomorrow night. It will make you want me more on our wedding night."

Paul takes her hand and replied "Mags, I will always want you. No matter what night it is but I understand you want it to be special and I agree. We can wait for Monday night. Did you want to try on your new nightgown for me?" Paul was looking at Maggie and drooling. She knew he couldn't wait for her to put that on.

"Well, this might be a good time to tell you something."

"Please don't tell me you're pregnant!" he said laughing at her. "Do you know how many people asked me that because we are getting married in such a hurry?"

"As many people that asked me Paul. The surprised look on their face when I would say—no, we are not pregnant is what makes it kind of fun!"

They both smiled at each other and Paul continued. "Ok, what do you have to tell me?"

"Sit down first." and it baffled Paul. What could she have to say? "I'm a little claustrophobic and cannot wear clothes to bed. They choke me and I can't breathe."

"That is what you have to tell me? Did you think I would be upset?"

"No, but I want you to sleep naked too."

"I have no problem doing that Mags and look forward to Monday night even more now." He is laughing and smiling looking at her which makes her laugh too.

"Is there anything else?"

"Nope. That will do it. How about we take the couch again tonight.
I will get us a blanket and pillows."

CHAPTER 26

It's Here!

Paul and Maggie did not think Monday night would ever arrive. Time seemed to be going in slow motion. Paul slept in his dorm room with Nicky Sunday night. Maggie was ok with it because Molly and Judy stayed at the apartment with her. Everyone knew— no one would be getting any sleep unless they passed out from sheer exhaustion. Lois and Sarah arrived with breakfast around 9 while everyone was starting to get ready. Hair had to be done, nails painted and the pampering took hours. It made Lois laugh at the circus going on with those 3 girls.

Maggie pulled up her long brown hair into a loose bun and Lois brought some baby's breath from the florist where they put some here and there in her hair. It came out just beautiful!

They all fussed over her makeup too. They bought some water proof, smudge proof mascara from the drug store. Actually they got some for them all. They knew many tears would be shed but at least they would be happy tears. Her beautiful blue eyes shown so brightly to match the smile she couldn't get off of her face all day.

Finally, it was time to start getting dressed. Molly and Judy dressed first to be ready in time to get Maggie in her dress.

When she took it out of her closet and unzipped the garment bag everyone gasped again at how beautiful it was.

They got her in the dress and it hugged her body so tightly—there would be no reason anyone would think they were getting married because she was pregnant. She slipped on the pumps she bought from the Bridal Salon which made her legs look longer than they were because truthfully, she was so short—only about 5'. Then they put the chiffon skirt on her and Sarah tied the most beautiful bow in the back with the satin hanging to the floor. It came out perfect.

The flowers arrived and the girls carried a dozen yellow roses each with navy and yellow streamers to match their gowns.

The box with her bouquet was separate and she couldn't wait to see what Paul picked out for her.

When she opened it up, they all almost died. The bouquet was simply gorgeous. Little petite white stephanotises with pearls in between some greens for filler. Maggie tried not to cry but was losing that battle. Then Nicky knocks on the door and walked in just as they were looking at the flowers. He stops dead in the kitchen, just gawking at Maggie and the girls.

"Maggie, I cannot wait to tell Paul how beautiful you look. There aren't enough words to describe how you look."

"Thank you Nicky. What are you doing here?" smiling so much at him.

"I have a gift from Paul for you" as he hands her a beautifully wrapped box with a silver bow.

"No Nicky, I didn't get him anything. We didn't talk about it."

"Paul said you would say that and to tell you to stop. He said the only gift he wants from you is to see you walk down that aisle to him and say I DO!"

Well . . . Molly and Judy were crying and so were Lois and Sarah. "He also said I couldn't leave until you opened the gift so I could tell him if you liked it or not."

Maggie unwrapped the beautiful box and opened it to see the most beautiful double strand pearl bracelet she had ever seen. She knew she would have it forever and she would wear it forever.

Tears streamed down her face because she just couldn't control her emotions any longer. They had been building up all day with all the activities and she needed that release. No one even yelled at her to stop because she was ruining her makeup, they were all doing the same.

She walks over to Nicky and kisses him. "Can I say how good you look in your suit too?" Nicky is just smiling away at her.

"Will you take this message to Paul from me?" Nicky just nods his head.

"Tell him, I'm counting the minutes until I see him. Tell him, last night lasted forever without him being here with me. Tell him, I need him . . . as much as he needs me. And lastly, tell him how happy I am and how much I love him!"

Nicky smiled at Maggie and hugged and kissed her again. "Nicky, I have a message for you too!"

He looks at her confused as she just says "I know Paul is your brother and now I'm your sister too!" She kissed his cheek and saw how pleased he was with her comment . . . then turned to leave being so happy for them both.

CHAPTER 27

Finally

Everyone arrived at the chapel and there were people not invited to the reception that wanted to see them, so the chapel was fuller than expected. All of Paul's team mates were there in full force too!

There were hurricane lamps standing next to each pew and they were lit—adding so much romance to the ceremony.

The music started and Molly and Judy walked down the aisle together. The doors to the chapel closed and Mike said to Maggie "Are you ready to become a Tanner now?"

She just smiled and nodded her head to him and leaned up to kiss his cheek which made him so happy. She took his arm and someone in the back of the chapel fixed her train so it would flow as she walked.

The doors opened and she looked straight up the aisle and saw Fr. Neilson smiling away at her and next to him was Paul with the biggest smile on his face. As she got closer she saw tears running down his cheeks and he quickly wiped them away but everyone saw them.

When Fr. Neilson asked "who gives this woman away to marry this man" Mike proudly and loudly said "her mothers and I do," referring to Lois and Sarah which brought tears to most in the chapel and sent goose bumps up and down her arms when he said that. He handed her over to his son, who took her hand smiling, being so happy.

20 minutes later it was over and they were married.

Fr. Neilson finally said "Ladies and Gentleman—I would like to introduce you to Mr. and Mrs. Paul Tanner."

Everyone clapped and yelled and it was amazing. Something neither would forget.

They received congratulations from everyone at the chapel and even received some gifts which shocked them. They gave them to Mike to hold for them.

Off to the dinner they went and once in the car they finally had time to be alone.

"You look so beautiful. I'm so happy Maggie. I couldn't wait for tonight."

"Thank you so much for saying that. I wanted to look so special for you. How can I ever thank you for the beautiful bracelet. It matches my earrings and I will wear it always. I love it!" as she shows it to him on her wrist.

"Can I say how good you look too in your suit? You clean up nicely Tanner." It put a big smile on his face. She saw how good he really did look. The circles were gone under his eyes which were now clear beautiful blue and not blood shot any more. His hair was tamer because he got it cut for the wedding and his blond curls seemed to fall perfectly around his face. She couldn't stop looking at him and they both couldn't stop smiling.

There was more! When they got to the restaurant—Lois helped her take off her skirt and when Paul saw . . . that body . . . in that dress . . . with her legs . . . in those heels—he near passed out. Nicky came out just then and near dropped too.

"Oh . . . My . . . God . . . You are one lucky man Tanner" as he is patting him on the back smiling away at him.

Paul just smiled at Nicky and replied "Yes I am!" Then shook his head back and forth just gawking at his wife.

"Mags—I thought you looked beautiful before and now there aren't enough words. I can't believe you said you did this for me! How lucky I feel right now!"

That was the reaction she wanted to get from her husband. She wanted him to feel she was beautiful to him. She was so happy he did because she *did* do it *all* for him. She took his face in her hands and kissed him so softly as he held her around her waist and she loved feeling his hands on her body.

Maggie always wanted her wedding to be exquisite. It didn't have to be big but she wanted it to be intimate and elegant. That is just what Lois and Sarah delivered to her. When they walked into the reception they saw how busy those two were. They had white roses tipped in navy in big vases on the tables and in between the greens, dropped big pearls and crystals making the centerpieces look unique and so beautiful. There were tea lights lit on every table and everywhere for that matter and when the lights were dimmed they looked like stars. Every chair had a white cover with a beautiful big navy bow tied in the back. Navy linen napkins adorned each plate, set on white damask tablecloths. The crystal, silver and china completed the elegant look Maggie always dreamed about.

They were announced by Nicky and everyone clapped and cheered. His boys were all there in full force and one girlfriend turned to Antoinette and whispered "There is no way she is pregnant in that dress" which made Antoinette laugh. She knew they weren't pregnant but everyone was afraid to ask her.

Paul took Maggie's hand and turned her around in a dance move in front of everyone who was smiling, so happy for them.

They ate and visited each table thanking them for coming and cut the cake which was Maggie's favorite kind, white, with tons of buttercream icing. The cake top was covered in flowers from Mary's Flower Shop which mimicked her bouquet with pearls in between the little white flowers. Everything was perfect. They smiled all night and Lois and Sarah saw it and were so happy for them.

Once it was time to go, Paul swooped her up catching her off guard and ran out the door with her to the screams and whistles of all their guests. One last comment to Nicky on their way out from Paul "Don't call me Nicky, I'll call you" which made the three of them laugh and off they went.

CHAPTER 28

Honeymoon

Paul and Maggie's honeymoon consisted of one day. The Tuesday she had off of work and then Paul had classes and practice.

He didn't want to waste a minute so once they got to their apartment he picked her up and carried her over the threshold. He knew they had been there before but felt—she should get the whole deal for their first night as a married couple. She giggled and laughed all the way to their bedroom. So did he!

He releases her with the biggest kiss and she smiled at him slyly. He asked "What? Do you want to say something?"

He put her down and she started undressing him. "I just want to help you get naked for me!"

He gives her the biggest grin back while she took off his jacket and tie and unbuttoned his shirt pulling it out of his pants. "Sit down." And he obeyed . . . as she took off his shoes and socks and kissed his feet. "Don't get too used to me kissing your feet" and she laughed when she told him that. She gets up and unbuttoned his trousers and gently pulled them off. She turned around and asked for help getting out of her wedding dress. He carefully unzipped it and kissed her bare neck and shoulder sending shivers down her body as he slipped his hand around her waist inside the dress. She loved feeling his hands on her body. "Sit here and I will be right out" as she heads into the bathroom closing the door. She was so nervous and she doesn't know why because it wasn't like this their first time was having sex. She just wanted the night to be something they remembered for their whole lives. She pulled down her hair and brushed it out and got that 'special gift' his boys gave him as a shower present and pulled it over her head letting it drop to the floor. It really was beautiful and so sexy being so sheer. It left nothing to the imagination, but she knew Paul would drool.

"Maggie, I'm getting older by the minute here!" Paul anxiously told her laughing sitting on the edge of the bed.

Just then he heard "Oh no Paul!"

"What's wrong? Are you alright? "Paul, you are not going to believe this but I just got my period. We won't be able to have sex for at least 4 days!"

Paul's head dropped and thought—*well—welcome to married life.*

Maggie opened the door and he lifted his head and she was smiling at him. He knew then, she was playing with him but couldn't even get mad because she looked like an angel in her new nightgown. It came complete with thong and she pirouetted in front of him for the full affect and just then he got the biggest hard on he ever thought he had. She goes to him sitting on the edge of the bed and sees his dilemma "I think I can take care of that for you Mr. Tanner."

"Mrs. Tanner—I *know* you can!" He gently lifts the gown off of her and places 2 fingers on both sides of her thong to remove it, sliding it down her legs and giving her goose bumps. Then he picks her up and lays her down in their new bed with their new sheets and they were in heaven as he kisses her softly, then deeply, feeling her body under his hands, listening to her approving sighs every time he hit a sweet spot. He thought he was going to explode "I can't wait any longer Mags. Will you let me?" She nods and she couldn't wait either as she moved her legs to welcome him. She stroked him but he stopped her, fearing he would explode if she touched him again. He looks down and whispers "I love you Maggie" and she replied "I love you too" while looking into his beautiful blue eyes. She couldn't look away and neither could he as they both exploded at the same time losing their breath. He fell into her arms where she pulled his body down on hers. He knew she loved holding him after sex and he loved when she did. He was in heaven and knew life with Maggie would be like they *were* in heaven. He never imagined he could love someone, like he loved her.

"What are you thinking of?" She softly whispers.

"I'm thinking about how much I love you and how surprised I am about that. I never knew you could have feelings like that about one person and it is overwhelming and scary."

"Scary because it makes you afraid?"

"Yes, maybe afraid is a better word."

She nods her head "I know—it makes me afraid too."

"Are you afraid our marriage won't work out?"

"No, no, I know it will. I'm afraid because it is so good so far. Our apartment is like brand new. Everyone was so generous with all the gifts we got. I still get to speak to my brothers and can't believe how much you love me. I see it and I feel it from you. You hover over me like you are protecting me from a big monster or something." Smiling down at him still in her arms. "I could never ask for anything more. I feel I have everything I ever wanted or dreamed about."

"I know what you mean. I feel the same way. That is how I knew we were doing the right thing and making the right decision getting married. It felt right and when everything started falling into place—it was like a confirmation. This is what should happen. This is what I want and you're right—it was like dreams came true."

"I wasn't sure if guys dreamt about their future like girls do. So you had a thought about how you wanted your life to go?"

"Yes, and I am looking at her and lying in her arms. You are exactly the way I wanted my life to go. I never expected it to be so soon. I always thought I would be older. But I know one thing. If I didn't make you my wife—I would have missed out on my dream."

Maggie teared up when Paul told her that and bent down to kiss him. It didn't take long for them to get their blood boiling again and again and again. It was certainly a night they never would forget.

"In between 'sessions' with her lying in his arms he told her "I have to thank the guys for that gift. It was more than I could ever have imagined. You are so beautiful and I will always tell you."

CHAPTER 29

Back to Normal

Paul's next game was Wednesday night and they were both happy about it. They wanted to spend Tuesday together and get their routine down before she had to go to work and he had to go to practice and back to classes. They went to get groceries and invited Nicky for dinner. Paul asked and Maggie didn't have a problem with it. She put some pork chops in the oven and was going to fry some potatoes on the stove. She got a big salad ready and Maggie wasn't fond of salad unless it had every item you could think of in it. Tomatoes, strawberries, cucumbers, olives, croutons and cheese. The more the better. Then she sprinkled sunflower seeds on it and it looked complete to her. She made dressing with raspberry vinaigrette, oil, salt and pepper and some sweet basil. She was all set and so was her table with her new dishes and silverware she got for a shower gift along with new drinking glasses.

Everything looked perfect for her first dinner and everything smelled so good.

Paul is in the shower and she was waiting for Nicky when she heard a knock on the door. She thought it was Nicky and was just going to tell him to come right in and not knock. She wanted him to feel at home with them. But she was shocked when she opened the door and standing there was Paul's coach, Coach Barrows and his wife with a gift in hand. She flashed the biggest smile at them and invited them in wholeheartedly.

"I'm Maggie Tanner." She held out her hand to introduce herself to them. They shook it but Mrs. B, which is what everyone called her, gave her a warm hug. They both were anxious to meet her and see how Paul was. Coach knew his life was going down the tubes. He saw it on his face and on the court so they couldn't wait to see what was going on with him. They also wanted to see if she was pregnant and that is why they got married so quickly. Then coach was worried, now that Paul was married—how it would reflect on his relationship with Nicky. They were the top point guards in the nation and he wondered now that he was married—if he and Nicky would be at odds. He knew they were close friends off the court and needed to see for himself.

Nicky comes in next and didn't knock which made Maggie smile. It looked like she didn't need to tell him that. He was already going to make himself at home. She flashed him a big smile and went to him immediately for a hug as Nicky picked her up and said "It smells so good in here. I'm glad I saved my appetite." We have company Nicky and then he looked and saw coach and Mrs. B there. He shook hands with coach and kissed Mrs. B, "I didn't see you standing there". He was so intent on seeing Maggie and Paul. "Please go get your brother out of the shower and tell him we have guests. I have to stir something on the stove."

He smiles and goes down the hall to get him yelling—"come on you old married man. Speed it up, you have company" and they all laughed at him. Then they heard him yell, "Nicky, you are not company. You are family."

"Not me old man! You have company waiting in your living room to see you." Right then coach knew he didn't have to worry about his relationship with Paul. He saw as plain as day it was stronger than ever.

Paul dries quickly and dresses, wondering who was there and when he came out he was shocked it was coach and Mrs. B. He went to Mrs. B and kissed her and then shook coaches' hand as he told them both "Congratulations on your wedding. We're sorry we couldn't make it but wanted to come give you a gift and meet your wife." Just then Mrs. B handed her a beautifully wrapped gift and she asked if she could open it now and she replied "yes, I hope you like it." It was a beautiful crystal frame and she showed it to Paul who immediately told her "we could put our wedding picture in it. We don't have any frames." Maggie was smiling to him and went immediately to Mrs. B to hug her. Just then she heard something sizzling again on the stove and they got up to leave. "No, don't leave. I made tons of food. I am not taking no for an answer. You have to stay for supper."

Coach looked at Olivia and she nodded and said "Great, now *I* don't have to cook tonight" making them all laugh. Paul offered to get everyone a drink while Maggie and Mrs. B went to the kitchen to get ready for dinner. Maggie gave her two more place settings for the table while she tossed the salad. "I thought we would start with salad and then have the main dinner. "Ok my dear, that sounds perfect,"Mrs. B told her. She calls everyone in and she sat Paul at the head of his table and Coach B at the other end. Mrs. B sat next to her and Nicky on the other side. She passed the salad to everyone and they took what they wanted. Paul was looking at the sunflower seeds and she looked at him and said "eat them, it won't kill you." He didn't say a word and did as he was told while everyone laughed at him. "I see you are already a smart man Paul and getting the husband thing down right!" Coach teased him. "Yep, do as I am told, that is what all the 'how to be a good husband' books said to do". Again Coach and Mrs. B. laughed at him and so did Nicky and Maggie.

She put the potatoes in her new corning wear dish, and brought out the pork chops, placing them on the new serving platter that matched her dishes and quickly made gravy for over the chops. She strained it and served it in a gravy bowl the set came with too. She was all set and could now sit and eat and relax. The pork chops were tender and practically fell apart and the potatoes came perfect. Everyone complimented her on the dinner and wondered why she made so much food. "I thought there would be leftovers in case Paul got hungry after practice or classes. Better to have more than not enough."

Everyone cleaned their plates and Paul and Nicky had two helpings of everything. She was so happy they liked what she made. When they were done, she got up to clear the table and Mrs. B. started getting up and she told her to just sit and relax while she looked at Paul but he was already getting up to help her. He kissed her smiling and whispered. "This was so great. I am going to be so fat if you keep cooking and feeding me like this." She smiled at him patting his cheek and lifted her head for another kiss.

"We have ice cream for dessert if that is ok with everyone." No one had an issue with it as she warmed up the hot fudge syrup for Sundays. Paul scooped the ice cream and she drizzled the hot fudge while Nicky put the whipped cream on. Coach and Olivia smiled at each other seeing the three of them in the kitchen working together and knew his point guards were going to be fine. Especially since Paul looked so good and healthy, but mostly, because he looked so happy.

They told them about all the rumors going on about them. Maggie told them she gets firsthand information about what is happening with her and Paul in the bathrooms at various places. "First I heard I was his girlfriend, then the next week, I was his sister and the week after, when Paul's parents came in to see him—they said I was pregnant and they came in so we could tell them. That sent me over the edge and I ran up to the people saying that and told them. Please spread the word. I am not pregnant and that is not why Paul's parents are in. I can't imagine what they will be saying next. Maybe stunned we are married or getting divorced already." Paul said, "No Mags, divorce is in a few weeks. Give them some time" as he laughed saying that.

Maggie showed Mrs. B around the apartment and she loved it. She loved how big it was and how it seemed like more of a home to her, not an apartment. Then they went out on the deck and saw how big it was. Paul and I are going to get a grill and a table and chair set. I think we will eat out here a lot when the weather is nice. I love it." Coach said "If you get a grill, I would chain it to the porch fence so no one steals it from you. You never know if someone would do it as a prank or just to be mean."

"Good idea Coach. I never thought of that until you just said it." Paul commented with Nicky shaking his head agreeing.

"Well, we have to go but thank you so much for the delicious meal. You are an excellent cook Maggie and now I know where to come when I want a good meal." Mrs. B said making Paul smile so happily at his wife. "Why don't you sit with me at the games? I would love to have you sit with me and will save a seat next to me."

"I would love that Mrs. B but my two friends come to all the home games with me. Would you save a few more seats for us all? Maybe some of the players' girlfriends would want to sit near us too."

"Yes, that's fine Maggie. I'll save the whole row for all of us. Sounds like a plan."

Maggie and Paul kiss Mrs. B goodbye and shake coach's hand again as did Nicky who was heading to the couch after they left.

"One more thing" Coach asked Paul before he left. "What's with those little kids making baskets during practice? What is that all about?"

"Coach, one of the fathers asked us a few games ago and now every game kids are lined up with their fathers wanting to dunk the ball. They love it and their fathers are so happy. One even said now his son will want to play basketball after he just made that basket. So maybe we could scout them for future U ball players." Paul laughed as he said that and Coach smiled. "Is it OK coach? Can we still do it if someone is waiting?"

"No problem, as long as it only takes a few minutes and you don't get any more elaborate with the play."

"Great, thanks. See you tomorrow at practice."

Coach and Olivia talked all night about the evening they just spent with Maggie, Paul and Nicky.

"Olivia, I don't think we have to worry about Paul and Nicky being at odds now that he is married. I see they are fine and closer than ever. Maggie accepted their friendship and its clear Nicky adores her too."

"I think that case is closed and I also think Maggie and Paul will be fine too. She is so good for him and he looked so great. I'm happy for the both of them. Their apartment is beautiful too. I was impressed with everything this whole night."

"I think you're right. Everyone will be just fine now and maybe better than ever. *I have a good feeling about this year Olivia. A real good feeling.*"

Paul was so happy with the way the evening turned out. He was happy coach visited him and Maggie would be sitting with Mrs. B during the games. It made him worry less for some reason. Maggie was cleaning up the kitchen and almost done because Paul helped her out while Nicky was napping on the couch. "Nicky, get off my couch!" Paul yelled to him and they both laughed. Nicky jumped up and said "I'm going to get back to the dorm. I have to study for a test tomorrow anyway." He went to Maggie and hugged her thanking her for the best meal ever. Then he hugged Paul and went on his way.

"I had no idea you could cook like that. It was the best meal I think I ever ate. I am in big trouble now. I won't able to resist your cooking and now will really be packing on the pounds."

"I'm so glad you liked it. What a surprise we had tonight. I think coach and Mrs. B had a good time. I think they probably wanted to see if I was pregnant and we answered that too." Paul nodded.

"I have some studying to do too, so will you be alright?"

"Paul, do what you have to. I'm fine. I have stuff to do here and now you will be out of the way!" She laughed and kissed him. "How can I get any studying done when all I want to do is kiss you?" She smiled and kissed him again then slapped his butt. "Get moving and leave me alone until we get to bed later." He nodded and went to get his laptop to get his work done.

The next day at classes everyone clapped when he entered the room. They saw the wedding band on his finger and all congratulated him. "Before anyone asks, no, we are not pregnant." Everyone would laugh but saw how happy he was.

Maggie opened the shop and Sarah came in right after her and they hugged immediately. She thanked her again for everything she did and they talked about the wedding and how perfect everything turned out. She told her about Coach and Mrs. B showing up at her door and how they stayed for dinner. She was beaming telling Sarah all of that. Then everyone started arriving and she got back to work and life returned to normal for her.

CHAPTER 30

First Game as Mrs. Tanner

Maggie spoke to Molly and Judy and told her where their seats were going to be. Paul still waited for her to get to the gym and little boys were still lined up with their father's beaming, waiting for Paul and Nicky to have them dunk the ball in the basket. They had the OK from coach and Bobby and Nicky played with the ball then tossed it to the little guy where Paul would let him dunk it. Every time the crowd would go wild making the boys feel like they won a championship.

She told Antoinette where she would be siting and she spread the word and before they knew it they would all sit together with Mrs. B. She even joked and said she felt like a mother hen with all her little chicks sitting around her. She was so happy about it.

Maggie worked late until 9 on Thursday's so she didn't have to get to work until noon. She loved being home with Paul whose classes always started later. She got to do stuff around the house or just rest in bed because the schedule she kept with Paul was exhausting. She even went to practices with him and soon all the girlfriends started coming and they all sat together. They were a tight bunch that year and everyone got along and everything went smoothly. Coach didn't even care they were there, they never bothered anyone and coach felt the guys were calmer; they weren't fighting with their girls because they were always at practice and not with them.

Another tradition started between Paul and Maggie at the home games. Right before a game, he would find her in the bleachers and go to her. He would take his wedding ring off and give it to her to hold where she would place it on her ring finger alongside her wedding band. Then he would take her hand and kiss it, giving her a big smile. Everyone around her would go wild whenever he did that and even Mrs. B laughed, every time. Once that started happening- it seemed the game couldn't start until he did that. Coach was even ok with it. His point guard was happy, healthy and played hard when his wife was there, so he couldn't ask for more. All the Assistant coaches, talked privately of course, about how Paul played better when she was there and they always looked to make sure she was there, sitting with Mrs. B.

After that first game she went to, being married to Paul, they both went to the party at the Commons Center with all of their friends. Again she was in the restroom when she heard 2 girls talking.

"Did you see Paul and his wife here?" A girl named Stephanie asked. "Yeah Steff, I noticed they were here with all the players and girlfriends and some of their other friends too." Lisa replied.

"I brought his jersey he left at our dorm that night he stayed with us. Remember? Then he didn't even remember us, when we went to his dorm to get him to party with us the next day. I want to see the look on her face when I give it back to her."

Stephanie flashed back to the night Paul spent with her and Lisa. He was stoned and drunk to top it all off. He had some pills with him and they each took one off of him when he dosed off. He was too wasted to even get a hard on, so whatever they were thinking would happen for them that night—wasn't going to. He fell asleep on Lisa's bed and they let him sleep it off. When he woke, he found himself naked and with 2 girls sleeping besides him naked too. When they woke—he was gone, but when they went to his dorm room—he didn't even know them. Stephanie said "you told us to come get you today. You said you could get more pills for us. We partied in our dorm together last night." Just then Nicky came home and threw them out.

"Steph, why would you do that? That was before they were married!"

"I don't care Lisa. I want to hurt her the way he hurt us that day."

"Steph, he is a different person now. He straightened his life out and I give him credit for that. I heard if it weren't for her and Nicky helping him—he might be in bad shape today!"

"I DON'T CARE . . . !" Stephanie yelled.

Then they left and Maggie came out of the bathroom and told all her friends—"I just heard something in the ladies room. I'm going to start holding it in, until I get home anymore. Sometimes it's ugly in there."

"What did you hear this time" Antoinette asked.

"Two girls are going to come over to upset me about something that happened with them and Paul before we got married. I will handle it and if you want to do something—just laugh at them."

They all nodded and were shocked someone was going to come to deliberately hurt her. Right as she said that, don't you know she sees two girls walking over to her and one holding a jersey?

"Mrs.Tanner right?"

"Yes, do I know you?"

"No, but we wanted to give you Paul's jersey back. He left it in our dorm one night."

Maggie smiled at them, took it, looked at it and then ripped it in half, right in front of them. "Would you mind throwing it in the garbage over there? I don't have any room in mine at home, from all the girls delivering Paul's clothes back to me."

Well, both their faces dropped and turned white while everyone standing there just laughed at them. Then she leans into the both so they could hear her as she said "Do you believe in Karma?" They both just looked at her. "I believe in Karma and two days after you are both married—someone is going to come to your door and deliberately try to hurt you. When that happens, you will think back to what you just did and know how it feels. Then and only then will you ever be sorry." She picks up her head and says, "It was nice to meet you Stephanie and Lisa." They both were shocked she knew their names because they never said them. Maybe Paul told her about them they thought, but knew she couldn't have known them. Maggie stuck her nose up in the air and turned to all her friends who laughed again making those girls look like idiots.

As they walked away Lisa said "I told you this was a bad idea. Now the only one with egg on their faces is us."

Paul saw Maggie rip up his jersey. He knew those girls were trying to hurt her too and saw she could handle herself with them. Actually he was surprised how bold she was. He walks over to her and kissed her forehead. "Do you need me?"

"No, I took care of it." He smiled at her but she didn't return the smile. It was getting late and Maggie liked to be home early when she had work the next day so he said bye to all his friends after giving them all a 'boys club' handshake /hug and went to get her.

"Are you ready? It's almost 11 and we have to get you home."

She smiled and said "yep, ready to go now." He held his hand out and she took it and as they were walking to the door she came face to face with Lisa and Stephanie and said "Thank you for taking care of that for me. Enjoy the rest of your evening."

Paul asked "What did they say to you?" She told him and he was shocked. "Maggie, I'm so sorry you had to go through that. I hope my past doesn't come back to haunt us."

"I think we should be prepared because for some reason—I don't think your past is over."

"You told them our garbage at home was filled, with girls dropping my clothes off?"

"Well I heard them in the ladies room gloating over how they were going to hurt me. I don't know how that shit even came out of my mouth."

He puts his arm around her as they headed up the small hill home. "My wife is a badass . . . remind me to never piss you off" as he smiled at her. "Yes, don't you ever forget it Mister!" Again he smiled at her "would you like to take your frustrations out on me tonight?"

"Oh . . . that isn't even a question. I am definitely going to, so be naked and ready when I get out of that shower." Now she started laughing and Paul knew she couldn't be mad at him if she tried.

While he was lying in her arms he whispered "I am really so sorry Mags you had to go through that."

"Let's forget it. I handled it and don't want to think about it anymore." She said that but it did still bug her.

CHAPTER 31

Life Goes On

Maggie and Paul were loving life together. She was never so happy and so was Paul. She even went to the gym with him to practice his foul shots. One thing she knew was how terrible he was with his foul shooting and once he started practicing with her— his ranking improved dramatically. They smiled constantly and were together always. He brought her lunch when he was off and it was usually something he grilled for her. He was terrible in the kitchen but he was a great grill master. That was his field of expertise. He and Nicky cooked together when Maggie was working late and always had something waiting for her when she got home. Nicky spent many nights on Paul's couch as promised and Maggie even cooked some of Nicky's favorite meals for him. He never felt like a third wheel—Maggie always treated him as family which thrilled Nicky. Paul would even get mad every now and then when she paid too much attention to him but she knew he was only teasing her. She never wanted to leave him out and Paul appreciated her accepting Nicky like she did. He realized everyone might not have had the same thought about his friendship with Nicky.

The Holiday's rolled around and they were both happy they would be heading home to Paul's mom and dad's. Maggie loved Christmas and couldn't wait to spend it with a family that also felt like she did. At her Dad's, they did have Christmas Eve dinner but nothing more. He never gave them anything and always opened his gifts when they weren't around. He left Maggie and her brothers alone to celebrate without him. Paul and Nicky went and picked out a tree and Molly and Judy came over to help decorate their apartment but the comedy show Nicky and Paul put on trying to get that tree in the stand was too funny. Then once they got it in there—they looked and saw how crooked it was and that even make it funnier because they had to start over. "Nicky, do you know anyone in the architect class? Maybe we can call someone for help." Then they both laughed and after struggling—they finally got it right and carried it in.

Maggie decorated and the place looked beautiful. She loved baking too and every time Paul came home from practice or late classes— something sweet smelling was always in the oven. He loved being the taste tester.

They both decided to set a budget for Christmas gifts for each other and promised to stick to it. She bought him all new University gear because his things were ratty looking. Sweats, t-shirts and a jacket. She had left over money so she bought him beautiful Henley's for dress. He loved all his gifts. Paul bought Maggie a beautiful cross necklace and she cried she loved it so much. She couldn't believe he thought of something like that, but in truth, Paul knew his wife all of his life. He wished for her forever and felt God granted him that wish which is why he gave her that cross.

The Team was on a roll that sophomore year. The girlfriends had the same thing in common. They were Basketball widows—but because of their friendships—it didn't even bother them. They had each other and when the guys had away games—they piled over Maggie's where they all brought food for supper and listened to the game on the radio. Again Coach noticed how well things were going between them.

It was nearing the end of the season and then playoffs would begin. It was a no brainer that they would be in the playoffs and the University would be the site where they would be played. When they put in the bid to host the games years ago—they had no idea they would actually *be* in the playoffs. Coach B did amazing work in the off season with recruiting and the whole community knew—it was only a matter of time before the teams would start to be successful. This was the first of many to follow.

After one game they all trucked over to the Commons Center for a party. Everything was going fine and then something unbelievable happened. Maggie was coming out of the restroom when someone grabbed her and pinned her body against his. There was a small hall where no one would see them. He grabbed her breasts rubbing them and slid one hand down her abdomen and rubbed her private parts. Then he whispered "I just had to see what was so special about you—to turn Paul's head like you did. Now I see, you really *are* so sweet." Maggie thought she was going to pass out but then she got so mad and grabbed his hand holding her so tightly and twisted his fingers. She heard them cracking. He yelled and released her but she wasn't done with him yet. She was able to turn and kick him in his balls which dropped him to the floor. She was just getting ready to kick him again when 4 guys rushed over to him and dragged him out of the building.

In the meantime, Paul was looking for her and she was missing.

He thought she was in the bathroom and watched the door for her. She came out and he saw someone grab her. He dropped his beer and tried running to her but the place was so packed he couldn't reach her in time. All the while his eyes were on her as he saw what was happening. It was only a matter of seconds. Everyone saw Paul running and ran after him wondering what happened. The girls noticed too and followed. Maggie was sheet white and when Paul got to her she collapsed in his arms. He was holding her up when Paul told his friends what happened. "I'm taking Maggie home. Go find those guys" he yelled to his boys. Nicky was shaken too, shouting. "We'll find them Paul. I promise you." Off they all went—shocked at what happened. Molly, Judy and Antoinette went with Nicky and Bobby.

Paul had to practically carry Maggie home. He put her coat on and buttoned her up talking so softly to her. She was almost incoherent. Then he wrapped one arm around her and held her hand with the other, slowing walking up the hill to their apartment.

Once they got inside—he took off her coat and brought her to sit on the couch. "Maggie—can I get you anything to drink? Do you need water or anything?" Maggie didn't reply as she stared straight ahead.

Paul paced back and forth in front of her—running his fingers through his hair being so frustrated. Then he screamed at the top of his lungs because he couldn't take it anymore. He couldn't believe someone molested his wife. He was out of breath and knelled down in front of her. She flinched when he touched her knees and backed away from him. That drove him even crazier. "Please, let me touch you. I have to help you. Can you tell me what I need to do for you? What can I do Mags? You are my wife and I wasn't there to help you!" Tears were streaming down Paul's face as he dropped his head in front of her. She finally looks down at him and raises her hand to run her fingers through his hair. He lifted his head and she saw the tears and his face was so red she thought he could have a stroke. "I don't know how you could help me right now" she whispered. "I should cry but I'm so numb. Maybe I could take a shower and scrub his hands off of me. I can't get that feeling to go away. I'm trying to imagine you touching me and his hands keep popping up."

"I'll help you. Let's get you in the shower and maybe you will feel better. Can we give it a try?" Maggie nodded and he helped her up and helped her get to the bathroom because she was still white. "Did you recognize him?"

"No, I never saw him before but he said something cryptic to me. I don't know how I'm going to forget it?" Paul looked at her confused. "What did he say? Can you tell me? Maybe I will recognize him if you tell me what he said." Paul didn't think the guy said anything to her. He was so intent on getting to her he never thought to ask.

"Please, take a deep breath and tell me. It's ok Maggie. Just tell me!" She looks directly at him and repeats," 'I just wanted to see what was so special about you—to turn Paul's head like you did. Now I see you really *are* so sweet', as he was rubbing me . . . between my legs" and she could barely get out those last words and then she started crying. Paul screamed "NOOOOO! NOOOOO! I did this to you, again!

Again, I hurt you!" and he couldn't even look at her but she was in no condition to go to him to help him.

Then he turns to her and pulls her body into his—wrapping his arms around her. "We have to call the police. You were molested and this guy shouldn't get away with it." Maggie nodded and he made the call. "Lay here and I will handle everything. Then I will come back and we will take a shower. I want to wipe all of him off of you. I want you to remember only my hands on you Mags. Will you let me? I know it will help. Trust me Mags. Please!" he pleaded with her and he did feel if he washed her with his hands—it would erase what happened to her. Again she nodded and it relieved him, to an extent. The campus police came and they felt they should alert the city police and they came right over. They heard it was Paul Tanner's wife and they were intent on finding that person who did that to her. Paul told them what happened and the City Police asked "Paul, do you think it was someone you played against? Do you have any beef with anyone or does anyone have any beef with you?"

Paul answered truthfully, "Not that I know of. I don't have any issues with anyone I play against."

"Ok, we had to ask and wanted to make sure, so we knew where to start looking. Just then Coach and Mrs. B arrived. They saw the police there and Mrs. B was in tears. "Where is she? I have to go to her."

"She's lying down. I want her to calm down—she's a mess."

"Did you think to call your mom or Sarah from her shop?"

"No, we didn't have time to call anyone yet except for the police. She is too upset to talk to anyone. How did you hear about it so quickly?"

"Nicky stopped and told us. He said not to be upset with him. He knew you needed support here, while they were all out looking for that guy."

The city policeman told Coach "I hope I don't have to arrest your whole team Bob. I hope they are going to be sensible if they find him!"

"I hope you don't have to also, but couldn't blame them if anything did happen to the guy." Paul nodded and went to coach who hugged him. He knew he needed that hug. Something terrible happened to his wife and he could see on Paul's face—he was just as upset.

Mrs. B walked back to see her and when Maggie saw her she started crying again. "Maggie I didn't come to upset you more. I came to help you" as she sat on the bed holding her in her arms—rocking her back and forth. The City police asked Paul, "Did you want to take her to the emergency room? Maybe they could give her something to calm down and let her rest tonight. She should get checked out and make sure the baby is fine."

"We are not pregnant officer. I know everyone thinks that, because we got married so young, besides, she won't go, and she won't take anything so it is a moot point." Mrs. B came out "She fell asleep. I think you should go back there in case she wakes. She will be upset if you are not there Paul."

"Good idea." Paul said thanks to the police, Coach and Mrs. B and told them—"I have to get back there in case she wakes."

The police told him they would call if they had anything.

After only 10 minutes, Maggie woke and Paul told her about the police coming. "Let's get you that shower now. How about that?" he smiled to her. She nods and gets up but was wobbly. He held her around her waist and walked her into the bathroom. He helped her undress and she told him "Please throw them in the garbage. I will never wear that sweater or jeans again." Paul opened the cabinet where the garbage can was and threw them in there. Just as they were ready to head in the shower the doorbell rings again. "Mags, turn on the taps and get in. I'll be right back" as he kissed her forehead.

It was Nicky and the boys. Antoinette, Molly and Judy were with them. Nicky looked defeated as he told Paul, "We thought we saw someone trying to get away but they lost us. We drove around the whole town and down the interstate—even through the park on the hill thinking they could be hiding there, but we lost them. We didn't find them. How is she?"

"Broken up." He looked around at them all and saw they wanted to know so he continued "The guy held her so tight she couldn't move. She grabbed his hand and thinks she might have broken some fingers because she heard something crack. That's when he released her and she was able to turn and kick him in his balls." Paul's head was down "He grabbed her breasts and then" . . . he hesitated . . . "he rubbed her . . . between her legs. He said to her 'I just wanted to see what was so special about you—to turn Paul's head like you did. Now I see you really are so sweet'." Just then they heard her crying and Paul turned his head back towards their room.

Nicky could feel Paul's grief. He saw it on his face and heard it in his voice. He knew he was trying to keep it together in front of all his guys.

"You should go. Maggie needs you. I will call you or you can call me if you need me." Paul just nodded but before everyone left, he lost it and broke down as he said "thank you all so much. It means the world to me and Maggie." He turned and walked towards the bedroom to get to his wife. Everyone let themselves out and Nicky closed and made sure the door was locked. Before he did he called back to Paul and went to hug him. "Do you want me to stay? I can stay here with you." Paul just shook his head no. "Nicky, I know you did everything you could. Thank you." Instead of heading to the shower Maggie did something even she couldn't believe. She called her father. It went to voicemail after only 1 ring. She knew her father rejected the call but she needed her dad right then so she left him a message.

"I know you won't call me, but I have something terrible to tell you. I was assaulted tonight. We called the police and they are looking for the guy. He touched me dad"! She was crying leaving the message but continued, "Where only my husband should touch me. He said something terrible to me. I am trying to erase what he said but I can't get it out of my head. I need you so badly daddy. I wish things were different between us. I want you to know, my husband Paul, is a great husband and is doing everything he can to help me. Well, that's all I wanted to say. I needed you to know in case it is in the paper about what happened. I love you daddy!"

Frank Sr went wild just then! He got her message and went crazy thinking someone did that to his daughter. He was so sorry at that moment he wasn't speaking to her and remembered his wife's message to him during his dream; she needs her own life with her own children. He knew she was right but didn't want her to leave. He realized it could have been different if he wasn't so stubborn. He could still be in her life and enjoy her and his sons but there was that mean streak that just never gave up on him. It's almost like he enjoyed being so miserable. He also knew his wife was an angel and the only one that could handle him and those thoughts always melted his heart every time he thought about it and how much he missed her.

He was going to wait to see what was in the paper, if anything, and then plan something, but he had to find out first who did that to her. He would get revenge for her and promised himself he would.

Paul sees Maggie didn't make it to the shower yet and he bent down and softly kisses her and she lifted up her head to kiss him back. It relieved him a bit as he quickly undressed to join her. He turned the water on and took her by the hand leading her into the shower with him. He squirted her liquid lavender soap on her very pink sponge he teased her about all the time, as he slowly washed down her whole body. He wanted to make sure she felt his hands on her and he bent down and kissed both breasts after he ran the sponge over them. He lifted up her leg and hitched it on his hip as he got her sweet spot and it seemed to start to relax her. "Turn you head under the shower so I could wash your hair Mags." She did what she was told and Paul washed and rinsed her hair, then rinsed it out with her cream rinse and she seemed all set. He got a towel and dried her hair first, then another towel and slowly dried off her entire body. He took her lotions and he knew which ones she used because he watched her every day while lying in bed—when she got ready for work. He loved the show she put on for him daily, as she applied her lotions, put on her makeup and fixed her hair.

He dried her hair and asked "Do you want at shirt or anything to wear to bed tonight?" She just shook her head no and he went and turned the bed down, coming back to pick her up and lay her under the covers where he joined her.

She immediately cuddled in his arms where he held her tightly. "Are you feeling any better now?" She nodded her head and then fell asleep in his arms. Paul didn't sleep a wink, he just watched her all night until he saw it starting to get light out. He couldn't even close his eyes. He kept trying to think who would do that to her or say that to her. He didn't have any issues with anyone on the court so it baffled him. Then his face dropped and his heart sank as he thought, *Maybe it was someone from Louden House!* The only players he knew that frequented that place were on his team and once he stopped going, so did they. It had to be someone else that went there. Now he decided he had to be on the lookout for someone or anyone who used to go there that he might recognize.

Maggie was quiet all week. She called Sarah and Lois to tell them what happened and she handled telling them without breaking down. Paul saw how strong she really was. He knew she wanted to get past it and every day he saw her getting better and better but she was still off. In between classes he walked down town to have lunch with her and she barely ate. Sarah told him, "she has said less than 20 words to all of us here. She stays in her office and buries her head in her work and she barely eats. I don't want to bring it up and felt she would say something to me—but she hasn't. She keeps saying she is fine. Do you think we should get her to talk to someone professionally? I don't know how to help her."

"I don't either Sarah. She comes home and we eat or should I say, I eat and watch her move her food around her plate. Then we clean up and she'll go shower and I study. I'll ask her to help me and she comes over and I lay on her lap but she just closes her eyes while I study and just sits there. You're right. I don't want to bring it up but maybe I will have to. I'm going to wait for the game Saturday. If she is not better by Sunday, I will tell her she has to speak to someone about what happened to her."

"That's a good idea. Give her some more time. She might snap out of it by herself. What did you bring her for lunch? She won't eat."

"I'm calling her bluff. I brought her 3 pieces of white cake with buttercream frosting. Her favorite and if she doesn't respond to this— then we are in trouble. This is her all-time favorite and she would take this cake over sex!" He smiled telling Sarah that while she laughed at him.

"Well, she is in her office, so go for it and good luck." She kissed him before he went back.

Paul knocks softly on her office door and she smiles when she sees him. "I have a surprise for you" he happily told her. "What is it?" He held the box out to her and her eyes lit up. She knew it was from a bakery and she gasped like a little child as she opened it up and saw the beautifully decorated pieces of cake with pink flowers all over each piece. "OMG! Where did you find this?" She asked as her face lit up for him. He started relaxing immediately. She took out a piece and he teased her "Where is my piece?"

"You gave them *to me*! They're mine!" she told him as she took the box to hide it from him and started laughing. He laughed at her but he really wanted to cry. She was smiling and joking and he missed his Maggie all week and all of a sudden—she was back.

He lowers his head and his face is all red and her face drops when she sees he is upset. "What is it? Did they find that guy?" He shakes his head no. "Well, what is it? Do you have something to tell me?"

He looks at her and said "I want my wife back. I saw your eyes light up with the cake and that is my wife again. I miss her and don't know what I can do to make her well again. I want her to know, I am so so sorry this has happened to her and wish I could carry her pain for her."

Maggie's face dropped and Paul saw it and hoped he didn't say too much and ruin everything.

"What time is your next class?"

"I'm done and just have practice from 3 to 5."

Sarah is walking by and she calls out to her and she stops. "Would you mind if I went home now for the day?"

"No, not at all. I'll lock up tonight and balance the register. Go now. It's not a problem."

Maggie gives Sarah a big smile and then hugs her. "Thank you so much mom, for everything this week."

Sarah almost cried and didn't want her to see that so she said "Go on now, before I change my mind" laughing.

Maggie grabbed her purse and turned to get the cake box and grabbed Paul's hand, practically running out of the shop.

She flew up the stairs to their apartment dragging Paul with her. He had no idea what was going on and thought *I hope she is not going to yell at me for bringing her this.*

Once they got in the door she kissed him and wildly. She started undressing walking backwards to their bedroom, all the while watching the expression on his face. She laughed every time she threw a piece of her clothing at him especially when her bra hit him in the face.

"What are you doing? Get those clothes off!"

Paul thought he was hearing things and stripped as fast as he could. His wife was sitting in bed—naked—waiting for him. He thought he was dreaming.

Maggie climbed on top of him and kissed him deeply. Then her kisses were wild driving Paul crazy. She slid up and down on him as he got hard and kept it up until she almost was ready to explode but she waited until he filled her up. Once she had him, she moved her body up and down until he was ready but he grabbed her and flipped her on her back to continue. Their breathing was heavy and rapid and before they both knew it—they were coming together like they always did.

Paul collapses in Maggie's arms both out of breath and she wrapped him up in them as she ran her fingers through his hair the way he likes it. Neither was saying anything until she starts to laugh.

"What is so funny?"

"I'm not done with you yet and what is so funny is how you will be dragging at practice this afternoon while I am here eating my three pieces of cake!"

Paul started now too, and said "I think *you* should come to practice with me so *you* could tell Coach why I am dragging my feet since it is *your* fault."

"Well, maybe we should stop now, if you are afraid of Coach!"

"Oh no you don't! You don't make a promise and then negate on it." He lifts his head to look at her and she is smiling at him. "Ok, no going back on my promise, so . . . are you ready again or do you need coaxing?" She moved her hand to find him and saw he was soooo ready for her again and she bent down and kissed him softly as they started all over.

CHAPTER 32

Next Game

Paul didn't want Maggie to go to the next game. He felt she should stay home and recover more until she was strong enough to handle being in front of the crowd at St. John's Center. He knew everyone knew what happened because it was in the paper. His parents couldn't come in and that stressed him out even more. *And* Sarah was going to be away too, so he called Mrs. B and asked her to take care of Maggie for him. Then he asked Bobby to have Antoinette look after her too, which was no problem. All the girls got together and decided they would surround her at the game to make her feel safe.

"Paul, I know you don't want to go to the Commons Center after the game, would you like to invite everyone here for some pizza and I know there are some good games on TV."

"Do you think that would be too much for you Mags? I don't want you to get stressed out."

"No, I'm good and would feel better being here tonight after the game. If no one wants to come, it's OK. But could we just come home after the game?"

"Yes, of course. I will see if anyone wants to come over and let you know as soon as I can." Maggie goes over to Paul "thank you so much for this week. You took such good care of me and I know I would be in a much worse place if it weren't for you." She wraps her arms around him hugging him tightly and it stressed Paul out thinking she was still shaken over the whole incident because of the way she was holding him. He wrapped her up and walked her backwards to their bed. It made her laugh as he plopped her down with him on top of her. He was fine as long as she was smiling at him. "You know I have to go to the game, right? Otherwise you will suck tonight if I'm not there!" She laughed at him— "Really? Well, we'll see about that. How about I show you something I know I don't suck at" as he is lifting her shirt over her head and kissing her deeply. "I don't think you are supposed to have sex before a game."

"Who told you that? It's not a proven fact and we'll see how I play tonight after our session here now!" They both smiled looking into each-others' eyes and Maggie lifted her head for a kiss which Paul was more than happy to give her. "I forgot to tell you. Mrs. B is picking me up for the game."

"Good Mags. I feel better with you going with someone. Are you sure you don't want to come with me? I know it will be early but you could get your seat and be all set."

"Please stop stressing out. I will be fine. Life is going on for us and I will not go backwards. How about you tell me how much you love me. I know it will make me feel better."

"Maggie, there aren't enough words or ways for me to tell you and show you how much you mean to me. I love you more than my own life. You are my angel and will always be. I would be nowhere without you and I want you to believe me."

"I do believe you love me more than you can say because it's how much I love you Paul, and always will."

Kiss me again Mags and then I need to go. She lifts her head up and he kisses her softly then deeply and she breaks away. "Better not start anything again, but we can pick this up tonight after everyone leaves?"

"I'm already looking forward to it Mags."

At the gym she walks in surrounded by Antoinette, Mrs. B and all the girlfriends including Molly and Judy and all of a sudden everyone sees her and gives her a standing ovation. The warmth she felt from every-one at that moment was overwhelming and when she lifted her hand and waved and then put it on her heart showing how much she appreci-ated it—the crowd went wild again. She lowered her head and Paul was watching her every move making sure she was ok and also was moved by what everyone did. Nicky came over and put his arm around him and once they saw she was in her seat with everyone—they turned and went back to practice. Maggie was nervous and everyone sensed it. She got so quiet and then Antoinette said, "Maggie, it looks like we are coming over after the game. Can I pick up some soda and chips?"

"That would be great. I'm going to order the pizza at halftime so it will be ready in time." Then everyone chimed in and said they were coming too. She immediately felt better and more relaxed.

The game was getting ready to start and the 10 players are on the court when Bobby notices something while on the bench. He quickly calls Nicky over. Bobby is Nicky's substituted when he comes out for a breather. "Nicky—do something for me. Don't ask why now. I will tell you and you will see. Come out after a few plays. Say you twisted your ankle. Please Nicky—do this for me." Nicky was shocked. "Ok Bobby, I'll wait a few plays—then limp off the court."

"Thank you and you will see why. Trust me." Nicky nodded and went out to the court. Coach saw them and was wondering what was going on. Finally everyone was lined up and the players went to shake hands and they barely shook Paul's or looked at him. Paul just thought they were trying to get in his head for the game, throwing him off so he blew it off. After a few plays, Nicky pretended he twisted his ankle and as planned, Bobby went in for him. Paul walked Nicky over to the bench and he told him not to worry, it was nothing. They went back to play and all of a sudden Bobby ran down court and threw himself at a player from the other team, taking him down with him, after throwing him the biggest elbow right in his ribs. Everyone watched and couldn't believe what he did and wondered why . . . until . . . everyone saw the player on the floor with two fingers taped together like they were broken or sprained. The guy on the floor was also holding his balls. The light bulb went on and Paul's face dropped and turned to look for Maggie in the stands. She stands on her seat so he could see her and looked at the guy on the floor and nodded to Paul. Then at the same time they all knew, that was the guy that assaulted her. Paul went to him as he was just getting up and threw the biggest punch at him and he went down again. Everyone knew what was happening. Even coach who quickly called the police and security at the gym. There would be a riot and he had to stop it before it got bad. The refs were blowing their whistles and trying to break up the fight but Paul went after him again and his players were holding him around the waist and his arms. His face was so red they thought he would have a heart attack. Nicky had him and said "Paul, let's go. The police are coming. They will arrest him." Paul pretended he was going back to the bench but got away from Nicky and went after him *again*! They all had to practically carry him over to their bench. In truth—they all wanted to take a whack at him. Coach walked over to the visiting coach and explained what was going on. He was in the dark about everything and was so shocked. "It all makes sense now Bob. This week he said he sprained his fingers when he fell and he had a groin injury from the last game." Coach told him what a rough week it was for Paul and his wife. When that guys teammates didn't even come over to help him, his coach knew something was wrong. They all backed away and let him take whatever was going to happen to him.

The two coaches and the ref's got together and declared the game forfeited in favor of the U.

The local police arrived and 22 State Police cars also came, in fear of a riot. The Troopers lined the sides of the gym so no one could go out on the court and so they could control the exit. The announcer came on and told everyone the game was forfeited and for everyone to leave the arena peacefully. Luckily they all did as they were told but not before the local Police Chief himself, came in, and took that kid out in handcuffs. Right in front of 10,000 people. They all cheered when that happened. His 4 team mates came over to Paul along with their coach and asked if they could speak to him. Coach nodded and Paul and Nicky came over to hear what they wanted to say.

"Paul, we are so sorry about what happened to your wife and want you to know we had no idea he was going to do that. We would not have condoned what he did and want you to know that." Paul looked at Nicky and Nicky said "I believe them Paul. No one could have agreed to do a thing like that." Then Nicky looked at those players and his face was beet red "What were you thinking, coming into our house and bringing him here to shake hands with us all and Paul especially. Do the right thing and testify against that leach before he assaults someone else's wife. Maybe even one of yours!" The four just looked at Nicky and were shocked he said that because none of them even thought of that and it could very well happen. Some of the players were married and they knew he was a womanizer. "Paul, we couldn't say anything because none of us could afford to lose our scholarships. We see we made a mistake not reporting him. We are so sorry. Can we please apologize to your wife?" Paul's eyes got wide and he looked like he wanted to choke all four of them and again Nicky held him around his waist and all his team mates came back over thinking they would have to hold him back again. "*Never* will I *ever* let you near my wife. *Never*! Maybe if you make sure that pig gets put behind bars, I will let you *look* at her, but that is all. You will *never* speak to her . . . EVER!" Paul's face was all red—*again* and they pulled him away from those guys. Just then he looked for Maggie and she was still standing on her seat wrapped in Mrs. B's arms and Paul couldn't take it anymore. If he didn't go to her, he would have attacked those guys, so he ran to where she was sitting. She sees him coming and meets him at the steps where she jumps in his arms. Everyone watched them and cheered when they saw that. She had her arms wrapped tightly around his neck and he had her wrapped in his. "Paul, please calm down. I'm fine. Really. It's quit liberating now that they found him. Please, I'm fine. It's ok now." Paul couldn't stop hugging her and she told him again "Please, for me. Calm down. I'm fine. Please! I can't wait to get you home with me. We have a houseful coming and now lots to talk about." She flashed him a big smile and it immediately calmed him down. He kissed her and Nicky came and got him but not before he hugged his sister first. They went to change and go back to their apartment to have some pizza with all their friends.

CHAPTER 33

Frank Sr.

It was all over the news that they got the guy who assaulted Maggie.

> *"Near riot situation at the University tonight as they appre-hended the person who assaulted Maggie Tanner, wife of star Point Guard Paul Tanner last week."*

Maggie's father was wild when he saw that. The next morning he got up early and headed out somewhere. He told Frank Jr he would be late getting to work and Frank knew better than to even ask.

He drove 2 and ½ hours somewhere and when he walked into the old building of offices—it almost seemed like they were waiting for him. He was announced and brought to an exquisite office with leather couches and chairs and big oak desks with bookshelves lining 2 of the walls. He immediately held his hand out to shake the person behind the desk who spoke first.

"Frank, we are so sorry about what happened to your daughter Margaret. We have been watching her since she was born and know what a beautiful young woman she turned out to be. We checked on her husband—Paul Tanner. He comes from a good family. We also found out he was going down a dark path until he met Margaret. His best friend Nicholas Newman and your daughter helped him straighten out his life and now we see he is doing better than we expected. I thought you should know that."

Frank just nodded like he knew all of that. He actually did, but he didn't know about Paul and now see his daughter was on a mission to save him. That is why she wanted to get married so quickly.

Again the person spoke without Frank even saying a word yet. "We see they got the person who assaulted her. We strongly suggested at the time, the Police Chief, arrest that person himself and see he did. We were pleased."

Frank just nodded and the man behind the desk signaled for him to sit down, so he did take that seat in front of the desk.

"What would you like from us? I know if it were my daughter, I would want to do something . . . harsh shall we say? But then once I calmed down—I would reconsider my choice. We have information on him and see he is not a nice boy. He has previously molested a handful of women. Some of them, have been paid off! I think once the trial hits, more of his conquests will come out of the woodwork, about what he did to them, too. In fact, I'm sure of it! The trial will be hard on Margaret. She will have to recap what happened and it will be painful, especially once his attorney gets her on the stand. He will tear her apart and make her look like she deserved it."

Frank's face got so red—he was so hot thinking about someone doing that to her as he sat there gripping the arms on the chair like he could rip them off.

"We have already decided to reach out to his attorney—before that happens. That will be our gift to her. She really is a beautiful girl Frank and we don't want to see her upset again and we don't want to see her husband take any backwards steps, if you know what I mean. We know he is just as upset over this. We have been watching. He is quit talented and smart! Coach Barrows from the University worked hard to recruit him and Mr. Newman and built his whole team around the both of them."

He stops and hesitates before he said more and Frank wondered why. Then he continued.

"Frank, we also know you don't speak to Margaret, but that doesn't matter—professionally speaking of course. Personally, I will tell you this.

I don't understand. She is beautiful, hardworking and a kind person. Everything I would want my daughter to be. She has done everything you ever asked her, from what we can tell, so it puzzles me on your reaction to her and frankly to your sons too. They are both good boys and have always been. It's none of our business—I know—but we suggest you let Joseph go out on his own. He should have his own job with better pay and benefits. He is very smart and we know someone has been after him to work for them. Let him go and then you could take better care of Frank Jr."

"Now, pardon us, if we overstepped our boundaries and back to business at hand. Again I will ask. What would you like from us?"

Finally, Frank spoke. "Thank you for seeing me. I appreciate all of your advice and will take it into consideration. Thank you for what you are doing for Margaret. I don't know if I could take seeing her so hurt and upset all over again. I also don't want to see her husband going down the wrong path again and didn't think about that. So again, thank you for reminding me. You're right. At first I wanted you to kill him for what he did. Now, I just don't know, but he has to pay. If he did this to my daughter and so many others as you already stated, he will do it again. Can you help me decide?"

The man searched Franks face to see if he really meant what he said and he saw anguish and pain all over it. He also knew all about Frank Sardo. He was a miserable man who basically mistreated his 3 children ever since his beloved wife died. So in their eyes, he deserved to have that pass.

"Would you allow us to make another suggestion Frank?"

Frank nodded and the man continued. "He is a ball player! None of his team mates like him from what we noticed. No one came to his aid at the gym that night they arrested him after your son in law went after him. He landed a really nice punch, from what we heard. His team mates had to carry him away from going after him again. The fury he had over him hurting his wife, suggested how much he cared for her. That should bring you much comfort, as it did for us. We would not be sorry if that person . . . took a little tumble and broke one or two wrists during that fall. It would humble him we feel—having to have someone feed him, dress and wash him. We believe some humiliation would be a good lesson for him. Of course, if he was planning on continuing his basketball career—that would be over too."

Frank lowered his head and then replied "I will accept your suggestion and agree." He slipped an envelope across the desk, where the man placed his paper over it and just left it there. He never touched it in front of Frank.

Frank got up to leave and extended his hand to him. "Thank you for your concern over my children. I will take your suggestions under consideration. Thank you for Margaret also. I am more than grateful!" The man took Frank's hand and held it until he was done speaking.

Then he let it go and Frank turned and left satisfied with accomplishing what he came to do.

Frank went over and over the conversation he just had all the way home. He couldn't explain why he was so hard on his children and he remembered how much he hurt his daughter when he had her in his arms—dancing with her during her cousin's wedding. He just wanted to keep her there and never let her go. His fury kicked in when she talked about her wedding. That would mean she would have to leave him and he couldn't help his reaction. He lashed out at her telling her no one would want her. He knew how beautiful she was because she looked just like his wife—he missed so much. He couldn't help himself. Then when she said she was getting married, he felt she was doing it on purpose. One thing he did know, was that he was the one that pushed her away. He did that, and was too arrogant to see or admit it, until just then.

CHAPTER 34

Stunning

It was after three when he got back to the shop and Joseph and Frank Jr were just getting back from some deliveries.

"I need to talk to you both." He said to them and it stunned them as they came over to him.

Frank's head is down and then he lifted it up and looked at his sons. Frank Jr looked just like him and Joseph had his father's face but his mother's blue eyes. He thought that, every time he looked at him.

"I think you should take that offer that keeps coming your way Joseph." Joseph turned white and noticed his father did not even yell about it. He didn't even know he knew about it. "It's for more money and benefits. You will be happy there—I know you will. If you do that, then I will be able to raise Frank's salary and sign him up for benefits too. You both need medical insurance and a pension. You should start one now, while you are young so you could retire comfortably."

Well, they both were shocked. Their father was talking to them and not yelling about something. They were having a normal conversation and they thought maybe he was sick and that is where he was all day, having tests at a hospital.

"Dad, this is such a surprise and so overwhelming to us." Frank Jr said.

"Well, don't get used to it. I'm having a weak moment and you both should take me up on it before I change my mind." He barked like the father they knew.

They both nodded their heads and Joseph stepped away and immediately made a call and just like that, he was going to start with a new company. "Dad, they hired me over the phone. Is it alright if I start next month?" Frank just nodded and turned to walk away. "I'm going home now. I'll see you both tomorrow. Maybe we can go to dinner tomorrow night. Maybe! And *maybe* you could call Mark and her husband and invite them too!" Frank Jr and Joseph almost passed out when he said Mark and her husband and just looked at each other as if to ask *how he could possibly know.*

"Dad, is everything alright? Are you OK?" Frank Jr asked.

"Yes, now it is." He turned and left leaving Frank and Joseph stunned while they just stared at each other. They couldn't figure out what just happened. They called Paul's phone to tell Maggie immediately and she was so happy and thrilled for them. "Maybe something is wrong with him. Is he sick?" she asked. "No, he said he is fine and Frank and I are stunned. There's more! He said to ask Mark and her husband if they want to join us for dinner tomorrow!"

"What? Holy cow! How could he know it was me?" Maggie was shocked and Paul saw her color turn. He was trying to figure out what happened. "We don't know. He was gone all day today and when he came back he looked . . . different. We can't figure it out."

"OMG Joseph. Do you think he really means it? I don't want to get my hopes up if he is going to rescind the offer."

"Well, let's make it tentative and I will call you tomorrow if he comes to work and doesn't mention it again."

"OK! I'll tell Paul now. He is anxious to hear what is going on."

"Talk to you tomorrow Maggie."

Paul cannot wait to hear what that was about and when she told him he was stunned. "Maggie, I was hoping for so long that this would happen for you. You can see your brothers now. *And* your father wants to see you too!"

"He wants to see us Paul! The both of us!" Paul just nodded. "I will be nervous meeting them all."

"Don't be. You speak to Joseph and Frank all the time so you are already brothers." Paul just nods and pulls Maggie in for a hug. He knew she needed one just then.

CHAPTER 35

Reconciling

Well, the next day Frank Sr came in to work and told Frank to make a reservation at Arcaro and Genell's for them all. Again, both sons almost fell over. They were wondering and worried about what his demeanor would be that next day. They were relieved he was still speaking to them and still nice. He also told them to make the reservation for 5. They knew the 2 extra were for Maggie and Paul. Joseph told his father "I'll call Mark now and tell her what time and where." His father actually smiled when he made that joke, again throwing both sons off.

Maggie couldn't believe it. She was going to have dinner with her family and husband. She was leery about it. She wanted to believe it was all with good intentions but then thought about how mean her father was and wasn't sure how to approach the dinner. She didn't want to get her hopes up and think everything would now be fine when he could turn quickly back into that monster. She told Sarah and Lois and they were both shocked and told her to go, but with caution. They were also worried about Paul. They didn't know how Frank Sr would react to meeting him but hoped for the best.

Maggie was nervous the whole day. Paul was going to come get her at work and then walk across the street to the restaurant for dinner. He had to admit—he was a little apprehensive too, but knew this night was important to his wife.

Right at 5:30 Paul arrives to get her and she locked up the shop. He saw how nervous she was and made her stop to take deep breaths. Then he bent down and kissed her, but what he didn't see was Frank Sr watching them. Paul flashed her a big smile which relaxed her and took her hand as they made their way to the restaurant. The table was in the back and the walk seemed like miles to Maggie, just trying to get to her family. Her brothers get up immediately when they see her and Joseph went to her first and embraced her. Then she introduced him to Paul. He shook his hand and then hugged him. Frank Jr did the same thing. Their father was not there yet but as soon as she realized it, he comes walking back to them. He looked at Maggie and surprised her. He opened his arms for her and everyone's mouths just dropped. She walked into his embrace and was stunned when he wrapped her in his arms and held her. Frank felt he had to hug her after everything that happened to her. Then she lifted up her head and kissed him on his cheek which almost made him cry as he tightened his arms around her. Paul, Joseph and Frank were all smiling away at them and couldn't believe what was happening.

Once he let her go she said "Dad, I want you to meet my husband,

Paul Tanner." Paul extended his hand to shake and he took it and gave him a really really strong hand shake back. "It's nice to finally meet you Sir."

"I read about you all the time in the sports section. It seems you play really well."

"I only play well because of Maggie—Sir. If it weren't for her, I don't know where I would be today."

"Maybe someday you will tell me about it then." Paul was shocked. He wanted to talk to him. He just nodded his head and didn't say more.

Frank Sr. said "Well, let's eat because I'm starved and I also discovered I am a terrible cook!" Paul chimed right in "So am I sir. But I'm really good at grilling." Everyone laughed at him.

"Do you like where you are living now?"

"Dad, our apartment is so nice and it's pretty spacious. The landlord replaced the rugs and painted. He bought us a new mattress and had the whole place professionally cleaned before we moved in."

"I know, I saw it when I installed your new washer and dryer." Maggie almost passed out when he said that.

"What? The washer and dryer were from you? All along I thought they were from Joseph and Frank. You gave me that card and message too?" Looking at Paul now he told him "Yes, Your mother and Sarah backed me into a corner one day and *ordered* me to just deliver them. I knew they meant business and I would never want to piss those 2 off, plus, I wanted to do it, so I stopped for the card and signed it from your mother and me. I have to admit—I was so hot at the 2 of them but after I cooled off, I saw how they were really looking out for you both."

Paul was shocked. "I had no idea she did that. She never said a word and I believed they were from both her brothers too."

"Well, that's enough now. All this it too much for me. I'm not used to emotions and want to stop now."

They all nodded their heads and started talking about what they wanted to order. They talked about food and Paul's games—staying away from Maggie being molested. They didn't want to upset her that night. After dinner Frank Sr got up to leave. They weren't surprised so they let him go. They knew he already showed more feelings to them in one night than he had their whole lives. "I'll see you tomorrow" he said to his sons. He turned to Paul and Maggie and said "I'll see you sooner or later". He looked at Paul and said "Thank you". Paul looked at him confused until he continued "for taking such good care of Maggie." Paul nodded to him and off he went leaving them all there stunned. None of them knew what to say. "Does anyone know what just happened?" She asked. "He was so nice. If he could have just been like that his whole life—it could have been so nice." Both her brothers agreed but couldn't say what happened to him to make him turn like he did.

CHAPTER 36

Who Is She?

It was one thing after another with Paul and every time they felt peaceful in their life together something else happened. She knew he came with baggage, but that much? Maggie could have never imagined what she would be up against, marrying Paul. While she wanted to help him pull his life together and turn it around—it seemed something else would happen and she was weary and tired from all of that drama. She had her own drama with her family and that always went on the back burner so she could concentrate on Paul.

Once again something happened at the Commons Center, after another game one Saturday night. Maggie started feeling like she was going to boycott going to those parties because they were more upsetting than fun anymore.

While standing with Molly, Judy, Antoinette and some of the other player girlfriends, some girl runs in yelling Paul's name! Maggie turned to see who that was and what was going on. Paul and his friends were standing right next to the girls.

All of a sudden this girl yells: "Paul, I'm back!" She jumps into Paul's arms and wraps her legs around his waist and arms around his neck and is kissing him.

Maggie's face just dropped. She really didn't know what to do and to top it all off, all of her friends were just looking at her with that same expression she had on *her* face!

Paul tries to free himself from her, pushing her away with his arms—trying to get her off of him.

She looks at him and is confused. "Paul, why are you pushing me away? I thought you would be happy to see me. I have been away for months now. Aren't we going to party the night away like we always did?" Paul's face was purple but if he looked over at Nicky, he would see,

So was his. Nicky knew who she was and was happy she left the country for all of those months. She is the one who introduced Paul to that drug dealer and got him going to Louden House. She is the one that kept him drunk and stoned all of those months before she left. Oh, they never dated, at least that is what Paul always said but he was always out of it, so Nicky never really knew. Those two just hung out—trying to destroy their lives together.

In the meantime, Paul immediately looked for his wife. He saw her looking at him and steam practically coming out of her ears. He knows very well all the shit she has to put up with when it came to him and his life before meeting her. He also knew he had a lot of explaining to do and could see the hurt on his wife's face when he looked at her. He wondered himself how much more she was going to put up with. In truth, he forgot all about that girl, wanting to erase his past from his memory. He only wanted to move forward, and with Maggie he felt he was. Except now, another thing she has to go through.

"Marion, what are you doing? Leave me alone" Paul is still holding her at bay with his arms out, stopping her from coming near him.

Marion was pissed. "What do you mean, leave me alone? I thought you would be happy to see me."

"Why would I be happy to see you? You near destroyed my life when we hung around. I couldn't even spell my name some nights after partying with you. I don't want that life anymore. I told your dealer to leave me alone and never contact me again and I stopped going to Louden House."

Again she tried to go near Paul and again he held her back, away from him. "Paul, you can't be serious. We always had a blast together. I thought we were friends. Friends with benefits!"

"A friend doesn't do what you did to me. Keep me oblivious to everything going on around me. *And,* don't give me that 'friends with benefits' line, in front of all my friends. We never had sex and you know it. I pulled my life together and will never go down that path again. Not with you or anyone else."

Everyone around Paul knew that was true. He did pull his life together and they all admired him for doing that along with respecting him and Maggie.

Marion was stunned. She did not think Paul would react like that, until, she notices something on his finger. A ring! Oh no! It's a wedding ring.

"I see now, why you are pushing me away. You got married. I see the ring on your finger. So, someone trapped you. She's pregnant isn't she?" Then she says something that almost made Paul want to slap her. "I know someone that could take care of that for you. No one has to know. We can either get her an abortion or they can give you something so she will miscarry the baby and then you could be free from her."

Paul couldn't believe what she said. He was stunned and it actually made his stomach turn, it was that bad. He immediately goes to Maggie and takes her hand pulling her over to meet Marion.

"Maggie, this is Marion. Marion—this is my *wife*, Maggie Tanner." He said her whole name to her.

"Before you are nice to her Maggie, there is something you should know. Marion is the one who introduced me to that drug dealer at Louden House. She is the one who got me started and not to mention the one who kept me drunk and stoned all last quarter. She went to Paris to study and just got back today thinking we could pick up where we left off. She also just told me, if you were pregnant, she knew a way to get rid of the baby, so I could be free of you."

Then he turns to Marion, "As you can see, we are not pregnant. And when we are—it will be something we both planned. Something we will *never* want to get rid of. Suggesting that is low . . . even for someone like you." Marion stood there shocked.

Maggie was white. She couldn't believe that girl suggested something like that and really didn't know how to react to what was happening. Just then, the band played a slow song and her favorite one. Paul knew that too and thought it just saved them both from lunging after that girl.

"Marion, I am married and happily married to this beautiful girl. She is the reason I straightened my life out. I will never go back to the way it was with you. Never!"

Paul took Maggie's hand again and escorted her onto the dance floor where he wrapped his arms around her holding her close to his body. He was upset and Maggie sensed that girl really shook him. She brought her hand up to his face and held it there knowing he would like that. His head is bent down to hers and he whispers, "thank you Maggie, for not going ballistic on me. I know it is just one issue after another with me. I am begging you not to give up on me. Please! I love you too much to survive us not making it. Please, look at me so I can kiss you. I need to right now!"

Maggie hesitated as her head is buried in his chest and then looked up at him and smiled trying to make him see she was fine. Then she reached up and took that kiss because she needed it also. They kept on the dance floor wrapped in each other's arms and tried to calm down, all the while Marion is just seething. Once the song was over she just asked "Can we leave now?" Paul nodded and thought it was going to be a rough night at home trying to explain more until Maggie said "I just want to get naked with you in our bed" and flashed the biggest smile at him. Paul immediately calmed down and thought *this is what she does for me, keeps me on a straight path and calm.*

Once home they did go to bed but she would only let Paul hold her. It threw him and he tried not to panic. She felt she couldn't have sex that night but didn't say why to him although he could have guessed. She was so fed up with everything and just wanted to calm down. Once he fell asleep she wiggled out of his arms and hit the couch. She was trying to process everything that night and everything since she met Paul. While she knew she loved him with everything she had—she was distressed over her life with him at that moment. *How many more things are going to happen to us* she thought. Paul felt her gone and got up immediately to see where she was. She pretended she was sleeping so he wouldn't talk to her but he shocked her and picked her up—carrying her back to bed. There was no way he was sleeping in their bed without her. Once he did that—she remembered . . . I do love him that much and know he feels the same about me. She rested her head in his shoulder and went back to bed—safe and secure in his arms.

The next night Paul was at practice and when Maggie got home from work she found Marion sitting on her deck at the table. Maggie's stomach dropped and she just froze there on the top of the stairs. There was no way she was letting her in her house, so she approached her on the deck.

"What are you doing here?" She asked Marion.

"I came to see where Paul lived and to ask you something."

"Ask away. I will answer any of your questions."

"Why? Why did you ruin him? You turned him into a dull, boring person. You took his life away from him and put him in jail, with you."

"Ruin him? You are so blind! Open up your eyes and take a look at yourself. Clammy and drugged up. Are you happy with yourself? Did you see yourself in a mirror lately? Do you know you forgot to put most of your clothes on, when you crawled out from under that bridge you live under to come here?"

Marion did not expect that from Maggie. She thought she was a prissy little thing and really didn't expect to get any answers from her. She just thought she would crawl back to her apartment and lock the door until Paul came home.

Maggie knew she stumped Marion and continued. "I'm calling the police right now. As far as I'm concerned—you are trespassing and I don't want you here. I'm also going to get a PFA against you so you can't come near me or Paul ever again. I am sure once the police see how strung out you are, they will haul your sorry ass in and lock you up until you come down off of whatever it is you are on. How would you like that?" She takes out her phone and dials 911. Marion knew she wasn't bluffing. She heard the phone dial and then the 911 operator answer.

"This is Maggie Tanner. 901 Quincy on the University Campus. There is someone trespassing on my deck that won't leave. Can you send the police immediately please? I fear for my life. This person is strung out on some kind of drug."

Marion's face just dropped and didn't know what to do, so she ran and ran like hell off of her deck. Maggie just screamed "come here again and I will call the police again." Marion just turned around and threw her the finger which made Maggie laugh.

Now that did it! Maggie was steaming mad. She felt she handled Marion the way she should have been handled. Paul came home in time to see her throwing stuff around. He froze in the doorway and wondered, *what happened now*. She was throwing his clothes, his sneakers, pillows and just stomping her feet all around the apartment.

"What happened? Stop right now and tell me!" As he follows her around the rooms trying to catch her. Her face was red and she was out of breath and seemed she didn't even notice him. Finally, he caught her and held her two arms forcing her to stop and look at him.

She was breathing heavy and tears were streaming down her face and she looked like she was furious at him and like she saw a ghost as he shook her to get her to come around. She broke free from his embrace and walked past him, now pacing back and forth in the living room, then the kitchen, running her fingers through her hair like she wanted to rip it out.

"Maggie, tell me now—what is going on. When I left today you were fine. *We* were fine. What happened? Please—my heart is pounding right out of my chest. Please!"

She sits at the table and her head is down still not saying anything.

Paul slowing walks towards her and kneels next to her at the table. "Please Mags! Please don't tell me we are over. It would kill me."

With that comment she looks at him and tells him "I love you more than I can say Paul. I want you to know that." With that statement Paul thought—*she is leaving me*.

"Please Maggie. Please don't say we are over! I am begging you to not give up on me. On us!"

She is staring at him, while her head is spinning and trying to regroup. Her heart was breaking because she knew she could never leave him. She was already too deep in her marriage and loved him more than she thought possible. In truth, she loved Paul and loved being married to him. "I could never give up on you or us. I need a release Paul. I need to just throw something or hit someone. I don't want to yell or take it out on you or anyone. I don't know how to process stuff that happens to us anymore. It seems to be never ending! Can you tell me how to get over this?"

Paul felt somewhat relieved with her last statement to him and lets out a huge sigh, dropping his head for a moment and then looks back up at her.

"Tell me what happened so I can help you. Help us."

"I came home from work and Marion was sitting on our deck. She said I ruined you and I'm keeping you in jail with me. Boring and useless . . ."

Paul was shocked and did not expect to hear Marion was at their apartment and he was upset and wondered *is she going to keep coming here?* He thought he made it clear he was married and to leave him alone. "I'm so sorry. I am always apologizing to you. How much longer are you going to suffer from my mistakes, my past? Even though it would kill me if you left . . . I don't know how you handle all of this."

"How come you didn't tell me about her Paul? Were you waiting for her to come back to you? I just don't understand why I didn't know about her."

"I never think about her even though I think about my past. Yes, she is the one that I partied with and introduced me to her dealer, but we were never in a relationship and even though she claims we were friends—we weren't, really. I just saw her at parties and wound up hanging out with her. We never had sex. It wasn't like that. I don't know what she thought coming back here. Was she really expecting me to continue hanging out with her or did she want more at that time and I didn't see it—I really don't know and certainly don't want to ask her. The way she reacted when she saw me—I think she thought I was waiting for her to come back. I don't know where she would have gotten that idea from. I haven't spoken to her since the day she left. What else did she say to you?"

"She was strung out on something and had half her clothes on. I told her I was getting a PFA against her for you *and* me, so she couldn't come near us. Then I called 911 and she thought I was bluffing until she heard the 911 operator answer. I told them there was someone trespassing on my deck and wouldn't leave and I feared for my life . . . Send the police. I told Marion if she was still here, the police would lock her up because they would see she was on something. That is when she ran away as fast as she could." Maggie's head is down and then lifted I asking "do you think she will keep coming back here or did my threat about calling the police get to her?"

"I don't know but if she does we will get that PFA against her. I don't want her near you or me. I just don't understand it myself. Maybe she has no friends and thought I was the only friend she had here. I wish I had an answer for you but once again—I don't. Please forgive me Maggie."

'Forgive you?" Asking with a questioned look on her face.

"Yes, please forgive me for what I did to you. I got you into some kind of nightmare . . . marrying me." Paul's head is down now and she grabs his face in her two hands and kisses him. Then he responded with deep, wild kisses which she loved and noticed he was holding her tighter than ever before. She didn't want to blame him. She knows he wanted to straighten out his life and realizing now, how deeply their feelings actually were for each other. So once again, she tries to calm him down. After all, she thought, that was her job as his wife.

"Did I ever tell you how much I love your kisses?" Smiling at Paul trying to make them both feel better.

Paul flashed the biggest smile back at her and it seemed to calm both of them down. "How about we go out to dinner tonight. I think we could splurge on something for *us* this month." Maggie nodded—agreeing.

CHAPTER 37

Old Habits Surface

Marion never showed up again, and neither saw her or had any contact with her after that police call.

February passed and the team was on a roll. They would make it to the playoffs easily with their record and not only was the whole school buzzing about that—but the whole community was buzzing about it. The newspapers were very kind to the team posting article after article about them and their success because it was a success for the whole area—not just the team. Everyone supported them and tickets for the games usually sold out days before.

March madness arrived and the last games being played were tough ones. Teams with similar records all vying for the same thing—a ticket to the big dance.

Everywhere any of the players went they were treated like rock stars and they were all loving it! Coach B had to continuously remind them to not let it go to their heads or it would ruin their game and friendships within the team. The 10 players were closer than best friends. They were brothers that year and supported each other fully with whatever was going on in each of their lives.

Every now and then on a Sunday afternoon you could find them all at Paul's where his wife would cook up a mean dish of pasta and meatballs for everyone. After everyone would leave Maggie and Paul would just lie in bed—arms around each other feeling so happy and content—not being able to take that smile off of eithers face.

So, they made the playoffs and the games were set. The final game for the championship would be 2 hours away and they had the dates for those games but Maggie couldn't ask for the time off because she didn't know if Paul would make it that far. She certainly hoped so, but they had to wait until each game was played. The tournament was one and done!

Again—tickets were at a premium. There were only so many seats in that gym and it was the biggest gym in the area. So Paul made sure he got tickets for Maggie, her family and friends and of course his mom and dad.

First playoff game came and went—having won decisively. They advanced to the next round and won that one too by 6 points. Maggie thought that was too close for comfort and sweated it out sitting in the bleachers with Sarah, his parents and Mrs. B. She couldn't wait for that one to be over.

If they won the next game—it would advance them to the final two. There was so much hope out there from everyone that they would make it. Paul was a wreck knowing what a big game it was. They were so close to the championship they could practically taste it.

On his way up the hill to his apartment after practice one night, his old drug dealer followed him. Then he surprised Paul and hugged him. Paul turned white. He didn't want to be near that guy and the dealer recognized that look. "I left you something in your coat pocket. No one saw us. I thought you might need something to help you take the edge off." Paul backed away from him and turned not even saying a word to him and just walked away.

Maggie didn't know what she could do to calm him down. He was so nervous—she worried he would look for something on his own to help him. It scared her to death thinking he might slip back to *those* days.

She thought *I will have to tell him how I am feeling so he knows how afraid I am for him and us.*

Paul comes home from practice and he is so wired and wound up, he couldn't sit still. She fed him dinner and after she cleaned up she went to find him so she could talk to him.

He is just pacing in their bedroom and it confuses her about what he was doing.

"Can we talk about something?" She asks.

Somehow he knows what she is going to say. He reaches in his pocket and pulls out a baggie with two pills in it. That dealer sought him out and gave it to him.

She turned white and he saw her look like she was going to pass out—almost confirming all of her fears about Paul slipping back down that black hole. At that moment—he hands her the bag.

Looking at the contents she quietly asks—"did you pay for this?"

"No."

"Is anyone else on the team going to take this?"

His head is dropped and he is looking at the floor as he sits on the bed.

"Does anyone else know you have this?"

"Just the person who gave it to me."

"Marion's dealer?"

"Yes"

"Do you think that person would turn you in?"

"No, he has too much to lose. He would never say a word." Paul almost whispers his answers to her.

"Do you want to tell me who he is?"

"No Mags. I don't think you should know. If by some slim chance any-thing should happen—you will be able to say honestly—you had no idea where I got it."

She kneels down in front of him placing her hands on his knees while still holding the bag.

"Do you remember when we were discussing our relationship and said we would talk everything out so there would be no issues between us? Or causing us harm?"

He nods his head yes and gets emotional, lowering his head to meet hers.

She lets him go until he could compose himself so he could explain to her why he felt he needed to do this.

"If you tell me . . . you need this *more* than me . . . I will give it back to you" now holding the bag so he could see it.

Now he is really upset and distressed—shaking his head no and she sees his heart breaking. Again she lets him go.

She puts the bag down and pulls him on the bed with her where she wraps him in her arms.

He calmed right down but still wasn't speaking. "I will talk first. OK?"

He nods his head yes.

"You are so worried and nervous about the next game because it's a big one. Maybe you thought you needed something to take the edge off of you because you are so wired."

He nods his head yes again.

"Did you forget how you almost died the last time someone gave you a pill to take? Or what was decided on, if you got upset or anxiety ridden?"

He did not respond.

"I'm here to take that edge off and help you. I'm here to stop you from ruining your life. Most importantly—I'm here to stop you from ruining *our* life."

"Will you let me?" She says it with tears streaming down her face and she starts shaking now—feeling so scared she cannot reach him.

Once he feels her trembling in his arms—he realizes everything she just told him or asked him. He seemed to snap out of the turmoil he was in and now wanted to help her.

He lifts his head and kisses her softly and wraps her in his arms holding onto her so tightly.

"I was pacing because I was debating on whether I should tell you or not. That one little voice in my head saying *she won't know. It's just one pill.* But I *did* remember we promised we would talk everything out. That is why I hesitated and I did remember the last time I took a pill and what it had done to me. I almost died. But thank God for Nicky! I feel you shaking in my arms and know I did this to you. I'm making you shake and I scared you. I will not do anything to jeopardize our marriage—our relationship or my love for you."

They both are crying now and holding onto each other and wouldn't let go.

Paul tightens his grip on her trying to help her. He thought how calm she was talking to him. She didn't yell or scream at him. She just calmly talked to him about what he was about to do. He again realized all the harm he could have done to himself, to his wife and to his life.

After a few minutes he feels her melting into his arms. She looks up and kisses him. He responded and kissed her back wildly. He starts undressing her and she pulls his T-shirt over his head and unbuttons his jeans. They both quickly remove what was left of the clothing on their bodies. This was just for them—for all of the anxiety building up between them. They had to have that release—to calm them down. It was wild and wonderful and full of passion like they had never experienced before. She pulled at his hair and bit his lip while reaching to stroke him up and down all the while breathing deeply and moaning when his touch was not as light as usual. He kneaded her breasts with his hands and his fingers held her nipples while he sucked and nipped at them in his mouth. She threw one leg over his hip trying to pull him down on her and it totally worked as he broke away from their wild kisses and positioned himself between her legs. She wrapped them around him as if to hold him captive until she was ready to release him. Again they were so ready for each other and again they exploded together at the same time taking their breath away while moaning with pleasure. Paul collapsed on his wife's body where she kept him there with her arms and legs wrapped around him, holding onto him so tightly.

Once they caught their breath—she released him from her grips and

He wrapped her up in his arms pulling her on top of him so he could hold onto *her*.

Again she starts kissing him but this time the kisses were soft and so full of love. He responded the same and when they were ready again—it was full of feelings and love for each other. They took it slow and enjoyed every caress, every kiss, every moan with the pleasure and love they felt for each other. Again when they were finished—she kept him wrapped in her arms—sighing at the way she felt about him.

She whispers "right now with you in my arms—I cannot describe all the feelings I have for you. The one I *can* make out is how much I love you Paul. It almost hurts it's so much. That feeling is so powerful!"

"I almost destroyed that Mags. I almost destroyed us!"

"No! You stopped and I believe your love for me caused that hesitation. It worked Paul. Our love for each other stopped you."

She gets up and finds the bag with the pills in it and takes it to the bathroom—flushing them down the toilet.

They crawled under the covers and slept like babies—so peacefully through the whole night waking the way they fell asleep—wrapped in each other's arms.

CHAPTER 38

Getting Ready

Well—the game Paul was so wired about came and went with them winning decisively. Paul and Nicky were so in tune with each other—it seemed they were unstoppable. Some of the plays they made together where heart stopping—amazing and unbelievable. The crowd was wild from the time the buzzer rang to start the game to the final seconds.

Then it became official. They were heading to Philadelphia to play for the national championship. The final two. The town was buzzing, the community was buzzing and the campus was buzzing. Everyone in the state it seemed was excited about the game. How lucky they were that the game would be played in Pennsylvania. It was the first time ever a National Championship would ever be brought to their home state. The support they had was unheard of for our little University. They were the Cinderella story of the year.

Paul and the team would be gone 2 days before the game to get ready for it. They needed to practice on that court at the arena and be rested rather than travel the night before or day of the game. Coach B felt that would be too much. So on Thursday they headed out.

That morning before Maggie had to go to work—Paul was moping around the house. She saw a different look on his face. One she never saw before and it concerned her.

Going to him and kneeling in front of him sitting on the couch she takes his hands in hers.

"Do you want to tell me why you look like you are going to a wake? Smiling so widely at him.

He just flashes her a big smile back and answers "I should have known you would see it."

"Tell me what's on your mind."

"I won't be home for two nights."

"That is what you are worried about?"

"Yes, I'm leaving my wife alone for two nights. It bothers me, along with the fact that I won't be with you for two nights. We have never been away from each other since the day we got married. I'm finding . . . I don't like it."

She just kisses both hands one at a time and replies "how sweet of you to worry about me. I will be working until nine tonight so it will keep my mind off of you not being with me. When I get home I'm planning to go right to bed so I don't think about you not being in our bed. Then on Friday I will have my meltdown—being so anxious to get to you. That's my plan . . . how do you like it so far . . ." Laughing, to try and ease his mind.

He starts laughing too and she sees his expression change.

"Please don't worry. Molly and Judy are going to drive to the game with me. I won't be alone and I have my room confirmation too. I have the directions to the arena and will see you there. I will text you every minute I get to let you know how I am and what I'm doing."

"Mags, I feel better you are all set. I know you told me about your plans before—but I feel better hearing them again."

She lifts her hand to his face and tells him "I love you Paul. I will be with you always, every time you just think about me."

"I don't know if I would even be going to this game if it weren't for you. Thank you Mags. Every day I see what I could have missed if I continued on the path I was on."

"Paul, if you feel yourself slipping again, calls me immediately. I will help you. Call me for or about anything. Do you hear me?"

He just nods his head agreeing.

"Now, I have to get to work and you have to get to the bus before they leave without you. Tell Nicky I said good luck."

"I will tell him Mags. I'll see you Saturday but will talk to you as soon as I get there."

He lowers his head to hers and kisses her softly first and then like it could have lasted an hour. Finally breaking away from that kiss he looks at her and sees her eyes well up with tears.

"Not to worry. They are happy tears. So happy you love me so much."

"I do Maggie. I love you so much. I'll talk to you later." She nods she heard him and turns to leave. She can't look back or she will run back to him and never make it to work so she just keeps walking to her car to get to work.

CHAPTER 39

The Big Game

As promised Paul texted Maggie as soon as he got to his room in Philadelphia. The smile on her face when she got it was unmistakable to all of her co-workers in her office. They knew she just heard from her husband. They all smiled to each other because they saw how she glowed every time she heard from him.

Thank God she had work until 9 that night because she was so anxious being without him He was right when he said they hadn't been apart since they got married 7 months ago. She didn't know how she would get by on Friday night. That night she was sure would be one of the longest of her life, just counting the hours—minutes—seconds until they left on Saturday for the game.

Many businesses in town were closed Saturday and so was her shop. Everyone including Sarah was headed to Philly for the game. After all, they knew the two point guards and couldn't wait to see them play. Joseph, Frank and Maggie's dad were all going to watch the game on TV because it was going to be televised.

Once Saturday finally arrived -she gathered up her two friends and headed to Philly. They were so excited and talked and laughed all the way to the hotel to check in. They met Paul's parents in the lobby. It turned out they were waiting for them which she thought was so nice. It made her so happy.

Lois hugged them also saying "I'm so happy to see you again Molly and Judy." Everyone was thrilled at how things were going.

"I will take us all to the arena if that's Ok with you. I promised my son I wouldn't let you out of my sight today Maggie" now smiling at her. "That's ok with us" looking at her friends for their approval and they both said it was.

Maggie was shaking she was so anxious for the game. She got quiet and everyone noticed. Molly asked "What's wrong? Is everything alright?"

"Yes- I'm just so nervous about the game. I can't seem to calm down."

Judy chimed right in "I am too. I don't know why *I'm* so nervous about it. It's not like I'm playing out there or *my* guy is out there."

They all laughed and it seems to calm the three of them down a little.

The arena was massive and packed with fans already and they looked for Mrs. B and found her and the seats she saved for them.

"I was lucky to get these. It's just crazy here" she told them. But the seats were good and they could see the whole floor and they looked right down at the bench.

Finally the music the team practiced to, blared through the loud speakers and everyone went wild waiting for them to come out onto the floor for their warmups.

With everyone now standing, Maggie looked and looked and Molly finally said "there he is Maggie" and following Molly's finger—she saw Paul coming out.

Her body was shaking she was so nervous and really didn't know how she could calm herself down. Lois just took her hand and squeezed it realizing her daughter was in such a state. Maggie held onto her hand and it seemed to work.

When she looked at Paul on the court she could see something was wrong. Then she looked at Nicky and saw the same thing.

She turns to her mother and said "something is wrong."

Lois did not know what she was talking about. "What do you mean?"

"Look at Paul and Nicky. They aren't just nervous about the game. They look wrong. Off!"

Lois looked and her face dropped and she turned immediately to Mike and told him. Mike then looked and he said the same thing. "You're right Maggie. Something is wrong."

Mike quickly went to see the trainer to see what was going on. Mrs.

B even saw that something was wrong.

Maggie saw Mike's head slump and knew it wasn't good. Whatever the trainer told him, could not have been good.

He comes back and everyone including Mrs. B huddled around him to see what happened.

"Someone told the committee that some of the team members were doing drugs for the games and that they were on something tonight. They drug tested 5 of the 10 players. Nicky and Paul were two of them." Maggie turned white and at that moment they all saw that and thought she was going to faint. Mrs. B grabbed her around her waist to hold her up not wanting to cause a commotion in front of everyone.

Then Mike told everyone—"they were all clean."

Maggie just started crying and couldn't stop. She lowered her head in the little huddle so no one could see her. Mrs. B and Lois kept rubbing her back and patting her hand. Molly and Judy were so stunned they were speechless.

Then Maggie lifts her head and said "Someone set them up. I know that's what happened. Paul came home last week with two pills someone gave him. One for each remaining game. We flushed them down the toilet. That person set them up. I asked Paul if anyone else on the team got them too and he wouldn't tell me. Someone wanted them to lose either last game or tonight. Whoever gave him those, knew he took them before. This is just too much! Oh my God! The most important game and this happens" she said still crying and upset.

Mrs. B asked "Maggie, Can I tell Coach what you just said. It might help the boys knowing this was a set up."

She looks at her father and asked "Dad, what do you think? Will it make matters worse?"

"No Maggie. I think the truth has to come out and you know also—that my son was clean. What a win for us all. Don't you see that?"

She nods her head to Mrs. B and off she went to tell her husband as they all went back to their seats to wait and see what Coach tells her. People sitting around them saw Maggie being upset and Mike just told them she is just so nervous about the game. "We were just trying to calm her down." Everyone bought it and commented, if it were their husband or son on the floor—they would probably be just as anxious and nervous.

Preliminary warm ups were done and they all headed back to the locker room to regroup until 15 minutes before the game. Everyone stood and cheered as they left the floor. She stood on her seat trying to catch her husband's eye and when she did she tried to flash the biggest smile at him to try and make him feel better. He smiled back at her and put his hand on his heart patting it. It made her smile even bigger to him.

Mrs. B came back and Coach B agreed it was a set up. Not naming anyone in the locker room he is going to tell the team just that. They both felt by mentioning it—it would make them play harder. She said they were all shook when the committee came into the locker room and called out those 5 players for drug tests. Coach felt even though they were clean—it shook them up enough to disrupt their game coming up. Because Maggie and the rest noticed it immediately that they looked off—he felt whoever wanted this to happen accomplished their goal. They all looked shaken.

The music starts and the team is getting ready to take the court again and this time they all looked at their faces on the court and could tell they came out with a different attitude. Mrs. B said "It looks like it worked Maggie. Whatever Coach said to them worked because I could tell they look different now."

Everyone all nodded their heads—they saw the difference.

Keeping up with the tradition—Coach nodded to Paul that he could leave the court and he came right to Maggie. He ran up the steps to their seats and kissed his Mom and Dad and took off his wedding ring and gave it to his wife who placed it alongside hers. Then took her hand and kissed it—sending everyone over the top. Mrs. B just laughed as she always did and everyone around them clapped and screamed. Then he bent down and kissed her lips, surprising her.

Touching his face she quickly told him "Good luck. I know you will have a great game today. I love you Paul!"

With that, he put his hand on his heart and pretended he was falling backwards at what she said and they all laughed about it. He quickly kissed her again and went back to the court.

The buzzer rang, signaling it was time to start the game.

Maggie was a nervous wreck and wondered how she was ever going to make it through the whole game. She was nervous sweating and kept wringing her hands until her mother in law grabbed hold of them both trying to calm her down. "Doing that is not going to help your husband Maggie" saying as she smiled at her warmly. That helped her a little, but not much.

Every time one team scored, the other countered. It was like that the whole first half. There were hardly any fouls either. Both teams played hard as soon as they got over the jitters in the first few minutes of the game.

With only 2 minutes left to the half and the score tied at 40 apiece— Nicky inbounded the ball from Paul and took it down court. All of a sudden Paul was left alone under the basket which Nicky saw and quickly looped the ball to him where he caught it . . . feet off the ground and slam dunked it through the net for 2 points. That was their signature play. The crowd went wild. It was so loud you couldn't even hear the buzzer sounding off for a time out the opposing team called. They all ran over to the bench to get instructions from Coach B. He always had a poker face and he rarely smiled. They knew if they won tonight—he would finally be happy.

Maggie was screaming so loudly all night that she practically lost her voice and they still had a whole second half to go yet. The buzzer sounded again and they all went on the court where the opposing team would inbound the ball.

Nicky and Paul were so in tuned with each other after that shot that just happened. The point guard threw the ball to his player where Paul stole it and threw it to Nicky under the basket for another 2 points and this time he was fouled!

Again everyone was screaming and standing and clapping. Nicky took his place on the foul line and threw the ball up and in it went to finish off the 3 point play. So now they were up by 5 points but that still was not enough to make everyone breathe any better.

The opposing team again inbounded the ball and took it right down for a quick 2 points which narrowed the lead again to 3 points and that is how the half ended with the University ahead by 3.

Maggie sat down and tried to regroup as Paul's mom and dad and Mrs. B all breathed a sigh of relief for the moment. So many fans kept coming over to Maggie and telling her good luck with the second half as if she were the one on the court. She just said thank you or joked about not knowing if she could survive another half like the first one. Something else happened. The TV Network carrying the game found out Paul was married and started focusing on her in the stands. Every time something happened they showed her reaction. Joseph and Frank were stunned they kept showing her on TV. They texted her and told her and she was stunned. She had no idea the world was watching her have a nervous breakdown—so she tried to watch what she was doing during the second half. Everyone around her was stunned when she told them too. Even Mrs. B because they were focused on her too!

The team came out—the buzzer sounded off and everyone went on court and shook hands to start the final half. Again it was a see/ saw game. One team scored—the other countered. They kept up with each other throughout the whole game. Finally with a minute left and the score tied, a time out was called by the other team. Coach B told them—if they scored more than 2 points, their opponents would likely start to foul his players—hoping they wouldn't make their foul shots so they could try to get the rebound and ball back. He told them to try not to foul anyone and give them that chance to score. Let them really earn their next points. So off everyone went back on the court and again Paul inbounded the ball to Nicky who saw their center standing all alone under the basket so he flung the ball practically the whole length of the court to him and up he went—dunking the ball for 2 points. The visitors quickly tried to inbound the ball to catch everyone off guard and the only people they caught off guard were their own players. Paul intercepted the pass to one of the point guards and up he went for an easy layup for another 2 points. Everyone was crazy in the stands. People were clapping and screaming and so were Maggie and Paul's parents, Molly, Judy and Mrs. B all holding onto each other jumping up and down.

Now they are up by 4 points with 30 seconds left. 30 seconds in basketball time . . . was a lifetime. Coach knew the visiting team only had 1 more timeout left while he had 2. They inbounded the ball again and Coach couldn't believe his opponent didn't call a time out after that last play which is what he would have done. They got the ball past half court and proceeded to shoot a three pointer which bounced off the rim and landed right in the hands of our big senior center. He saw Nicky go down court and threw it all the way down for him to get and he did, as it bounced right in his hands, where he jumped up for an easy layup. Now up by 6 points with 20 seconds left the visiting coach called his final time out. Everyone knew what he would instruct his players to do. Foul whoever gets the ball.

The 10 players walked to the end of the court where now Nicky was instructed to inbound the ball to Paul instead of Paul inbounding it to Nicky. Everyone knew why too. Paul had practiced his foul shots and had an 84% rating for foul points. Everyone on the team knew—he practiced his butt off and his wife used to rebound for him. So that was the new plan and did it ever work.

Up by 6 points—Nicky inbounded the ball to Paul where he was fouled immediately. Maggie was so worried and knew if he missed and something happened like they lost the game—he would blame himself. So up to the line he goes while his teammates all slapped him on the back or fist bumped him. Everyone took their positions and the ref threw the ball to Paul who bounced it twice at his feet before he threw up the first shot. Right through the net! Not even hitting the rim!

The place was going crazy. Everyone was standing now on their seats.

Next shot—2 bounces then up and right through the net again! People were jumping up and down and screaming at the top of their lungs.

The ball is inbounded again and coach told his team not to foul anyone so they let the point guard take it right down for an easy layup. Still up by 6, Nicky inbounds the ball to Paul with 8 seconds left.

He is fouled immediately, *again*.

Up to the line he goes and the ref bounces the ball to him where he again bounced it twice in front of his feet. Then he threw it up and Oh My God! It went right in. All net—not even banking it off the backboard or hitting the rim.

Second shot went up as everyone held their breath—only to see it go right in again! The noise was unbelievable and the electricity was amazing in that place.

8 seconds to go and again they let the team take it right down for an easy shot and that player . . . *missed*! It was wild out there! . . .

It was unbelievable and with 3 seconds left—Nicky inbounded the ball to Paul and before he could even be fouled he threw the ball straight up into the air as the buzzer sounded the end of the game and it was complete bedlam out there on the floor.

Nicky went right to Paul where they hugged each other jumping up and down. Then the starting 5 were in a group hug with each other while the rest of the bench emptied and went out to join in the celebration. Even Coach was finally smiling while hugging all of the assistant coaches.

Confetti and streamers were falling from the rafters in the ceiling of the arena and it was the biggest party any of them had ever witnessed. Music was blasting and the team was lying on the floor jumping on each other, celebrating.

Maggie was crying and just couldn't stop the tears from coming. Mrs. B was crying and so were Paul's parents. They just all kept hugging each other; all with camera's capturing it.

Mike said to Maggie "thank you Maggie. If it weren't for you—I don't think we would be here today . . . in this gym . . . watching the most amazing thing happen to my son." Then he and his wife just grabbed her and they all cried together.

When the players got off of each other on the floor they went to shake the hands of their opponent and congratulated them on a great game played. The sportsmanship they demonstrated made her so proud of all of them.

After that they all went to look for their families and Paul was trying to get through the crowd to get to his wife and parents. Mrs. B already went down to find Coach and they lost track of her, there were so many people now on the court.

Paul finally finds Maggie who is standing on her seat crying while looking for him. She sees him coming to her and she jumps down and ran to him, jumping from the steps right into his arms where he hugged her swinging her around and around. He was crying too and he just kept hugging her. He was so emotional at that moment he couldn't even speak.

His parents found him and they just put their arms around the 2 of them feeling so much love for their son and daughter.

Paul puts Maggie down and lowers his head to meet hers. You just couldn't get that smile off of his face or anyone else's for that matter.

The ceremony for the presentation of the Championship trophy was next and he had to get back to his teammates to get his medal and see the trophy be presented to Coach B.

He kissed her "I cannot believe how much I love you Maggie. At this moment—I cannot believe all that has happened to me."

Nicky came and kissed and hugged Maggie and then had to pull Paul away from her—walking to the podium—arms around each other—where the rest of the team and coaches were all gathered.

The trophy was presented and each player got a medal which Maggie didn't expect. It was like the Olympics she thought. She watched as Paul's name was called 2nd to last and cried when the commissioner put that medal around his neck. Then Nicky's name was last and again she felt so proud as everyone screamed when they both got their medals. No one was leaving that gym until the team left the court.

Finally after about an hour of celebrating in the arena they all went to shower and change. The University was throwing a big party after the game. Win or lose they were so happy with the way things turned out that year for the season. Everyone was just so proud of the whole team and they had so many sponsors. It seemed every business down town and around the area donated to the trip.

As they always did, they waited in the lobby for Nicky and Paul to come out and when Maggie saw him she couldn't contain herself. She ran right to him and jumped in his arms where he was waiting for her. He just kept hugging and hugging her until his mom said "my turn to hug my son now" while laughing. She let go of him and he hugged his mom and dad while they both cried as they had their arms wrapped around their only son. It was so moving—everyone just watched the warm moment between them all. Then they hugged and kissed Nicky like he was their son too and you could tell Nicky was loving it. Molly and Judy became good friends with Nicky and were so happy and proud of him. They both went to him and hugged him together knowing his parents weren't there to see him. They wanted him to feel special too and did he ever appreciate their friendship.

Off to the dinner and party everyone headed and what a party it was. There were at least 500 people in that ballroom of the hotel they were all staying at and everyone was still clapping and screaming as the team entered the room. It was an amazing site and one they would never forget. The ballroom was decorated with streamers and balloons in the school's colors of blue and gold and was so big—none of them ever expected to see that many people and that big of a ballroom filled. Everyone wanted to talk to Paul and he stopped to talk to everyone who approached him but never let go of his wife's hand. He wasn't going to let her out of his sight or this time be pulled away from her to talk to someone.

He whispers in her ear "Let's sneak out for a while. Do you think we could disappear for a half hour?"

She just smiles widely at him and nods her head and they snuck behind people and out the side door where they ran to the elevators to get to her room on the 12th floor, running down the hall and laughing so much they couldn't stop.

Once she opened the door they locked it and barricaded it in case anyone saw them or followed them.

Now secured in their room—Maggie started undressing and Paul followed her lead. Their kisses were wild and passionate. She pulled him onto the bed where she crawled on top of him grabbing his hair and positioning herself over him getting ready to take him in. Once she consumed him they both moved to the rhythm of their bodies— moaning with desire . . . while Paul caressed her body. Again they exploded together and afterwards she fell on him where he held onto her tightly waiting for the spasms to stop so they could catch their breath. Then he picks her up in his arms and gently lays her under him where he was ready again for her. She just laughed and the moaning started all over again as he looked down at her and whispered "I love you Mags."

While lying in Maggie's arms Paul told her "I didn't think I could survive two nights without you. It was so difficult. Nicky was a big help.

I told him how I felt about leaving you and I think he was stunned at first. Then he said—he was so happy for me. He saw how happy and content I was and knew it was because of you. He said he loved you for it. Our talk was getting a little too heavy so I lightened the mood by just warning him to stay away from my wife. We both laughed so hard and then it kind of settled us both down and we were able to fall asleep." With that she leans down and kisses his head wondering if she were dreaming or did everything that happened to her the past 7 months . . . really happen. She tightened her grip on him and he knew she was thinking about something and lifted his head to kiss her softly.

Maggie didn't mention the drug test not wanting to spoil the night. She felt he would tell her when he was ready—if he ever was going to tell her. She left it up to him.

After a while they felt they had to get up and rejoin the party before someone looked for them. So they showered quickly and headed back to the ballroom.

They sat with their family and friends and ate being so hungry— neither had an appetite the last few days. It suddenly came back, now that everything was over.

As they watched everyone and everything happening around them they both smiled at each other and knew they were both thinking the same thing. What a ride the past 7 months had been!

CHAPTER 40

Shocking

The team had a State Police escort all the way back home to Northeastern Pennsylvania. Not *a* State Police escort—many police cars escorting them. Two in front of the bus, two in back and 2 two down the side. Then once they hit the county line—local police from all the towns around the University joined in—waiting for them on the highway. So many people were waiting for the team to come back. They opened up Memorial Stadium so everyone could fit—there were so many. Sirens were screaming right up to the time they arrived to thousands of fans and alumni. To top it all off, the weather even cooperated. It was so beautiful and warm the day they came back. No one would ever forget how special that week end was for eternity.

The paper had a whole section devoted to that championship game and pictures of all the games leading up to the big one.

There were so many articles about the players and coaches you would think they were interviewing players from the NBA. The reporters from other areas also loved talking to the players and taking pictures. They were so happy for the team.

There were multiple pictures of Maggie and Paul and some of Maggie with Paul's parents. Pictures of Paul and Nicky on the court and on the sidelines talking about what they were going to do. They were very popular and once again they were voted the top 2 point guards in the nation. It made everyone so proud of them. Not to mention they were only sophomores.

Maggie's father saw all of those pictures and noticed she looked so happy. *Paul Tanner credits his wife Maggie for helping him during the season and keeping him calm during the playoff games.* Then they had a picture of him swinging her around after that last game.

Frank went to bed early that night. He felt so calm and never remembered feeling that way before. Well, he did remember, his wife always made him feel calm. She meant the world to him. He was well aware of all of his demons but she was the one that kept them in control. Right from the first day they met. Why he couldn't bond with his 3 children was something they both always wondered. She wanted children and he wasn't going to refuse her that pleasure. She totally enjoyed her two sons and then when Maggie was born—she felt complete. Maggie was always dressed nice when she was a baby, in girly—girl clothes and every time Frank came home from work—she always had her looking so cute for him. He never admitted it but he loved it and she knew it.

While in a deep sleep, Frank is dreaming again. Once again his wife visited him in his dreams. All she said this time to him was "Thank you my love!" Frank knew exactly what she meant and just smiled at her. He knew she could finally rest in peace and believe it or not, he felt peaceful too. He also knew for some reason he would be with her soon. He didn't know how he knew that but felt, he would see her soon and maybe—he would meet her in heaven and be with her forever there.

The next day Frank and Joseph were a little leery about coming into work because it was Joseph's last day with them. They never knew if their father would turn back into Dr Hyde or Jekyll. It worried them until he came in with coffee for the 3 of them. The brothers just looked at each other and relaxed immediately. "Joseph, you are starting your new job Monday right?" He asked. "Yes Dad, Monday."

"I hope you are not worried about it. You will be just fine there. Frank, let's talk about your salary and fill out the benefits paperwork. Can you do it now before you go on the road with deliveries?"

"Yes dad. Let's go do it now." He smiled at his brother and teased him "Load up the truck while I'm busy with dad and then we can go as soon as I'm done." Joseph teased him right back. "Ok, so you are going to make me work my ass off today because it is my last day. Nice! Very Nice." They both laughed and so did their dad.

When Your Past Comes Back to Haunt You 'Again'

Paul got a job that summer as an intern for an Advertising Agency down town and not far from Maggie's shop. That was his field at the U and when they heard he was looking for a job—they scoffed him up. He would drop Maggie off at her shop and head over to his office down the street. He never realized how hard it was for her, now that he had a job too—working and coming home and doing everything she did every day and it shocked him and embarrassed him. He realized he took her for granted with all she had on her plate and started helping out around the house more and more and certainly had a new appreciation for his wife. He went to school and played ball. She had a lot more going on.

They even put some money aside to take a little vacation to the shore. They never had a honeymoon and felt this would be it. Paul's parents and even her dad Frank Sr both gave them a check to take the trip and relax for a change with the schedules they both kept. Maggie loved the shore and Paul notice how much it calmed her down and relaxed her. He realized she needed that time away from everything and it seemed to rejuvenate her.

Fall rolled around quickly and before either knew it—it was time for Paul to get back to school in September and then practice would start up in October. Time was flying by for the both of them being as busy as they were.

Maggie still loved her job and she once again started practicing with Paul every chance she got. He loved when she went to the gym with him and then they would come home and have a light dinner. He was still terrible in the kitchen.

Paul's grades were great and even made the Dean's list which made Maggie and his parents so proud.

The season started as it ended last year with the team being so hot—every opponent wanted to knock them off of their pedestal. Nicky and Paul were both on fire and so in tune with each other—they were amazing to watch.

Paul and Maggie were in the gym one night in the middle of the season right after the holiday's when a girl comes in holding a child who seemed to be maybe 18 months old. She came right over to Paul with Maggie sitting right in the bleachers. She just watched to see what was going on not giving it a second thought. Then his head is slumped and his face was all red and she sees him looking at the baby.

Maggie gets up and walks over to them. Paul just looks at her—face still all red.

The girl spoke to her, telling her what was going on.

"I know you are Mrs. Tanner. I have a baby—her name is Kristin and she is 16 months old. I don't want you to think Paul cheated on you. I was with him before you even met but I'm thinking Paul is her father. I'm here to ask if he would take a DNA test to confirm it. If he is not my daughter's father—I promise I will never bother either of you again."

Maggie tried to stay calm. She knew Paul was wild before he met her and she knew that was one of the reasons he wanted to clean up his act. But neither, ever thought this would come back to haunt him.

"What is your name?"

"Elizabeth."

"Paul, we can talk about this when we get home."

Looking at Elizabeth "Can you give us your # so we can call you tomorrow? Paul will let you know what his decision will be."

"Do you have any specifics? Where would you like him to go for the DNA test and who will be reviewing the results? Is there anything else you can tell us regarding when you conceived your beautiful daughter?" Maggie was shaking and trying to keep it together but realized—so was that girl.

Elizabeth relaxed immediately once Maggie called her daughter beautiful and seemed to want to tell her more just then.

"I conceived her the week end of homecoming in Sept of last year. I partied with Paul and some other people in my dorm room. Honestly— I'm not sure Paul is my daughter's father. I had a very active weekend last year during homecoming and one that I will never forgive myself for. Don't get me wrong—I love Kristin, but I'm only 19. It's very difficult to say the least. I had to drop out of school and my parents are helping me but it is getting stressful there. I thought if I could find Kristin's father— I could get some help. I really am not expecting you to be involved in her life if you choose not to be. I am just as much at fault here."

So all her cards are on the table now Maggie thought. She told them what she was expecting from him or the baby's father.

"Can I hold her?"

Maggie saw Elizabeth was surprised she asked to hold Kristin as she handed her over to Maggie.

"You are so beautiful. Look at you!" smiling while talking to the baby. She kissed her and the baby was laughing and so happy. Elizabeth had her dressed in a beautiful pink jacket with a hood and when she took her pink cap off, she saw the baby had black hair and beautiful brown eyes that shined. Elizabeth had the same color hair and eyes and Maggie thought she looked just like her.

Paul just looked at her and the baby together and didn't know what to think or how he should be feeling. He was so stunned and just stood there.

She hands her back to Elizabeth saying "You are doing a great job with her. I can see how happy she is."

Again Elizabeth was shocked Maggie was so nice to her. She also thought how kind she was. She didn't know how either would react when she approached them but found them to be as gracious as they could— being thrown in the situation she just put them in.

"Thank you for your number. Paul will contact you tomorrow. I promise you."

She just nodded her head and zipped up the baby's coat and put her hat on her and left the gym as both Maggie and Paul watched.

"Let's go home now. I'm ready." She told Paul who wasn't saying a word.

They bundled up too and Paul put his hand out to Maggie to take which is how they always walked home—hand in hand. She hesitated and then grabbed his hand squeezing it. She went in for a kiss and he knew that is what she wanted when she lifted her head up to his. He kissed her softly and still didn't say anything as they walked up the small hill to go home.

Once they got inside she tells him "We have to talk about this. I don't want to be in a panic but my first thought is—I cannot afford to give that girl a check every month!"

"I am going to hyperventilate right now! We just get by ourselves! I don't know how we are going to do this." Paul sees Maggie starting to shake.

"I'm so sorry Maggie. I see how upset you are and have every reason to be."

"Do you even remember that girl Paul?"

Now his head is down and he just says "No, I don't remember that person or the week end she was talking about. I was stoned all the time and know on multiple occasions I woke naked with 2 or 3 girls lying in the same bed with me. I'm so sorry I have to tell you that."

"I knew you had drug issues and knew there were many girls but how stupid of me to just erase thinking about that. We are lucky she is the only one that approached you . . . so far!"

Maggie was wild but still not yelling and just paces back and forth in the kitchen and her voice is shaking when speaking to Paul.

"I don't mean to be mean right now, but did your father ever have 'the talk' with you about using . . . *condoms*?"

Her hands are flying all around talking to him and she is trying to keep her head while confronting him but she was about to lose it and she is realizing it so she takes a few deep breaths to calm down.

His head is down almost like he is afraid to look at her. He knows he just put her in the worst possible position ever.

"Are you going to say anything?"

"I'm going to say how scared I am right now Mags. I'm shaking I'm so scared and for many reasons."

"First and foremost I'm scared you will leave me over this. I'm petrified and my heart wants to beat out of my chest thinking that. I just gave you yet *another* reason to run away from me."

"Next, I'm scared that child is mine when I don't even remember that girl or that weekend."

"I'm scared because I have no idea how I am going to help pay for that child when I already put so much pressure on you during school and the season."

"I'm scared because you have to continuously help me take care of my mistakes."

"I'm afraid you will get tired of hearing about them or having to go through them because of me."

"I know I made many mistakes in my life before I met you. That is why I love you so much. You gave me my life back. The life I wanted to have and now do. I just keep screwing it up with my past always coming back to haunt me."

"I'm afraid you will fall out of love with me because of my past. I want *you* to be the mother of my child—conceived out of love for each other, not out of being drunk and stoned."

"I feel so sorry for that child. If I'm not the father—will she even have a chance at life? At a good life?"

"There is a flip side to every coin! What could the flip side to this coin be? That poor child is in a no win situation."

Now *he* is just pacing and pacing back and forth speaking to her.

She regroups and is calmer now. She is surprisingly stunned he was worried about the baby.

"Let's take one thing off the table Paul!"

Paul looks at her puzzled and wondering what she wanted to let go of.

"I will never leave you. I love you. So let's not include that in all of our worries right now."

"You have to get the DNA test. I will not negotiate on that."

Paul goes right to her and wraps her in his arms. He felt he needed to feel her and knew she felt the same.

"Let's wait to see what the DNA test says and then we could be in a panic—but I think you are right about the child. If you aren't the father, that poor baby is in a bad situation already. We can talk about that later too."

"Tomorrow go for the test. Let's get this over with and then we can make some kind of plans if it turns out Kristin is yours."

Paul holds her tighter in his arms. She let go of him and just told him "I have a terrible headache now. I'm going to lie down. I feel I need to rest and I'm not mad at you Paul. This all happened before us. Truthfully I don't know what I am. Weary maybe . . . that's how I feel right now. Just so weary . . . I can't describe it any other way and I want to just rest."

He releases her and she turns to go to lie down and stopped before she took another step.

"Will you come lay down with me?" And now she starts to cry.

Paul just nodded his head and followed her to bed. Once under the covers she rolled over to him where he wrapped his arms around her.

She couldn't stop crying no matter how hard she tried which made him feel worse. Then she stopped and when he looked down at her in his arms he saw she cried herself to sleep. He just rested his head on hers and fell asleep but not until he tried to think about that weekend and what happened. He didn't remember much except how he woke up. He didn't even know whose bed he was in when he woke. It was killing him trying to remember but it killed him more for being so stupid. Then he thought *what kind of shape would I be in today if I hadn't met Maggie?* Once again he had to acknowledge—he might not even be alive if it hadn't been for her and Nicky. He tightened his grip on her and kissed her head softly whispering "I'm so sorry Mags . . . so sorry . . .

Paul and Maggie both woke up early the next morning. They got the name of the lab where he had to go for the DNA test. The woman there said it takes weeks before the results come in and right then he knew his life would be turned upside down until they did. Maggie opted out of going with him. She felt she just couldn't. She kind of wanted to teach him a lesson. She wanted him to feel alone and to see how he liked it. She knew it happened before they even spoke, but his carelessness might have come at a cost—one that they would have to pay for, for the rest of their lives.

It seemed every time they were in a good place something always happened to set them back. That is why she was feeling weary.

Every time he got stressed she wondered if he would slip back into that drug world he was in when he met her. It was a constant worry. Then she had all of that drama last year with her father, being assaulted and of course, there was Marion.

She was just plain weary and felt she needed a break.

After only an hour Paul returns home and tells her about the test and how long it would take. Again, her heart just sank—knowing now, they had to walk on egg shells until those results came back.

Her brain hurt from trying to work out how they were going to handle it if he *was* actually the baby's father.

Once she realized it was going to be weeks . . . weary stepped up to the plate again—and was the frontrunner in all of her thoughts.

She sits and cries and told him "I'm so sorry. I don't mean to upset you any more than you already are but I just can't stop crying. I'm sorry Paul."

He goes right to her and picks her up and sits on the couch with her in his lap. He is so emotional too now and they both felt *we needed this release.* It has to all come out so they could relax and after a while—they both did calm down.

She pulls him off of the couch and just pleaded "Please!" Will you please?"

He knew what she was asking, so he takes her hand leading him to their bed. They help each other undress and start kissing like it would be their last time together. Then they slowed it down wanting to feel each other. Feel every kiss. Feel every caress as Paul touched every inch of her body. Kissing her neck and following down the length of her body. He rubbed her nipples between his fingers and listened to her sigh in approval. When he touched her, he felt how wet she was and knew he did his job getting her ready for him.

She ran her fingers through his hair knowing how much he loves when she does that. She hitched her leg over his, trying to coax him over her because she was more than ready to feel him inside her. She stroked him up and down slowly and smiled when he now moaned in approval. Then when he couldn't take it any longer his kisses became wild as he positioned himself over her where her hips met his so she could fully consume him. Together they moaned and groaned and felt the heat between them. It didn't take long for them both to explode—taking their breath away.

When they were done, Maggie kept Paul in her arms. She held him tightly and kept kissing his head which was lying on her shoulder. They both sighed and it seemed to calm them both down—somewhat.

"It's going to be hard trying to get through this, until the test comes back. It will be like a black cloud over our heads until we find out. I really don't know how to get past this. How to put this on the back burner until we find out the truth. Do you?"

Paul replies "I don't know either Mags. I don't know what to say. I don't know how to help you. If we could afford it I would ask you if you wanted to have a baby too. Maybe that would make you feel better—knowing we would be having a child because we loved each other so much. But we can't afford to yet. I could drop out of school and try and get a job and I would do that for you Mags, for everything you did for me."

"Don't even say that. I would work 3 jobs so you could stay in school. The only reason you would be done with school would be if you were finished and graduating. *That* is the only reason."

Now looking into her beautiful blue eyes he just asks "I wish you could tell me how to fix this Mags. How can I help you? How can I be a father? How are we going to manage? I don't see the light at the end of this tunnel when two days ago it was right there. Now, it is so far away again!"

She reaches down and kisses him. "Let's put it to rest now. We will have to wait to see what the test results are. Then we can talk it out like we always do. What do you think?"

Paul just nods his head agreeing with her. Put it to rest and then panic if it doesn't go his way.

CHAPTER 42

A Surprise

Two weeks go by and during those two weeks Nicky and Coach B notice something was wrong with Paul. He still played well but it seemed he lost the drive he had before. Nicky kept asking him if everything was alright and he just kept saying yes.

He went to dinner at his house multiple times to see if there was an issue between him and Maggie and everything seemed fine on the home front.

Even Joseph and Frank saw the same. Like something was wrong, but again—Paul and their sister looked fine. Like nothing was wrong. Both Nicky and Joseph talked about it but couldn't figure it out.

When Joseph had Maggie alone he point blank asked her.

"I see you and Paul are fine Maggie but I know something is not right. Something is off with the two of you. Just tell me what's wrong!"

Joseph sees his sister's face get beet red when he told her that and waits for her reply.

"Paul and I are fine. I don't want to say anything right now but thank you for being so concerned for us. I'm begging you to please, just let it go until I can talk about it."

Joseph panicked and immediately thought now, that one of them were ill?

"Are you ill? Is Paul alright?"

"Please Joseph. Please . . . let it be and I will explain once I can. Please do this for me and don't let on to dad that anything is wrong either."

Joseph nods his head acknowledging he will let it go until she is ready to talk about it.

Right after he leaves, Paul arrives with the mail and the lab results were in. As they both looked at the envelope—Elizabeth called at the same time.

"My parents want to come over so we could review the test results with you and Mrs. Tanner. We just got the results and would it be Ok if we came over?"

Paul was stunned she wanted to come over with her parents and then got upset they were going to let him have it, if he was Kristin's father—fully realizing he would deserve anything they threw at him.

Maggie was listening and she nodded her head yes then whispered "let them come over so we could get this over with."

Paul told them and impatiently waited for them to arrive, pacing back and forth in the living room.

Maggie goes over to him "it will be ok. As long as you love me Paul—we will be fine no matter what the test results say. Please believe me!"

He takes her hand and kisses it bringing it to his heart that was practically beating out of his chest. She touches his face and he gave her a faint smile. Then the doorbell rang and they both froze up.

She releases his hand and goes to answer it. Elizabeth was there with her parents and little Kristin. She invited them in and they all sat in the living room with their envelopes.

Paul said nothing and noticed how pissed her parents were when they saw him. He felt if it were his daughter he would react the same way—thinking *how could you have done this to my daughter or look what you did to my daughter*. He was so upset and shaking.

"Well let's not delay this any longer. Shall we open our lab results?" Maggie asked.

They both opened the envelopes and read the results. Paul and Maggie looked at the paper and he just cried and so did she. He was 100% *not* the baby's father. They both were so overwhelmed and hugged each other.

Then they looked at the stoic look on Elisabeth's parent's faces and their hearts just broke for her. She started crying and probably for multiple reasons. One being—she had no idea who the baby's father was and the second was how disappointed her parents looked to be with her.

Of course the main reason was—poor baby Kristin didn't have a dad and she would never have one or know who he was.

Even though they were so relieved—they just couldn't help feeling so sorry for Elizabeth.

Just as they were thinking that, Nicky walks in the door.

He looked at everyone in the room and wondered what was going on. Then he looked at Elizabeth and his face turned all white.

"Elizabeth" he called her name and everyone knew he knew her then.

"Nicky" she replied and she started crying.

Nicky went right to her and started speaking to her like they were best friends.

"Elizabeth—what happened to you? I searched and searched for you after that weekend. No one knew where you went or even remembered you. I looked for you for weeks and even went to the registration office to see if they knew you or could get me in touch with you. They were so annoyed when I wouldn't give up and threw me out of the building and told me never to come back."

Paul and Maggie were stunned at what was happening. It turned out Nicky, was the one she spent the weekend with—not Paul.

Maggie said "Elizabeth—why don't you tell Nicky why we are all here and who is with you. It's ok."

So she sits down and tells him what happened. She wanted to know if Paul was her daughter's father because she remembered nothing about that weekend. The lab results just came back confirming he was not.

Nicky was shocked and realized, that was what was wrong with his brother the past two weeks.

Nicky looks at the baby and notices it looked just like him. Then everyone saw him and Kristin side by side and thought the same. Maggie thought she looked just like Elizabeth, until she saw her next to Nicky.

"Elizabeth. I will take the DNA test. I will go right now. Tell me where. I had no idea. I am so sorry. If I had known I would have been there for you."

Elizabeth was crying and so was Maggie. Paul just kept looking at Nicky in shock.

"Brother, now I know why you have been off these past two weeks. If I knew I could have taken that burden away from you."

"How sad am I not knowing what happened that weekend or who I was even with. You all must think I am trash."

Nicky took her arm and said "You are not trash and don't ever say that again. It was a mistake and if I am the baby's father it will be both our mistake. I promise I will help you however I can."

"Please believe me Elizabeth! I searched for you high and low. I wanted to make sure you were alright and I wanted to ask you out on a real date. Those were the reasons I was looking for you."

Elizabeth's parents looked to be relieved now that Nicky was going to take the test and that if he was Kristin's father—he mentioned he would help her. That is all they ever wanted. Some support for their daughter—mentally and financially.

"Elizabeth, will you come with me to the lab? Can we bring the baby too?"

She looked at her parents and they nodded she could go with him.

Then she looked at Paul and Maggie and apologized. "I am so sorry for putting you through this—I can never apologize enough to you" as she turned and left with Nicky holding the baby.

They got the car seat out of her car and put it in Nicky's -then off they went. Maggie and Paul felt those two had a lot to talk about.

Everyone left with Elizabeth's parents finally shaking hands with Paul and Maggie. To say there was a lot of relief on everyone's faces was an understatement.

Paul closed the door and didn't know where to start as he is just staring at his wife.

"Can you believe all that just happened? I don't know what to say. Don't get me wrong Mags—I should still be in trouble with you, but what a turn of events. I have to go sit down, I am that shocked right now."

She nods her head in agreement and joins him just staring out into space trying to take in what just happened.

"Ok, so you are not the baby's father but Nicky most likely is. You have to admit she looks just like him. It's spooky on how much she looks like him. The fact that she sought you out and not Nicky bothers me. She didn't know which one of you she was with? And you mister! Not knowing if you were with her or not? Thank God those days are over Paul."

Paul's eyes lit up when she called him mister and hoped she wasn't going to yell at him.

"I feel so sorry for her though. Going through all of that by herself. Nicky can afford to help her out too. You know that. Maybe now she will get the support she so desperately needs."

Paul just nodded his head agreeing and was trying not to say too much but he did comment on Nicky.

"It kind of makes sense now. Last year before the season started—he was asking people if they knew a girl he was looking for. Now I know who he was looking for. He said he spent the weekend with someone and really liked her but admitted they were both drunk the whole weekend."

"Well, let's see first if he really is Kristin's father and then see what happens. I know one thing. We can finally put this to rest now. What a relief! I feel like a new person now." She says to Paul and Paul not wanting to let that go just picked her up and threw her over his shoulder laughing.

"I am going to take this new person to bed now and see if she is any different than my wife who I adore." All the while she is screaming and laughing to be put down.

CHAPTER 43

All Is Well Now

When Paul and Nicky were alone they talked about what happened. Paul told Nicky he would have to wait at least two weeks for DNA results to come back but it didn't seem to bother Nicky. He called Elizabeth a few times a day to check in on her and Kristin and even took them out for dinner almost every night. He took her shopping for baby things and seemed fine with the whole situation. Paul thought Nicky was hoping he *was* the baby's father to make it official. The fact that Elizabeth and Nicky got along so well added to the situation in a good way. In fact Paul and Maggie did see how well they got along. Almost like they fit together perfectly. Nicky was smiling a lot lately.

Two weeks later to the day the lab results came in and Nicky took his envelope and headed to Elizabeth's parents to open it. He asked Paul and Maggie if they wanted to come and they both declined and told him he should just be with them when they found out.

So once he got there and sat down they opened the envelope and it confirmed. 99.99% Nicky was Kristin's father. Nicky was so happy. No one could have imagined it turning out like it did. He had been thinking a lot about the end result if he was Kristin's father and had everything already planned out.

"Elizabeth, I can get housing subsidized because of my scholarship so you would have a place to stay. I have an income so I will take full responsibility for Kristin. I want to. Will you let me? I want to take care of you both. Will you move in with me?"

Elizabeth was stunned and so happy. He said everything she wanted him to say. Her parents were happy as well. They hugged him and said thank you to him. "Thank you for everything you are going to do for our daughter and for yours."

So, he went to the campus housing office and they just happened to have an empty apartment for a student with a child and off they went to see it. It was really nice and the 3 of them could fit with enough room for all the baby furniture.

In two weeks everything fell into place and Nicky was over the moon with his daughter. He took her to practice with him and no one raised an eye about it. Everyone supported him fully which made it easier on him. Even Coach and Mrs. B sent gifts for the baby which thrilled Nicky and Elizabeth.

Maggie and Paul babysat when they knew Nicky needed a date night with Elizabeth and even Elizabeth registered for school again trying to get back the time she lost.

They were finally able to tell Joseph and Frank why they seemed off those few weeks and it stunned them when they told them the whole story.

Little Kristin started talking away and called Paul—Uncle Paul which always made him smile when she did that. Of course she was Aunt Maggie and even Joseph was Uncle Jophas and Frank was Uncle Frank. It was so cute she couldn't say Joseph's name right. All was well again.

CHAPTER 44

Moving On

March madness came around again and this time Mrs. B was saving seats for Maggie and Elizabeth and of course baby Kristin. Many people always came by and asked to hold her or take her for a walk. She was so cute and everyone fell in love with her.

As the games got tenser Elizabeth left Kristin with her parents because the noise would be too much for her little ears and was there ever noise. Once again the electricity in that building for those games was amazing. Game after game, screaming and screaming, jumping up and down. Maggie wondered when Paul was finally finished after he graduated—how they would be able to adjust to a normal life from Nov through March.

The play offs were just around the corner and they knew this year would be difficult getting through them. They lost many players to graduation last year and the team did not have any height. The tallest player was 6'4" which was not really that big.

Once again the whole community supported them and followed them where ever they played. The papers again printed many articles about the games and players. Again they had an article on Paul and Maggie and this time, one on Nicky and Elizabeth, also with pictures of all of them with Kristin playing ball with her on the court.

They won the first round and then struggled during the second round but make it through . . . barely. They all knew they got lucky during that game. The games were an hour away also so the trip was taxing on everyone especially Maggie who had to work the next day. Paul's parents couldn't even make them this time.

In the third round to make it to the final two—they met their match. The team overpowered them in height. Coach B knew it—but what could he do about that? He didn't have the height and it had shown on the court. They rarely got the rebounds because they were towered over by players all around 7' tall.

Everyone played their hearts out and Paul and Nicky carried the team with their outside shooting but it wasn't enough to win the game and get them to the final two again.

Maggie thought they were just happy to get that game over with. It was a very physical game and many had bruises afterwards. Paul had a black eye and bruised ribs when someone elbowed him. The crowd was still so pleased with their team and wouldn't leave the gym until the players all came back to thank them for supporting them all year. Maggie, Elizabeth and Mrs. B all cried when they came back out on the court and Paul went right to her. She held him tightly and just smiled at him. There were no words she could say to him. He was just so exhausted, he hid his head in her shoulder and she left him there until he was ready to let go.

CHAPTER 45

A New Proposition

Life went back to being normal for the rest of the year. Again in May the Advertising firm offered Paul a summer job and he happily took it. They liked him and he felt once he graduated—they would offer him a spot.

He and Maggie took a trip to the beach for a few days. He always saw how happy she was on the beach. She loved going for walks—letting the waves crash around her legs. They got to relax some too.

While they were lying in bed one night Paul turns to her. She felt him and turned to look at him also.

"Maggie", he says softly to her.

She smiles at him wondering what he wanted to talk to her about. "I love you Maggie."

"I love you too Paul." She takes her hand and touches his face smiling at him.

"I want to show you how much I love you." She didn't know what he meant.

"Did you want to fool around again?" She's smiling and that brought a big smile to his face too.

"Yes . . . but no . . . that's not what I meant." Now she looks at him confused.

"I want to start trying for a baby soon. I want to be a father. I want us to be parents. I know we will be good ones." He said it with the biggest smile on his face.

It was so overwhelming to her because she never expected that from him. He had a whole school year left yet.

"Are they happy tears Maggie?" She just nods her head.

"Can we try after the new year? I will be graduating in May and I know the firm will offer me a good position and salary. It might take some time for you to get pregnant."

"Would you consider it?"

"Yes . . . yes . . . yes . . . yes "

She jumps on top of him and starts kissing him wildly as he picks her up and lays her beside him while he caresses her body—making her moan until she pushed him back where she laid on top of him—trying to feel him inside her—all while he is holding her steady. When they were done she lies down in his arms and stays there not wanting to leave.

She starts laughing as he is running his fingers softly up and down her back and hair.

"Why are you laughing?"

"I was just thinking maybe we should practice more so when we're ready to start our family—we will *really* be ready."

Now he is laughing too and just told her "I can't believe you think *I* would need practice. I think I know what I'm doing" pretending he is shocked.

He picks her up and lays her down next to him and they start all over again.

"Now you did it Mags. Now we have to practice *all* night until you think we got it right."

They both are smiling so much at each other, they really didn't know if they could continue but that thought came and went very quickly once she felt just how ready he *really* was for her.

CHAPTER 46

Heart to Heart

Senior year and last basketball season. Maggie thought—*when this is over I will have survived 3 years of college and basketball. How did I ever do it?*

Her shop was doing well and Sarah increased her salary to $40,000. She didn't expect that but she and Paul were always grateful for everything Sarah did for them. He would even walk to the shop when Maggie worked just to see Sarah and everyone, who were always happy to see him.

Nicky and Elizabeth couldn't wait any longer and wanted to get married. They did it before the basketball season started. Even his parents came to the wedding and once they saw baby Kristin they decided they wanted to be involved in Nicky's life. They apologized to him for never being involved in his life after his brother died and his mom and dad even decided to give their marriage another try. No one could believe it—but—yes—that all happened.

Nicky also found out when he, Elizabeth and Kristin visited his home that past summer—his parents had a whole wall decorated with pictures of Nicky playing ball. They had announcements framed when he and Paul were named point guards of the year—3 years in a row. It stunned him so much he decided to drop his beef with them and accept them for who they were—not who he wanted them to be. They also promised to come to as many games as they could. That was something Nicky craved and wished for and now it might actually happen.

Nicky and Paul were throwing balls around at the gym before practice when they kind of had a heart to heart.

"Nicky—I see how happy you are. You love Elizabeth and Kristin and anyone would have to be so blind not to see it. I know you are happy about your parents getting back together and promising you they would try and get to some games. I am so happy for you brother."

"I have to admit I was a little jealous when you found Maggie. I kind of felt you didn't deserve her seeing the way you were living your life. Then I saw what she did for you. Taking such a big chance on you like she did . . . turning her life over to you like that. You are my brother— and will always be and she is my sister and she will always be. Once we graduate . . . we will still be family. Will you promise me that?" Paul stops dribbling the ball and looks at Nicky. "I will promise you right now Nicky . . . you are my brother and will always be. Your family will always be mine and mine will always be yours."

"Thank you. I really don't know if I could survive life without you being in it."

Once again a statement from Nicky made Paul really think about how things are in his life.

"I will tell you a secret Nicky being that we just confirmed you will always be my brother!" Paul is smiling away.

"What is it? You know I hate suspense!"

"I asked Maggie if we could try for a baby after the Holiday's. I really want to be a father Nicky. I should have a good job once we graduate and I want to start a family."

"Paul, I see how you are with Kristin. I see your face light up when she is around. I should have guessed you would want to start a family."

"Let's try together to get pregnant. If they are boys—we can groom them to be the best point guards in the state. Wouldn't that be some-thing!" Nicky tells him.

"Paul Tanner Jr. and Nicky Newman Jr. following in their father's footsteps. Do you think Coach B would still be here?"

Paul is just laughing as Nicky is telling him all this. "Let me run that by Maggie and get back to you. I think you will have to check with Elizabeth too. Don't you?"

The rest of the players started coming in for practice so they had to put that conversation on hold all the while laughing at each other.

CHAPTER 47

Remembering His Promise

Paul and Nicky were so happy and content in their lives and it had shown on the floor during practice and during games. They were so mature . . . all the other players looked up to them. They were great role models and Coach B always appreciated that fact. Every now and then someone knocked on Paul or Nicky's door to talk out some issues they were having. Both of them offered tons of advice or helped with studying. They did whatever they could to help everyone out.

Maggie also had many visitors from some of the player's girlfriends. They always had questions for her about how she was able to handle them being gone always, either practicing or for games or on the road. She always made them feel better about situations they were in and it seemed everyone got along so well that year.

Once again Coach B *had that feeling*. The one he had that sophomore year when they won the national title. Because of that feeling—he kept his players close—to mostly keep them all out of trouble.

He was also able to recruit some 7' players which they so desperately needed. Things were looking good.

The whole team was on fire that year. Win after win. The whole community was once again buzzing about the team. Tickets for the games became a hot commodity . . . again!

Right after the holiday's Paul is studying while Maggie is puttering around the house trying to stay out of his way.

"How many miles have you walked around this apartment tonight Mags?"

"Am I disturbing you? I was trying to stay out of your way so you could study."

"How about you sit with me and help me."

Maggie just smiled and knew Paul wanted her to sit with him. She goes to the couch and just told him "Ok come here. You know you like it when you lay on my lap."

Paul goes right to her and lays his head on her lap and starts reading. She runs her fingers through his hair and he takes her hand and kisses it laying it back down on his face.

All of a sudden he closes his laptop. "I made you a promise didn't I?"

"Which one was that?" she is now laughing.

"The one where I told you we could start trying for a baby after the holidays!"

Maggie remembered that promise but didn't say anything to Paul. She didn't want to pressure him and just thought; when he was ready he would mention it again.

Now her smile is from ear to ear.

"Well, what are your thoughts on that?"

"I want to start trying Mags. I really want to be a father. I really want a family with you. Are you ready to try or do you want to wait?"

Maggie did not want to wait. She was more than ready and told him so.

"I'm ready and just waiting for you to say the word. I didn't want to pressure you and thought I would just wait until you were ready to talk about it again."

Paul gets up and takes her by the hand. "We better start practicing— you know how you want me to get it right!"

Now they are both laughing as they head to their bed.

"Stop taking your pills Maggie. I want us to have a baby. Will you?"

Tears are rolling down her cheeks as she just nods her head that she was ready.

That first month—nothing . . . and they kind of knew it wouldn't happen as soon as she stopped taking her pills so they just waited until that second month and again . . . nothing.

While she wasn't shook the first month after they started trying—she was shook that second month and she just cried and cried while Paul could do nothing but hold her until she would cry herself to sleep. "Maggie, it will happen. I know it. We just have to be patient. It might take a year and I don't want you to keep getting so upset every month. OK?"

"Ok. I don't want to let you down."

"You will never let me down. Let's just take it one month at a time and if necessary—one year at a time."

She just nods her head agreeing.

CHAPTER 48

The Final Game

March madness rolled around and their record was so good it was a no brainer they would be in the playoffs.

Once again the gym was wild during games. Then the road to the final 2 tournament started and the games were in New York at Madison Square Garden this time. They took buses upon buses to NY to the games. Maggie took a bus too because it was easier for her, Elizabeth, Molly, Joseph, Frank and Judy. They took the bus along with Mrs. B as did everyone at her shop. No one could wait.

Pauls' Mom and dad made the trip too; they were only an hour away so it was easy for them.

Nicky's parents flew into JFK because they lived in the middle of the state and it would not be an easy drive to the city. To say he was over the moon that his parents were coming to see him in the playoffs was an understatement, he was so happy. Not to mention—they got rooms for Elizabeth and Maggie so they could stay instead of going home and having to come back. The university secured rooms at a good rate for anyone that wanted to stay.

First game was over before the first half ended. They were leading by 30 points but they didn't back down because they all remembered previous games when they were down by 20 or more points and the second half was when they had a scoring spurt and came back to win the game.

So they never took it for granted that they would win. That didn't happen this time. The team just could not keep up with them.

Second game 2 nights later was closer but they won in the end. Nicky's parents couldn't believe how stressful it was sitting in the stands watching Nicky play. They couldn't believe how good he was and how in sync he and Paul were. They were totally shocked and amazed and felt so proud of their son which is all he ever wanted from them. They loved Elizabeth too and of course Kristin who was almost 3 already. Elizabeth and Nicky felt they shouldn't bring Kristin—because it would be too hectic—so Elizabeth's parents watched her that week and weekend.

Well . . . they won and were headed to the final 2 which would be played on Monday night. They all stayed and got to see some of the city in between practices. It was something to remember about the games and spending time with each other and families.

Maggie did whatever she could to keep Paul calm. They talked out his anxieties over the game and he seemed calm this time. Maybe it was because he was older.

Frank drove in with his dad for the final game. Everyone was shocked he wanted to see Paul play and come to the game. Maggie had tickets saved for them along with seats with them.

Maggie got there after everyone was already in place in their seats and as she made her way up the stairs everyone around her cheered. She gave them a big smile and warm wave and kissed Mrs. B. Next she introduced her to her Dad. She tried not to look shocked when she met Frank Sr. Then her in-laws came in and they both hugged and kissed her with Frank watching. Lois looked behind Maggie and near dropped when she saw him sitting there. Her mouth hung open and her eyes got wide but she saw Maggie smiling away. She knew she was so happy right then. She looks at Frank and said "Nice to see you again Mr. Sardo!" Frank Sr smirked at her but that is all he could muster up for her. Never in her life did she expect to see him at a game or with Maggie. She couldn't help how stunned she felt. That wasn't the end. Sarah came in next and near dropped when she saw him too. She looks at Lois and near lost it. But she looked at him and said the same thing Lois did. That is all she could come up with. "Nice to see you Frank!" turning to look at Lois with her eyes near popping out of her head. Frank smirked at her too as she sat down remembering how they both tricked him into giving Maggie and Paul their washer and dryer!

Everyone waited for the team to come out to practice before the game and once the music started blaring—all the players came out on the court and everyone yelled and clapped. They knew no one would have a voice by the end of the night.

The team they had to play was the one that defeated them in the 3rd playoff round last year. The one with giants for players.

This year they were prepared and were able to match them on the court. Not to mention, Coach B had one ace in his pocket that the other team could never match up with. That ace was having the top 2 point guards in the conference in his starting 5.

As usual, Paul found Maggie in the stands and went right to her, to hand her his wedding ring . . . taking her hand and kissing it, driving the fans wild. This would be the last time he would ever do that and everyone knew and just waited and watched—giving them a standing ovation. They turned and waved to everyone . . . faces all red as he hugged her this time and stayed there for a moment trying to take it all in. Cameras were on the both of them. The TV Stations knew he did that at every game and caught every second of it.

The announcer Frank Gills quickly caught what was happening and stated to the world: *Here we go! This is what everyone was waiting for! Paul Tanner does this before every game his wife is at and it drives the fans wild when he does this. This will be the last time this ever happens and everyone knows it. They are an amazing couple—married 3 years now and still beloved by the whole University Community.*

He quickly kissed her, then his parents and reached behind Maggie to shake his father in laws hand to acknowledge him also, and then went back to the floor to continue practicing.

Frank Gills again stated: *It looks like he acknowledged his parents sitting with his wife and behind him -that might be his father in law he also acknowledged. What a great player and all around person.*

The game went back and forth and back and forth with lead changes with every basket made. Maggie was so nervous because she knew this was the last game for Paul and wanted him to leave on a good note . . . with a national championship. Adding to that, was the fact that the game was televised nationally and Maggie realized the cameras were on her and Elizabeth every time one of them scored a basket. Both had to try and watch what they were doing—seated in the stands.

First half was over with the score tied at 38 points. She stood on her chair looking to see her husband going into the locker room and he looked up into the stands also trying to find her and once they caught each other's eye—they both relaxed and flashed the biggest smile at each other. Of course the cameras caught all of that too and kept replaying him looking for her all during the break. It was nerve wracking for them but the whole country fell in love with them after that. It was replayed everywhere on social media for days. Especially the time he kissed her hand after he handed over his wedding ring.

"Maggie, how do you and Elizabeth do this all year long?" Mrs.
Newman asked her.

Lois turned and just said "Maggie takes it well until we get this far. Then her nerves give out on her. If you ask her now to show you her hands—I guarantee they will be shaking."

Maggie just smiled at her mom and nodded her head agreeing because she was shaking like a leave. Lois wrapped her up in her arms trying to calm her down while her father put his hands on her shoulders to support her.

Again Frank Gills stated: *It looks like Mrs. Tanner is having a case of nerves. She is being consoled by her mother in law and father behind her. If I were in her shoes—I would be feeling the same.*

Second half started. The team was in a huddle and Paul and Nicky told everyone—"let's get going here! Let's show them how good we really are! Are you all ready to go out there and get that title?"

Everyone screamed "yes".

They broke huddle and walked out on the floor with so much confidence it almost looked like arrogance out there. Paul and Nicky had arms around each other and were talking about something. Probably a strategy.

Paul got the tip off and threw it down court where Nicky was waiting and he went up for a quick 2 points. The crowd approved by screaming as loudly as they could.

Even Mrs. Newman was yelling and so was her husband. They were so proud of Nicky—you could just tell by the smile they had on their faces every time he scored a basket.

Again they were only up by 2 points most of the second half and knew they had to pull away.

The freshman center standing tall at 7'4" got the next rebound and again found Nicky alone under the basket for another 2 quick points. Nicky stole the ball just then and Paul was waiting at the 3 point line and OMG it went right in! Another 3 points! The opposing team called a time out so they could regroup. You could tell when the team came out that they were going to play hard and so far they did.

Up by 7 now—the teams exchanged baskets again and our big center got the next rebound to Nicky, looping it to Paul, who caught it—feet off the ground—in the air and *dunked it*. That play was their favorite and they practiced it all the time. It was their *signature play* and everyone always loved it!

The crowd was wild! Wild—Wild—Wild!

2 minutes left and they were up by double digits. When that happened the other team started fouling them so they could try and get the ball back but I guess they didn't know about Paul practicing his foul shots with his wife. That year his rating was 92% and coach made sure only Paul got the ball so they would have to foul him.

He got 2 shots and they went right in.

Everyone could smell the taste of victory. They were just counting the seconds until the game was over.

Now with 25 seconds left, they let the team take the ball down court and score.

17 seconds left . . . Paul got fouled again. The ref passes him the ball where he dribbled it twice and up and in again!

Now everyone was standing on their seats waiting for the next shot. They felt that would be the icing on the cake. There was no way the opposing team could catch up.

Again they let them go right down court to score but he missed it and our big center threw it down to Paul where he went up in the air and dunked it again.

The buzzer sounded—the game was over and everyone stormed the court. Nicky and Paul hugged each other and wouldn't let go. The rest of the team came over and surrounded them both in hugs.

Emotions were running high right then.

They shook hands with their opponents and all jumped around hugging and crying with everyone especially the younger players. Streamers, balloons and confetti were falling from the rafters and the music was blaring.

Paul made his way to Maggie who was standing on her seat watching all the celebrating. He ran up the steps and grabbed her—wrapping his arms around her. The 2 of them just stayed there and cried and cried—they were so happy. Again with camera's on them.

His head was down resting on her forehead—they couldn't stop looking at each other.

Nicky was celebrating with Elizabeth swinging her around like she was a doll. He next went to his mother and father who were both crying they were so happy and proud of Nicky. When they told him that, it made him cry even more while they both wrapped their arms around him—kissing their only son. That is what Nicky always wanted from them and now— he got his wish. He was so happy—his parents finally told him they loved him and he had Elizabeth and his daughter. He just couldn't believe it.

Again they all got medals and coach got another huge trophy for the big case the U constructed to display all of the awards the teams got. There was another big dinner at the hotel but this time before they even went to the dinner Paul grabbed Maggie and they snuck up to their Room and *you know what they did*! And twice!

When they walked in the banquet room—the whole room went wild. He went right to Nicky and they hugged and everyone cheered and applauded in approval. They got a standing ovation—and everyone knew they would never see 2 point guards play like they did again, soon. They were amazing together on the court.

Appetites came back now that everything was over and they all ate like they hadn't eaten in months.

Once again Paul and Nicky were named top point guards in the nation which made them so happy. An unprecedented 4 years in a row. Everyone was so happy for them.

CHAPTER 49

Unbelievable Opportunity

Things took a while to settle down. The players were still treated like rock stars and the freshman players loved it. Especially the attention they were getting from all the girls.

One day not long after the last game—Coach called Nicky and Paul to his office for a meeting. Neither knew what he wanted to talk to them about.

"I just got off the phone with 2 scouts from the European Basketball league and they want to draft the both of you. Would you at all be interested? Let me tell you about the league first."

Nicky and Paul were shocked. It was never their aspiration to play after college so it amazed them when Coach told them.

"Why us Coach?" Nicky asked.

"Nicky, really? You and Paul were the top 2 point guards for 4 years straight in Division II Basketball. That is why they are asking."

They both just looked at each other and then back at coach. "This league has been active for 10 years now. There are a few reasons for this in Europe. First to get people interested in American Basketball. The second is so they could train potential players for the NBA. Scouts and teams feel some players are borderline, making it into the NBA so they send them to the European league to season them, so to speak."

"There is more. You will not be allowed to take your wives and children because they travel all the time. They mostly live out of hotel rooms and it distracts from the players if their families are on site. Think of it as intense practice sessions. But you will likely be in 3 countries in one week at a time!" At that moment Paul drifted off. It turns out he hated flying and this would require him to be in a plane almost every week. He let it go and let Coach continue.

"It will be very stressful, I promise you that!"

"Now . . . the salary is $150,000 to start and you could leave at any time if you don't like it or want to do it anymore."

He is looking closely at the both of them seeing how shocked they are.

"I have given you a lot to think about so go home and talk to your wives and really think about it. I have to give your reply by the end of the week. I know it's not a lot of time to ponder over it but—I think you should really consider it. It is a once in a lifetime opportunity for you both."

"It will be hard to leave Elizabeth, Kristen and Maggie but it is something you both should consider. If you were my sons . . . I would tell you to do it. You never know what will pan out from this experience. Don't forget—you can leave at any time. There are no penalties if you get there and a week later you want to come home."

Paul and Nicky walked out of Coaches office shocked and stunned. "Paul, I don't want to go but I will tell Elizabeth anyway. I have to tell her. It isn't something I want to do or even thought about."

"I don't know what to say Nicky. It is intriguing to me. I will have to talk to Maggie to see what she thinks but I can't say I don't want to do it right now."

"I think you should if you want to. I know Maggie will understand but there will be a lot of temptation for you also being without her. You know she calms you down and keeps you . . . let's say safe."

"I know what you mean Nicky but it has been so long since I went down that path. It's the furthest thing from my mind. I know I'm so different now. Don't you think?"

"I do brother and I don't want you to go. I don't want you to leave me. We have been together like glue for the past 4 years and I don't know what I would do without you with me. I'm planning to live here, just to be with my brother. But I will still be here waiting for your return if you choose to go."

Just then Paul did not know how to reply to Nicky except to just go to him and hug him.

"Nicky—if I go—when I come back—aside from Maggie—you will be the first person I seek out. You will always be my brother and we *will* live near each other. I promise you right now."

They turn to go separate ways when Paul calls out. "Nicky!" Now walking back to him.

He hugs him again "I don't think I ever thanked you for saving my life. Thank you for the past 4 years. For supporting me and Mags. You are my brother Nicky and always will be!"

Then as not to get too emotional they parted ways again.

CHAPTER 50

I Have News

Maggie was so sick that morning. There was only one reason she thought she would be and that was because she was pregnant.

She was flying so high she was so happy. She had the pregnancy test and took it and wanted to surprise Paul when he came home from his meeting with Coach.

When she saw the results it confirmed she was truly pregnant. Paul told her not to get upset every month and this time she didn't have to be. So many thoughts were running through her mind on how to tell him. Would he notice as soon as he got in the door because she felt like she was glowing she was so happy.

Finally she heard him come up the steps and was waiting at the door for him. She flung her arms around him and he returned the hug, picking her up and walking her backwards to the couch.

He kissed her so softly and tenderly which made her now wonder what was going on. He couldn't have known yet that she was pregnant so she pulls back from his embrace and just looks at him.

She saw he was smiling "What is going on? Why are you smiling and looking at me like that?"

"Did you want to go fool around before I have to go to work today?" Now she is laughing and so is he.

"Yes . . . but I have to talk to you about something first—Coach just told Nicky and I. I don't know how to start and truthfully Mags I'm still so stunned!"

"Well start at the beginning and let's see. I have something to tell you too!"

"Do you want to go first?"

"No, let's hear what Coach wanted first."

"Some scouts offered Nicky and me a chance to play in the European Basketball league. The salary is $150,000 to start. We can leave at any time if we don't like it."

"Oh my God Paul! That is amazing! Because you 2 were the top point guards 4 years in a row?"

"Yes. It comes with conditions though Mags."

"Well, what are they?"

"I can't take you and Nicky can't take Elizabeth and Kristin. The schedule is brutal and we live out of hotel rooms. We will be traveling to many countries in one weeks' time. They don't want the players to get distracted having their families there. Plus, it wouldn't be fair for you to live in a hotel room all the time."

Well, that is something she did not expect to hear. She turned white and he saw that. Then she got physically ill and ran to the bathroom quickly.

Paul flipped out when that happened and it upset him so much. He held her hair back and she told him to just leave her alone for a few minutes.

He moved away from her and let her go. Then she pulled herself together and washed her mouth out getting ready to talk about what he just told her.

"Maggie, I see I just upset you and for many reasons."

"Paul, don't worry about me. Tell me how you are feeling about that offer you just got."

He immediately thought—*she always thinks of me first* while he lowered his head not being able to look at her.

She takes his hands in hers "How about you tell me what it's all about before you make a decision. Let me ask you some questions."

He nods his head. "Do you want to go?"

"It's a great opportunity. It's a stepping stone to the NBA, but Mags, that is something I really don't want to do. But this offer is amazing. Look at the money I will be making even if it is only for a couple of months!"

"Yes good point—we have been paupers for the last 3 years." She smiles trying to make him feel better.

"It is a great opportunity for you—I can see that, but I worry so much about you and I won't be there. What if something happens—it will take me forever to get to you!'

"Yes, Maggie it would. But you will only be a phone call away and we could talk over the computer. We will be able to see each other that way too."

"I know you worry about me- but I'm hoping you know I'm a different person than the one you met 3 years ago. Your influences are all over me. Please tell me you can see that!"

"I do see it. Every day Paul. I'm so happy for you and so proud of you. You turned your life around and I really believe you are happy with how everything turned out. I'm remembering . . . when you were afraid to be without me for 2 nights . . . 3 years ago. My heart ached I loved you so much—saying you didn't want to leave me." Maggie practically whispers—remembering.

"Now you want to leave me for months or maybe longer. I'm trying to wrap my head around that."

He pulls her in for a hug and she barely hugs him back still being so shocked he would want to leave her. He pulls her in tighter and she couldn't resist and wrapped her arms around him tighter also.

"Let's sleep on it tonight. I have to get to work. When do you have to have your decision in?"

"Tomorrow."

"When will you be leaving?"

"Right after graduation."

"Ok. At least I have you home for a few more weeks."

"Thank you Maggie for listening to me. For not saying no, right off the bat."

"I would never want to stop you from doing something as important as this Paul. I just have to get used to the idea. But—again—I would never stop you. I want you to know that."

She turns to go get ready for work when he remembers she wanted to tell him something.

"Maggie, you had something to tell me too?"

She stopped dead and turned white again. He got up and thought she was going to pass out.

"What was it? Is it bad? What's wrong? What do you have to tell me?"

"Paul—truthfully I forgot. I think I'm just so stunned with your news right now—whatever I was thinking about kind of just escaped me."

"How about a rain check on the fooling around?"

"Yes, of course."

Paul saw how dejected she looked and thought *how can I ask her to let me go after everything she did for me.*

Maggie dressed and when she came out to go to work Paul did a double take. She felt like dressing up to put herself in a better mood. It was going to be a long night at work and she needed to talk to Sarah about what was happening. She knew she could help her mentally prepare for Paul leaving. That was the one thing. She knew he wanted to go and she did not want to stop him or make him feel bad about it. She just had to figure out how to do that.

"Maggie you look so beautiful! Are you sure you are only going to work?" now both of them laughed.

"I thought maybe my husband would like to come and take his wife out to dinner tonight on her break!"

"He would love that idea. 5 'clock?"

"Perfect!"

She goes to him for a kiss and this one was deep and passionate. Then she broke away because she had to go—knowing she was leaving him wanting more.

How Can I Do This?

Maggie paced and paced waiting for Sarah to arrive. She called her and was rushing right down to the shop. When she arrived she saw how pale Maggie looked and dragged her by her hand into her office closing the door.

"Tell me everything. Everything!"

When she was done Sarah was stunned. She couldn't believe what was happening.

"What are you going to do?"

"Let him go and like it!"

"Are you going to tell him you're pregnant?"

"No! He won't go if I do. He has to go and come home when he is ready. If he lasts longer than a few months—then I will have to tell him or he'll never forgive me."

Sarah nods her head. "I agree with you Maggie." That shocked Maggie.

"I know I just shocked you but you have to let him go or he will always remember you wouldn't let him do this and it will come up in every fight and get ugly."

"I'm just happy you didn't think I was crazy—letting him do this!""Maggie, how you married Paul in the first place was crazy enough for a lifetime. Look how that turned out. It's wonderful!"

For some reason that last statement from Sarah helped Maggie release the hesitation she was feeling and made her feel better about the whole situation. She even got color back in her cheeks and felt better all around.

At 5 right on the dot, Paul strolled into the shop to pick up his wife for dinner. He even dressed up putting on khakis and a blue oxford dress shirt which highlighted his beautiful blue eyes! She greeted him with the biggest smile trying to make him see she was fine. Everyone came out and kissed and hugged him being so happy to see him—even Sarah. "Don't worry Maggie if you are a little late getting back. I'm here for the duration . . ." smiling to both of them.

Paul holds out his hand to take hers and they both left just gawking at each other feeling so happy at that moment.

"You are so beautiful. How can I ever leave you?"

She just laughs and says "Are you trying to butter me up Tanner?"

They both laugh and smile like they are on a first date with each other.

"I've been thinking."

"Tell me and don't hold back on me."

"I think you are right about this being a good opportunity for you. I think you shouldn't let it slip away. If you do, you will always wonder 'what if '. I will never stop you from doing this and I will support you however you need me to."

Paul was shocked she said that. He knew she was on the wire about it and then knew she turned the corner once he gave her time to think about it.

"Maggie, I really want to go and try this out. If I don't like it—I will come back home to you."

"Even if you like it—you better still come back home to me."

"Are you worried I won't? That will never happen Maggie. Never!"

"No . . . I know I put that spell on you 3 years ago—making you believe you can't live without me and now I think it's wearing off. I'll have to find my spell book and do it again!"

Paul just shakes his head at his wife smiling away at her. "Do you feel better now about it Paul?"

"Yes. I will go see Coach tomorrow and tell him."

"I think you should."

"What about Nicky? What did he say?"

"He has no desire to do that. He is going to tell Elizabeth, but is not interested."

"Ok, I was just wondering."

CHAPTER 52

Paul Is Gone

Maggie tried to get up before Paul every morning he was still home because she did not want him to see her morning sickness.

She knew he would not leave if she were pregnant and felt he had to do this for himself or would always hold it against her even though he wasn't like that.

Lois and Mike came in for graduation and so did Nicky's parents. They all went to dinner and little Kristin was the center of attention. Nicky's parents doted over her which trilled Nicky and Elizabeth.

Paul's parents did not want him to go to Europe. They were so afraid for him and he knew why. They also knew Maggie couldn't go with him and that upset them even more and told them both about it. Maggie's father went wild when she told him what was going on.

She explained to him or at least tried to, but he was furious.

Once they were alone, Maggie told everyone why she felt he had to go. While they then started to calm down about it—they still didn't like it.

"I will make sure he calls you at least twice a week so you will know he is fine." She told his parents who hated the fact that he was leaving his wife home, feeling like he was abandoning her after all she did for him. They just couldn't get over it. But Maggie pleaded with them to just let him go. This was something he had to do and they finally caved and didn't say more about it. Lois saw how upset Frank Sr. was about it also.

She felt they all had the same thing in common. Protecting Maggie and making sure Paul was going to be fine.

After a tearful good bye they hugged him and told him to be careful. He told them on orders from his wife—he would call them twice a week to let them know he was fine.

Maggie and Paul had a lot of sex before he left. She even joked about it saying "I want to make sure you know what you are leaving behind . . . so you come back to me."

"I will always come back to you Maggie. You are my life. Do you understand this is something I think I should do? I don't know why I feel this way."

"I know what you mean. It's how I felt when you asked me to marry you. It was something I felt I should do." countering him with his same remark which threw him.

"Maggie, I will never stop loving you, if that is what you are worried about."

"I know and that is not my worry. My worry is—if you will be safe. My worry is- if you are healthy and will stay healthy. My worry is—if you find yourself going down that dark path—you won't call me for help. My worry is—how I won't be able to handle that!"

"Now you know—that is what I will be thinking all the while you are gone. So now—here is what you will promise me—to help me."

"I will promise you anything you want or need Mags."

"You will promise to call to say good morning to me every day or I will not survive the day. And you will promise me you will call to say good night every evening or I will never sleep a wink!"

Paul has tears streaming down his face as he promises his wife all she wants and knows he will keep them all because he had kept every promise he ever made to her when they got married.

That last night together was amazing and emotional. Maggie did not know how she was going to let him go. She tried to keep her feelings under control until he left. Then she would have her meltdown.

We are fooling around all night Tanner. Don't even tell me you're tired! . . . She laughed as she said that trying to lighten the mood. It was like a wake in their bedroom and she wanted that to stop. She wanted him to remember their last night together and when the morning came . . . she knew he certainly would. On her request—he left her while she was sleeping so he didn't have to witness the tears. That is what she told him but in hindsight what she didn't want him to witness was the major meltdown she was going to have—with him leaving. Nicky took Paul to the airport and when he got in the car, Nicky saw he probably did not get to sleep yet and his lips looked like someone punched him in his mouth they were so red and swollen. With Nicky just gawking at him and smiling, Paul just said—"Maggie's look just as bad"—as they both now smiled at each other. But Paul lowered his head thinking about the night he just spent with his wife and the lightbulb just went on. She knew he hates flying and with the long trip overseas coming up, he realized she kept him up all night so he would sleep the whole time on the plane. He couldn't believe he just figured it out. But he also knew—she was desperate for him to touch her, hold her and kiss her as much as he could before he left. He felt that is what *he* did for her. When she woke and found him gone—she near died. She cried and cried and cried. She hugged his pillow trying to see if she could smell his aftershave or just smell him on it.

For some reason she was so scared. Scared he left her alone, scared he would get caught up in old habits, scared he wouldn't come back to her.

She lay in bed all day—until Joseph found the spare key they hid outside under the grill in case they ever locked themselves out of the house by accident and let himself in.

He found his sister in the worst shape possible. He just sat on the bed and held her trying to talk her out of her meltdown.

"Maggie I'm here for you and will always be. Do you want to come live with me? I could get a bigger place and you could move in with me."

"No, I'm fine. I really don't want to move. I had my meltdown and now I have to get on with my life. My husband is on a business trip and will eventually come back for me. I know he will!"

"I know he will too Maggie. I'm sure of it. I don't have a single doubt."

"I have something to tell you Joseph."

"What is it? You know you can tell me anything."

"I'm pregnant. Before you go crazy—Paul and I talked about wanting to have a baby and try after the holidays but it was never happening. I found out the day he told me he wanted to go to Europe. I couldn't tell him because he would never leave me if I did. I couldn't be the reason he had to stay home. He has to do this and I encouraged him to do it. It couldn't come between us. I hope you understand and I don't want you to be mad at me or at him. No one knows I'm pregnant and I don't want anyone to tell him. I need your word on that."

Joseph started getting mad at his brother in law when Maggie told him she was pregnant but then couldn't be mad after she explained. He didn't know she was pregnant when he walked out that door and she was right. He never would have left and maybe held it against her their whole lives. She did not want to take that chance, which is why he felt Maggie couldn't tell him.

True to his promises—Paul called Maggie every morning and every evening. The time difference was a killer depending on which country he was in. His workouts with his team in Europe were brutal. It was more physical and intense than he ever had experienced. There was no time for anything except practice, play ball and travel. They were always on a bus, on a train or in the air. Now he knew why they said you could not bring your family. There would be no time for anything except basketball.

He reported to her daily on what he was doing and called his parents to check in with them too. That is what kept her going—those 2 calls a day. Sometimes it was 3 which she loved. He even called Frank to keep him informed on what he was doing. Frank being Frank—couldn't help his tone with him sometimes when he called, but Paul didn't let that bother him. Frank secretly loved when Paul called.

He set up his check to be direct deposited in their checking account to help her pay the bills. Each check was substantial so it filled up their account with just one paycheck.

CHAPTER 53

More Bad News

As mad as he was about Paul, Frank Sr saw how happy his daughter was. He knew Paul was a good husband. He saw how happy his two sons were too. They were dating Judy and Molly and he liked both of them. He knew Paul's parents loved Maggie and knew Sarah loved her too. He felt, everyone was all set and now—so was he. He knew they all would be fine and for only the second time in his life . . . He felt peacefulness.

That night when he went to bed—he never woke. For some reason he knew he wouldn't and was happy reconciling with his daughter and sons. He finally felt he did something right for a change but quickly realized the one thing he did do right . . . was marrying his wife Margaret. Now, he was sure she was waiting for him and truthfully he couldn't wait any longer either.

Life turned out good for his two sons and daughter. He and Margaret watched them together . . . from heaven.

Here we go again! Every time Maggie begins to feel settled— something happens. This time was no different! She remembered thinking and feeling the same way about her life when Paul was a junior. Just as they thought things couldn't be any better or loving the life they had— Elizabeth comes in to tell Paul she thought he was little Kristin's father. What a blow and setback that was. Luckily, everything turned out better than they could ever expected—but now this.

Joseph and Frank came over together to visit unexpectedly.

She flashes the biggest smile at them both but noticed they both had their heads down.

"What is it? OK, if you both don't tell me what's going on—I'm going to lose it!"

"Dad passed away this morning."

Her face dropped because she wasn't expecting to hear that. She had no idea what they both wanted until just then.

"He had a massive heart attack and the paramedics could not even revive him. They tried."

"I really don't know how to feel about him dying. I am so conflicted right now. He just started being a father to the three of us and now—he's gone! How do I react to that?"

Frank was just nodding his head. "Well, we are all in the same boat because that is exactly how I feel too. He made all of our lives so miserable and actually fed on it! That is something we will never find out from him. Why he was so unhappy and why he just couldn't love us. Then when things started to turn around, this happens. We didn't have enough time with him being the father he turned out to be in the end."

At that moment the three of them went in to a group hug and they stood there for a while, struggling with their feelings for their father.

"Do you want to come to make the funeral arrangements with me Maggie, Joseph?"

"I will go with you Frank. Maggie shouldn't upset herself too much."

"What do you mean? Are you sick Maggie?"

She lets out a big sigh and feels she has to tell him as she looks at Joseph who is nodding his head to her.

"Frank, I'm pregnant"

Frank was ecstatic. "You are making me an uncle? This is so great. Is Paul jumping up and down?" Then he realizes, Paul is gone and he gets mad.

"How can he leave you knowing you are pregnant? What's wrong with him? Is he crazy?"

Joseph pulled Frank out the door because he didn't want to upset Maggie, having to rehash why she let him go or why she didn't tell him she's pregnant. Maggie knew Joseph would explain to him.

CHAPTER 54

Arrangements

Funeral arrangements were all made and it turned out they were already planned for their father, by their father and it was even paid for.

It shocked them all. He didn't want a viewing—not even a private one. He just wanted to be buried next to his wife. Nothing more!

They did as he wished because the three of them felt—there was no way they wanted *him* haunting any of *them* for the rest of their lives! They already had enough bad memories of him and didn't need more.

His lawyer called them all for a meeting the next day and they went together picking Maggie up and going to his office downtown.

They were nervous because they didn't know what would be in store for them—knowing their father like they did. They thought and expected the worse!

Mr. Pantaloni his lawyer seemed happy to meet them.

"I am so happy to finally meet you. Your father spoke highly of the three of you!"

The three of them just looked at each other and then burst out laughing and it confused Mr. Pantaloni.

"Sir, our father wasn't fond of us for so long, so you have to excuse us for laughing when you said that." Frank explained.

"Are you sure we are speaking about the same person? Frank Sardo?" Joseph asked.

"The one and only and trust me—I know all about him. He was pretty miserable and I myself wondered how your mother lasted that long with him. I guess she really loved him. That is the only thing I could come up with."

Now they *did* know he was talking about their father.

"What did he used to say about us? Please tell us, because he just started talking to us a few months ago." Maggie asked next, anxious to hear about him.

"Well Maggie, he thought you were so beautiful. He would say—Maggie looks just like her mother—so beautiful!" Maggie was stunned and tears started rolling down her cheeks.

"Joseph, he thought you were so smart and knew you would do well working where you are."

"Frank, he fully expected you to be the glue—holding the 3 of you together to be a family and its leader."

Mr. Pantaloni gave them all a moment to grasp what he just said. He knew more about how our dad felt about us than he ever told us himself and it was overwhelming.

"Ok, down to business. Here are his bank accounts or I should say yours. He changed everything over to your names so you wouldn't have to pay inheritant taxes. He was pretty shrewd, but I don't think I have to tell you that."

Mr. Pantaloni handed each a savings pass book from the bank he did business with. It's a good thing they were all sitting down because when they opened it up they saw each book had $150,000 in it. Each one!

Maggie dropped hers and bent over having felt a sharp pain in her abdomen just then. Frank and Joseph got up and went to her immediately.

"Are you ok? Should we go? Do you need a doctor?" Frank asked panicking.

"No, no, I'm fine now. I don't know what just happened, but I'm fine."

"Can I get you some water?"

"No sir, really I'm fine. Just stunned I guess."

"Should I continue?"

"Yes please."

Everyone sat back down.

"The business now belongs to the 3 of you if you choose to still run it. You don't have to make a decision on it now. I will help you with whatever you need—should you decide to sell it."

"There is money in the check book to pay off any bills left and the house is in your names as well should you decide to sell that too."

"That should do it. It is pretty straight forward. I have copies of everything I just told you about for each one of you."

They all shook his hand and thanked him saying also they would be in touch and all headed back to Maggie's.

"Now . . . we have a lot to think about. What about the house? Let's talk about that first. I know I don't want it. I have my own place now and really don't need it" Frank told them.

"I have my own apartment so I don't want a house. At least not just yet. Not to mention the house is so old it will need at least $100,000 to update it." Joseph replied "Maggie what about you? Would you want mom and dads?"

"Never! Never ! Never! I'm buying my own house."

"So we all agree?" Frank asked.

"I will call Patti my friend who is a realtor and ask her to list it. Hire someone to clean it out and get rid of everything. There is nothing in there I want. Wait—moms Chrystal and china. I would like that if neither of you do."

Frank told her she could have it because mom would have wanted her to have it and it made her happy she had heirlooms from her mother. "Now what about the business. Joseph you could come back and we could run it together?"

"Frank—I'm so happy where I am right now. They would take you in a heartbeat if you want to sell the business. We might even be able to sell it to them. We wouldn't have to worry about the payroll, taxes or health insurance. That would all be provided. What do you think?"

"Do you really think they would hire me too?"

"We are so busy and if we sell the business to them—we will be even busier. So I think it would be a no brainer."

"Ok—I'll drop by there tomorrow to talk to the owner. How much is the business worth so I could tell him."

"Here is the paperwork from Mr. Pantaloni. I really didn't look at it until now . . . Oh My God!"

"How much is it worth?" Maggie asked. "$425,000!"

The three of them were once again stunned by their father never knowing the business was worth that much. He built up an empire for them and they just couldn't process that.

"He is looking down on us all right now and smirking at us. Probably thinking—I still got you in the end, stumping us like this."

They all just smiled and had a warm feeling about their father. This is how it should be, they felt and finally accepted—he did what he could for them but just didn't know how to tell or show them when he was alive.

CHAPTER 55

New Plans

Two weeks went by and Jimmy, Paul's advisor from the U came knocking on her door. She was happy to see him and remembered how much he helped them find the apartment they were renting. "Maggie we have to talk about the apartment."

"Ok Jimmy. What's up? Paul and I know his scholarship is up this month. I was going to call you because we need to know where to send out our rent check to."

"Maggie that's just it. You cannot live here any longer. You have until the end of June to find a different place to live. This apartment is allocated to the University and now that Paul has graduated—the landlord cannot rent to you anymore."

Maggie thought she was going to pass out just then. She was finally starting to get back to normal after Paul left, her father's passing and now this.

"Jimmy, the end of June?"

"Yes—I'm afraid so and I'm so sorry I didn't let you both know sooner. It's been so busy with the new students getting ready to come in and I have to apologize to you and Paul."

"Is there any wiggle room in case I can't find anything?"

"Of course! We will never throw you out on the street!"

"Ok. It seems I have a lot to do now. Find a place, pack, move . . ." she drifted off just then.

"Maggie, again I'm so sorry. I can see the place is in immaculate shape and I will tell the landlord. He will be sending your security deposit back. You will need it for your next place."

"Thank you Jimmy for everything."

The minute he leaves she calls her friend Patti again and made an appointment to see her. She didn't want to rent and knew that immediately. Now with Paul's checks coming in—they might be able to afford a small starter home. Then she called Joseph and Frank to tell them and they said they would help her check some places out along with Molly and Judy. She told them all, they had to rush because she didn't have a lot of time to find somewhere and close on a house. Everyone was on a hunt helping her find something.

"I would like a bungalow or something that looks like a cottage. It doesn't have to be big. But a nice yard and garage please. I'm tired of brushing snow off of my car every winter."

Patti knew exactly what she was looking for and went to work immediately trying to find her something.

"Sorry, one more thing. The house will be in my name only. My husband is in Europe working and will not be home in time. This is from my bank telling me what I could afford." as she handed her the paperwork.

It confused Patti about Paul but she just let it go because it really was none of her business. She was happy also that Maggie already had an amount she would qualify for a loan for the house so she got right to work.

The next day Patti called her and told her she found something that just came on the market in the hill section of the city. It was a beautiful section and Maggie always loved driving through it. The houses were all nice—the streets were quiet and it was next to a big park.

With Joseph and Frank in tow and Molly and Judy meeting her there she headed out to find it.

When she looked at it, she saw the outside was exactly what she was looking for. It looked just like a cottage and with the right paint and trim color it would look just the way she pictured a cottage to look like. So far so good.

The inside was in bad shape but Maggie could see the potential and so could her brothers and the girls. Their heads were spinning, looking around and thinking about what could be done with it.

When you walked into the house to the left was a beautiful staircase leading up to the 2nd floor. Up four steps was a landing with a beveled glass window that went right to the ceiling letting in tons of natural lighting. To the right was a family room with a fireplace on the far wall and built in book shelves on both sides. She imagined a big screen TV above the fireplace and some of Paul's trophies on the book shelves.

There were three bedrooms and Maggie said "I could take this bedroom and knock down this wall to make a bathroom and walk in closet. Then there would still be another bedroom for guests" looking at Joseph who knew what she meant. "I could work on one room at a time as I got money for repairs." Everyone was nodding.

Then she took her out to the back yard which was enclosed by a white picket fence and a nice size. There was a garage at the back of the property that you got into from an alley that went down the back of all the houses. The neighbors were not too close and with the fence it felt secluded and private enough.

"Patti, could I afford this? How much is it?"

"Maggie it is under your budget so you would have room for some projects too!"

"Can you give us a minute? I want to talk to my brothers and friends about it."

"I know this is the first house I saw but I love it. She is giving me everything I asked for. I could hire someone to start fixing it up immediately. What do you all think? Should I wait, or go with my gut feeling?"

"Maggie, I would go with my gut feeling. I will help you paint and do whatever I can. If you absolutely love it, then buy it before someone else does." Joseph commented.

"I know a contractor that can help you out." Frank told her.

Molly and Judy are nodding their heads agreeing. "We can see you love it. Your face lit up talking about what you want to do to it. I think it is a good move." Molly told her.

"You know we can help you paint too. I need a project anyway." Judy chimed in.

"Ok—Patti" she called to her.

"Let's get an offer in and see what happens. Getting the money is no issue and I would need to close as soon as possible. You know my situation. I have until the end of June, so the sooner the better."

"I will get right on it Mrs. Tanner and call you within the hour." As she shakes her hand.

They all decided to grab something to eat and Maggie decided to tell her friends her news.

"I have something to tell you both also, but you have to promise not to tell anyone. Especially Paul."

Joseph grabbed her hand as she told them "I'm pregnant and before you say a word let me tell you why I didn't tell Paul."

Their faces just dropped and after she explained they understood why Paul didn't know and why she wasn't telling him.

Before dinner was even finished Patti called with a counter offer for the house and Maggie just said "Ok. Let's do it."

Just like that, she owned a house.

CHAPTER 56

Getting Settled

Maggie and the contractor worked tirelessly on the new house. She had the outside painted dark steel blue and trimmed all the windows in white. She continued with the white picket fence that enclosed the back yard to the front also. It looked like she wanted it to look, just like a cottage. She didn't bother planting flowers because it was already late in the season so she just put planters everywhere to brighten the place up.

The inside was another story. She gutted the kitchen and picked out white country cabinets that went right up to the ceiling. She put in a big gas stove with 6 burners and a grill and a big refrigerator/freezer. She loved to cook and felt she wanted a big one. The contractor constructed a center island that was the same color as the outside of the house which broke up all the white in the kitchen and added some color to it. The drop lights over the center island looked like lanterns. She went to the counter top store and found beautiful marble slabs that had a trace of blue in them. They were perfect! Behind the dining room was the laundry room with a small bathroom she felt they needed on the first floor along with a small room she made an office out of. There was more room in that house than it looked like.

Off to the side of the kitchen she chose to put the dining area and dropped a beautiful but simple chandelier. She loved those too. French doors went out to the back patio along with a door from the kitchen.

She was able to save the hardwood floors that were there and had them sanded and refinished a rich walnut oak color.

As expected—Maggie knocked down the wall between her bedroom and a smaller one and made a master bathroom and walk in closet out of it. It was huge and took up half the house on the second floor. The second bedroom was not as large but a nice size—then one more bathroom for that 'guest bedroom '.

She did not want the renovations to take long and the contractor didn't run into any issues so everything went smoothly.

The only problem everyone worried about was that she wouldn't pick out any furniture. Not even a table for the dining room.

She did have to buy bedroom furniture because she needed somewhere to sleep. They knew why she was hesitating. She was waiting for Paul to come home so they could pick it out together. Everyone worried and hoped he wouldn't be away much longer. They knew she wasn't telling him anything that was going on or that happened so far. She didn't tell him she was pregnant yet either. She wouldn't even go for an ultrasound. Not until he came home. She told them time after time—not until her husband could take her and do it together.

CHAPTER 57

I'm Coming Home

Finally, after 12 weeks Paul had had enough. He missed Maggie too much and couldn't take being away from her any longer. He was doing well too on the team but everyone saw his heart wasn't in it. That life was not for him. Every time he tried to have a conversation with Maggie the time of day was off and the same with her. Every time she wanted to really speak to him—it was the middle of the night where he was. Their phone calls only lasted a few minutes each and they were both upset about that.

The lightbulb went on for Paul. He needed to come home. He needed his wife. He needed to feel her body lying next to his. He needed her so badly—it made him emotional even thinking about it.

Towards the end of his trip he thought—*how could I have ever left you*—when thinking about his wife.

He made plans to come home and wanted to surprise Maggie and once he had them—called Joseph to pick him up at the airport. Was Joseph ever happy to hear that he was coming home but more over so he could tell him all that happened while he was gone. Everything, except his sister was pregnant. He knew Paul would be upset once he heard all that happened and that Maggie never told him. Joseph knew exactly what to say to defuse him if he was angry.

Everyone is at the house and they are painting the fence in the back yard. It was around 4 and everyone but Maggie knew Paul was due in at 4:30. Frank and Judy were painting away like nothing was going on along with Molly and Joseph. Maggie was so happy her two brothers were dating her two best friends. It seemed everyone but her was all set. Right at 4, Joseph pretended he got an emergency call from work about a broken washer that just had to be fixed immediately. It wasn't unusual for this to happen. Every now and then one of them had to go repair something that couldn't wait.

Molly goes right to him smiling away and kisses him. She knew he had a tough task coming up.

"Good luck! Bring your sister's husband home to her!" He smiled back at her and kissed her again—then left.

Everyone was so nervous just waiting. Judy went right in the house and got a glass of orange juice ready for Maggie. When she got upset or shook, her blood sugar would drop suddenly causing her to turn white and almost faint due to her pregnancy. She knew once she saw Paul—she would definitely need it.

Joseph is so anxious waiting at the airport for his brother. He practiced and practiced what he was going to tell him so much; it made him a nervous wreck. Finally, he just told himself he would recap, as things happened.

Finally, Paul comes down the escalator to the baggage claim to get his luggage and he immediately sees Joseph waiting for him. They both went into a big bear hug and stayed there enjoying the moment between them.

"Did you tell Maggie I was coming?"

"No—you told me you wanted to surprise her!"

"Yes—I cannot wait to see her Joseph. I thought when I made my decision to come home—how could I ever have left her in the first place."

Joseph was so happy to hear him say that.

"I have so much to tell you and you are going to be shocked but you have to keep an open mind about everything I have to say." He tells him as they walk to the car.

Now Paul panicked and Joseph saw that. "Please Paul, just listen first. I have so much to tell you!" Almost pleading with him.

"Is Maggie alright? Is something wrong?"

"Nothing is wrong and let me tell you how proud I am of the way she handled everything that happened in her life since you left."

"Since I left? She didn't tell me anything. No one has said anything to me. Not you or my parents!"

"Tell me now, what is going on!" Paul was upset thinking something happened to Maggie and he wasn't there for her.

Joseph just nodded and started from the week he left.

"Jimmy told her she had to be out by June . . . she quickly had to find somewhere to live and decided to buy a house . . . went to the bank for a loan . . . hired a contractor to fix it up . . . our father passed away . . . sold the business and his house and split it 3 ways . . . had a savings book in each of our names . . ."

Paul's head was spinning trying to take everything in.

"Oh my God! This all happened in the 12 weeks I was gone?" Again he is just nodding his head.

"Your father passed away and no one told me?"

"Yep!"

"Are you saying—I have a house now?"

"Yep!"

"Maggie remodeled the house and hired a contractor *by herself* to do it?"

"Yep!"

"How could this all happen and I didn't even know?" Now he was upset.

"I left my wife home alone, with all of these issues and she never said a word or hinted anything was wrong! Why wouldn't she tell me? I don't understand!" seeming annoyed he didn't know anything.

"Really Paul? You don't understand? She knew you had to go. She knew she had to *let* you go. You had to see if that was what you wanted. She gave you the opportunity to make *that* choice on your own. You were the only one to say—I don't want to play ball anymore. I want a normal life. I want my wife. You and you alone were the only one who could make that decision. "

"I won't lie to you! When you left—we didn't know how we were going to help her. She was in bad shape. She had the biggest meltdown. She made us all promise not to tell you anything. Even your parents!

She had to explain to them why and they couldn't believe she was going to do that for you."

Paul couldn't believe all he put his wife through . . . again! It upset him so much but made him now all the more anxious to get to her and Joseph could see it on his face.

"There is one more thing—well two actually. I want you to know and realize—every thought she has—revolves around you. Every decision she made—was for you. I don't want you to ever think differently. She won't even buy furniture for the house. It's empty! She is waiting for you to come home so you could furnish it together. We had to talk her into buying bedroom furniture!"

Paul was so stunned trying to grasp everything his brother just told him. He sat quietly trying to take in everything and Joseph let him go. He saw how upset he was.

Then he was watching where Joseph was driving to see where he now lived. They pulled up to the front of the house and Paul just put his head down.

"This is exactly the house I would picture my wife choosing. It is just perfect and so her! I love it!"

Judy saw the car pull up and nodded to everyone. Maggie was taking a break . . . Judy ran in to get the cup of juice and told her—"you look a little pail. Drink this! Maybe you did too much today."

"Thank you Judy!"

Frank yells "Maggie—this fence isn't going to paint itself! Let's get moving!" They all laughed.

"Frank—the baby doesn't want to paint anymore today!"

Throwing her arms in the air she said "The baby wants a hot fudge sundae . . ." Just as they laughed again all faces dropped and just looked behind her and she followed their eyes turning around.

Her face dropped and she froze where she was standing and started crying. She saw her husband there crying also.

"I don't think I feel well. I'm hallucinating." Crying and crying and Paul ran to her and grabbed her pulling her into his arms.

"You are not hallucinating. I think *I* am!"

"Maggie, I don't know where to start. I'm so sorry I left you. Maggie, you're pregnant?"

He is crying so much he couldn't even talk.

He just looks at Joseph like he was asking *why didn't you tell me this?* "This wasn't for me to tell you. She found out the day you told her you wanted to go to Europe. You see brother. I told you. Everything was for you!" At that moment Paul remembered she had something to tell him when he told her about Europe. She said she forgot what she wanted to talk to him about. Now he knew, she must have *died* when he told her about going and felt how does she ever put up with me. That was the reason she got so sick once he told her his news too. That day all came back to him just then; as he was holding her like he would never let her go.

Everyone was crying now.

Judy and Molly went right to Paul and hugged him while he still had his arms around his wife. Frank came right over and hugged him too. "We're going to leave you two now. You have a lot to talk about.

Right now Maggie . . . I bet you are glad you bought that big bed . . ." Frank said teasing her and now they really laughed as Judy pulled Frank by the hand to get him moving.

"Judy" Maggie called her.

"Thanks for the glass of juice." She knew just then why Judy came out with it for her. She would have been passed out cold if she didn't drink that.

CHAPTER 58

Let Me See You

Maggie took Paul by the hand "Let me show you our house!" Paul is shaking his head no.

"I want to see you, not the house. I need to feel your body next to mine Maggie. I missed you so much. I love you so much. I can't tell you how much."

He touches her baby bump, still crying.

She takes him upstairs to their bedroom and she starts undressing him. Then she took her clothes off so he could see her.

"You are so beautiful Maggie."

He bent down with tears streaming down his face and kissed his baby saying "I'm your father and I'm promising you right now I will never—never leave you or your mother again."

Maggie cried as she ran her fingers through Pauls' hair and he just melted into her—kneeling in front of her with his arms wrapped around her and his child.

He gets up and pulls her over to their bed. His kisses were soft at first and then they got deeper and deeper. He caressed her body and felt her breasts were fuller from being pregnant and she moaned with pleasure when he touched them. He kissed her and her body until he couldn't wait any more.

Then he stopped dead which alarmed her.

"Why are you stopping? What's wrong? Is there something wrong with me?"

"No—no—can we still have sex? I don't know. Is it still ok to have sex with you being pregnant?

She cried and just said "Yes—right up until the doctor tells us we have to stop."

"And I won't hurt the baby at all—you know what I mean right?"

"No, the baby is not in any danger from you during sex. Look at me! Sex is fine and if you don't kiss me right now and continue . . ." she didn't have to tell him again—sex was still OK.

He was careful trying to position himself over her and held his body up so as not to *squash* the baby. That is what he thought so she let him go until they could *practice* how to have sex when you're pregnant.

When they were done he pulls her on top of him so he could hold her, both out of breath and enjoying so much finally being together and naked again!

"Maggie do you know what we're having? Do you want to know?"

"I didn't go for the ultrasound yet. I was waiting for you to come home. I wanted us to do it together."

She cries again. "I'm sorry. Raging hormones present and accounted for."

He holds her tighter trying to comfort her "I missed you so much Mags. I cannot begin to tell you. I craved seeing you. I craved you touching me. I craved hearing your voice. I can't thank you enough for everything you did for me. I know why you let me go. I know you thought the decision had to be mine to go and come home. How Mags? How can I thank you? How can I make it up to you? I don't know if I deserve everything you do for me."

"You want to thank me? I'm you wife. That's what spouses do for each other. I love you Paul and always will. You already did thank me. I am going to have our baby. That's thanks enough for me -along with you being home again!"

Paul gets up in the middle of the night—arms still around his wife and child. He carefully releases her as not to wake her. He kept her up more than he should have with him just getting home and all the emotions they both experienced. But it seemed he just couldn't get enough of her.

He walks into his bathroom and looks around to see what she did and materials she chose for the vanity and shower. He loved every single thing she picked out. The tiles for the shower were in all shades of blues and the marble counter top for the vanity had a trace of blue in it too which tied into the rest of the bathroom. The travertine tile flooring was just beautiful and he shook his head in amazement wondering how she thought all of that out.

Then he walks into another room and saw all of his things hung up in this huge walk in closet. It was separated into two sides—one for his wife and one side for him. She hung a chandelier also in that room and had a huge decorator mirror standing against one wall. He had drawers also and opened and closed them trying to see where she put all of his things. Again he was amazed.

He found a pair of sweats and put them on and wandered down stairs after checking on his wife first to make sure she was still sleeping.

The stair case banister was painted white to match the trim on all of the windows while the floors on the steps and living room were polished deep walnut. They were the original floors he thought and loved them. Then he wanders into the kitchen and saw the white cabinets noticing the same counter tops as the vanity in his bathroom. *She must have really liked these* he thought to himself, but saw why she did that. The island was the same blue as the house outside and then he realized she picked them out to break up all of that white and keep with the blue theme of the outside of the house.

He looked at the fixtures and loved them and another chandelier hung in the dining room was so her. He smiled to himself when he thought that.

He heard something just then. Maggie was crying and he ran up the steps two at a time to see what was wrong yelling to her "I'm coming Mags!"

He found she was crying in her sleep and got back in bed pulling her into his body—pushing her hair out of her face and around her neck.

She wakes and he told her "You were crying in your sleep! Are you OK? Were you having a bad dream?"

"Am I dreaming now? Are you really home or am I still dreaming. I couldn't make it out in my dream. I didn't know if you were really here or not!" Now tears are streaming down her face and Paul just tightened his embrace around her.

He kisses her lips and asks "Does that feel like I'm here?"

He leans down kissing her breasts—running his tongue across her nipples and smiling "Does this feel like I'm here?"

She leans back and moans in pleasure and grabs him trying to pull him on top of her. He was more than ready and able to as he tells her, "I hope you got some rest before because I think we are going to be awake until the sun comes up."

"I don't need any sleep when you are around. I hope the baby doesn't want any either!" She followed that up with.

It put the biggest smile on both faces when she said *baby*.

CHAPTER 59

Life Goes On

Paul and Maggie had some things to do now. She walked him around the whole house telling him what she was thinking when she was remodeling. They headed out to buy furniture . . . together.

Paul called his parents who were more than thrilled he was home and back with Maggie. They immediately said they would be in the next weekend to see them both. They couldn't wait to see their son and daughter and to see her baby bump.

Maggie made an appointment for her ultrasound . . . finally! "I almost forgot to tell you Paul!"

"What is it?"

"Nicky and Elizabeth are due 2 weeks after us. She is pregnant too!"

"Oh my God Mags! You are kidding me. What if they are both boys? We could teach them how to be point guards like us! Nicky and I always talked about that." He was just smiling away when he thought that and called Nicky immediately.

They were catching up and on the phone for two hours when she told him they had to go to her appointment or she would be late. He hung up immediately because he actually couldn't wait to see what they were having and make sure Maggie was going to be ok.

"Paul, are you going to be disappointed if it's a girl?" Looking at him with tears welling up in her eyes.

"No Mags—never! I will not be disappointed. I want to be a father. Girl or boy! But I will tell you this much. If it is a girl . . . she is never leaving the house!"

That made them both laugh as they made their way to the office for the exam.

Paul was holding Maggie's hand standing next to her on the table and was shaking so much being so excited about becoming a father and seeing his child being protected by his wife's body. That is how he thought about it. Maggie was harboring his child! He just couldn't believe it.

Doctor Burke, Maggie's OBGYN finally met Paul and felt better about him now being home. She always felt sadness coming from Maggie—going to her appointments alone and worried Paul would not be home in time for the delivery. She kept looking at the screen and then something came into focus, the baby and when they both saw it, they started crying. The Doctor was smiling also at them.

"Well, do you want to know what it is?"

"Yes" Paul just blurted out and then they both laughed.

She looked at them both and said . . . "Boy! It looks to be a healthy baby boy! I don't see any issues and everything looks fine. You are about 14 weeks along now—over your first trimester. All looks good so far!" Paul was on Maggie just kissing her head, her face and saying thank you to her over and over again all the while she is crying like a baby

Being so happy.

"I can't wait to tell Nicky!" he tells her on the way home. "I did my part and now it is up to him to complete us." Maggie just laughs at him and sees he is over the moon about having a son.

When they got home he drags her upstairs and starts undressing her and then himself. They crawled in bed and stood there almost the whole afternoon until he heard her stomach growling for food. He jumps right up "I will make you something to eat. You just rest. I don't want you to overdo it."

She is laughing at him knowing he is a terrible cook, "Ok, I will stay right here. Call me when you are ready and I will be down."

He heads to the kitchen and has to come back and back and back to ask her questions because he doesn't know where everything is and then realizes—she might not be able to eat everything. So she tells him she will help and gets up to join him in the kitchen.

This goes on for months and months and months. He just dotes over her and his son and she loves every minute.

Nicky and Elizabeth found a house that just went up for sale right down the street from Paul and Maggie! Everyone was just crazy when they bought that house. They were able to walk two houses down to visit. It made it easy for them to baby sit Kristin too.

One night when Nicky and Elizabeth were visiting—Paul was telling Nicky about befriending a man who owned an advertising agency in Paris. He said he told him all about how it works in Europe and how different it was from here in the states. He seemed excited when telling him!

Later that night—Maggie told Paul—"why don't you start your own agency. You and Nicky!"

"Really—you think I should?"

"Well what do you think? You learned a lot when you interned for the firm in the city and you learned a lot about advertising in Europe. So as not to upset the firm you worked for—why don't you and Nicky create advertising, for companies from here in the states, which want to advertise in Europe. That way you won't be stabbing anyone here, in the back, so to speak."

She could see Paul's wheels were turning and turning. He calls Nicky immediately and they talk again for hours about it.

"How much can you come up with Paul? I think I can tap my trust fund account for $50,000. That is all I could do after just buying this house and now with Elizabeth pregnant. If you could come up with the same we could start small until we build up clients."

"I will go talk to Maggie and see now and call you later."

"Maggie, Nicky is in if we can get enough money to start up the agency. He can swing $50,000. What can we afford?"

Maggie pulls him over to the office where she paid all the bills. She pulls out a savings pass book. It has $36,000 plus some interest. Then she pulls out her pass book from her dad that had $150,000 in it. She had one more but didn't show him that yet.

"Maggie, where did you get the $36,000?"

"I worked the corner while you were gone! You can never imagine all the guys who wanted to *do* a pregnant woman!" She can't control laughing at Paul whose face dropped when she said that.

Then he started smiling and shaking his head at her joke.

"Those are all your checks you direct deposited from playing those 12 weeks."

Paul is stunned. "I thought you used that money to help pay for the house or for the bills. You didn't touch any of it?"

"No—I didn't need to and kept it in case I did need it in the future."

"Maggie . . . I'm stunned. I can't believe you didn't spend it." Next she hands him the pass book from her father.

"This is the pass book my father set up for me. You can see the amount. You can use your money and take the balance of what you need from this account. I told you he left me some money but we were going over so much you probably forgot all about it. I have one more book and I don't know if you approve or not but the money Frank gave me from selling our dad's house and business- I put in this trust fund for our son. At the time I thought—where ever he decides to go to school—it will be paid for. You never know what could happen down the road and I don't want him to be strapped."

Paul is so stunned when he sees the amount in that book too—he pulls her into his body needing to feel her at that moment. She wraps her arms around his neck and shoulders and hangs onto him too. Then he kisses her softy feeling so proud of her for being so smart with their finances and for being his wife.

"I can't believe you did all of this. You're amazing and the fund for Paul Jr. just blows me away."

"Wait . . . Wait . . . Wait . . . What do you mean Paul Jr.? When were you going to tell me that is what his name is going to be? I think I have a say in this too!"

He is looking at her wondering if she is serious or not and then she bursts out laughing and so does he. He knew she couldn't be mad at him if she tried.

"Paul Jr? Really?"

"Please Mags. I want a Paul Jr.!"

"Oh my God! Men and their sons. Holy cow!" She is still laughing at him.

"Well . . . that is the name I would have picked out too." Now she is really laughing because she had him going thinking she wouldn't name the baby after him.

She pulls him over to the bed . . . and what is it with that bed anyway? Every time they pass it by they wind up in it . . . having sex. Not that she was complaining.

Later Paul spoke to Nicky and they had the money they needed—they were going to see a lawyer to set up the Global Advertising Agency. The GAA! Everyone was so happy and a lot of work had to be done to get it set up and apply for all the licenses. It was an eye opener. But over the course of a few weeks they were all set up. They even found an office down town, not far from Maggie's shop, so everything was falling into place.

Nicky and Paul made call after call and worked night after night and slowly they had a decent client base. Once word got around, the business took off quickly. They were both very good at it too. It came naturally to them and both were so likeable, which is why it was working so well for them with their clients.

All of those long hours and week end work paid off. When they couldn't help someone, they always referred them to the firm Paul interned for every summer. Did they ever appreciate that extra business. They weren't upset with Paul at all, once that started happening and they in turn started referring overseas clients to the GAA also. It worked out well for them both.

CHAPTER 60

Paul Jr.

Their first Christmas in the new house was just perfect. Maggie finally had her family to spend the holidays with and Paul's parents came in and stayed with *them* for a change. The tree was so beautiful and Paul loved coming home to all of the decorations and baking going on in the house. Something sweet smelling was always in the oven and he loved being the taste tester.

Right after Christmas, Maggie really started feeling pregnant. She was huge and waddled around the house when the doctor wouldn't let her go to work anymore. The shop threw her a baby shower right before her last days and once again everyone went over the top with the gift giving. Paul and Maggie were always so grateful to all the girls at the shop and especially Sarah who did so much for them.

Maggie was due the middle of January but on the 5th her water broke. She called Paul frantic and then he became frantic.

"Nicky . . . !" He yells to him down the hall in his office. Nicky came running and saw Paul was white.

"What is it? What's wrong?"

"Maggie's water just broke." That was all he had to say.

A big smile swept across Nicky's face and he just said "Let's go, I'll take you home."

He dropped Paul off and went home to get Elizabeth and wait until they got word they were going to the hospital.

Once he got home the contractions started. The doctor told her to wait until they were 10 minutes apart before she headed over to the hospital and did that happen quickly once her water broke. Paul was just pacing and pacing timing them, and when they hit 10—he said—"let's go Mags. It's time."

He helped her get to her car and didn't know how he was going to get her to the hospital he was shaking so much. He thought *thank God it was only a few blocks away from our house.*

They send a text to everyone and told them where they were going and why and everyone was so excited and worried at the same time. She was in labor earlier than expected but the doctor said everything was fine so they all calmed down.

Joseph and Frank paced and paced in the waiting room as well as Nicky. He was thinking he would be going through the same thing in just a few weeks.

Hours went by and no news. Once they hit 6 hours everyone started to panic, even Molly and Judy. Elizabeth told them it should never take that long, which made matters worse.

In the delivery room—Paul was so upset watching his wife go through that pain to give him a son. Once again he felt he didn't deserve her and all she went through and goes through for him. She saw that look on his face and just tried to smile at him—squeezing his hand. Squeezing his hand was an understatement. With every contraction Paul thought his hand would be broken she held it so tightly. He knew she was scared and in truth, so was he.

"How about you tell me how much you love me. Maybe it will ease this pain some." Trying to smile at him.

They were both shaking but for different reasons. He was so scared he would lose her because she was having such a hard time delivering Paul Jr. She was shaking because she was going into shock.

Doctor Burke finally said "We have to do a c section and knock her out now! She doesn't even hear us right now—if we want to save her and the baby we have to do it now. Do we have your permission Paul?"

"Yes—please save my wife and son. Please!" pleading with the doctor.

Before they knocked her out he told her looking into her eyes and squeezing her hand "I will tell you how much I love you. More than there are words to say. Go to sleep now Mags and when you wake you will have a beautiful son. I will be right here for you and for him."

With that she was out and they did the c section and rescued Paul Jr who was in distress. They quickly examined him and he hadn't made a sound yet. Then all of a sudden—a big cry came out of his tiny mouth and everyone breathed a sigh of relief. The nurse brought him right over to Paul to see and asked what his name was and he proudly but quietly said "Paul Tanner Jr."

Still holding his wife's hand—tears ran down his cheeks trying to remember everything that happened so he could tell his wife when she woke.

All of a sudden Doctor Burke put her head down and everyone else did too. Paul noticed immediately and asked "What is it? Is something wrong?"

The doctor looked at him and nodded yes and Paul almost passed out.

Now raising his voice and crying "What is it? Do whatever you can to save my wife. You have to save her. She saved me and you have to save her. Please . . . Please!"

She explained what was happening, barking out instructions to the nurses to get more blood for his wife and they all scurried around doing what she needed.

"I'm so sorry Paul." She said with her head down.

Why is she saying she is so sorry? Paul thought, hardly able to breathe. The Doctor continued "If you were planning on having more children— it won't be possible. I'm so sorry!" That was all she could say.

"Will my wife recover? Will she live?"

"Yes—a very normal life. She will be fine now. There was too much bleeding. It was like her uterus exploded and it's unrepairable. Sometimes things like this happen and for no reason at all. This is all her body could handle."

Paul cried uncontrollably at all that happened. He didn't know how he could repeat that to everyone waiting. The nurse agreed to go out to tell them with him. Then he said he wanted to go back to be with his wife. He didn't know how he was going to tell her too about what happened and worried how she would take it. In truth he didn't care about having another child. He just wanted *her* and wanted her to be well again.

He also asked that his son be brought in the recovery room to be with his mother. Paul felt when she woke it would help if he could be there so he could show her their beautiful son.

When everyone saw Paul and the condition he was in—they immediately knew it was bad news. His mom and dad arrived just in time to hear what happened and went right to him wrapping him in their arms where he wept uncontrollably.

Joseph and Frank were inconsolable too, but in truth—they all were. The nurse ended the report by reminding everyone that the baby was fine and in perfect health and now so was Maggie. She would make a full recovery. That seemed to help as she looked around and saw everyone nodding to each other.

When Maggie woke—as promised . . . Paul was right there and picked up her son for her to see.

"Look Maggie. Look how beautiful he is. Look what you did Maggie. Can you see him?"

Tears started coming down her cheeks and she nodded her head to him still being so groggy.

"The nurse asked me what his name was and I said Howard!" Laughing as he told her which made her smile back at him.

"No—I said Paul Tanner Jr. What do you think? Do you like him yet?" laughing again at her.

She just nods her head and reached out to touch her son. He was perfect and beautiful and she knew it.

He put Paul back in his little incubator crib and then takes her hand kissing it and resting it on his face. She ran her fingers through his hair and fell back to sleep. She saw her two men and felt better. She knew she could rest now.

CHAPTER 61

Maggie's Turn

Maggie flipped when Paul and Doctor Burke told her what happened. She let out the biggest scream and grabbed Paul by his shirt crying.

He tried to hold her but then she just punched his chest trying to get him away from her yelling.

"I don't understand. How did that happen? Why did it happen?" She asked but knew those questions would never be answered.

The nurse came in with a shot for her to calm down and she just looked at her and yelled. "Don't you dare give me a shot to calm me down! Don't you dare!"

Paul has never heard her speak to anyone like that. He felt as badly as anyone could feel trying to talk her off the ledge. The nurse backed away when she said she didn't want the shot and Doctor Burke nodded to take it away.

"Doctor Burke, please don't give her that! Let us speak for a while and I will call you if we need you."

The doctor just nodded her head and left their room.

Maggie was beyond mad. She was so angry. She felt she lived her whole life trying to please everyone she knew and remembered all she let Paul get away with. She just couldn't understand it.

Why did this happen? Now . . . she couldn't even have any more children and her heart was broken.

It seemed she was mad at everyone too. She barely smiled when she had visitors and hardly said a word. She did hold her son and tried to bond with him but she felt numb. She couldn't snap out of it.

The doctor sent a phycologist in to see her and she said less than ten words to her. Paul was beside himself not knowing how he could help her. He didn't know what he could say to her to make her come back to him and come back to their son.

It scared him and he felt he had to tell her that—but she already knew he was scared. She sensed it and then when she saw the circles under his eyes she knew he wasn't sleeping. He wouldn't go home either. He promised he would never leave her when he came back from Europe and that meant when she was in the hospital too. He slept in a chair next to her bed. He tried holding her hand and she didn't even hold it back but he never let it go.

Maggie was trying so hard to cope with the realization that she couldn't have more children and was having a hard time with it.

That final night in the hospital she finally spoke to Paul. Before that she barely spoke to him. She knew it wasn't his fault but she had to blame someone.

Paul wanted his wife back. He needed his wife back. He had everything he ever wanted and now he didn't know how to fix Maggie. Finally— almost like she gave up being mad, she asks in a whisper . . .

"Can you help me feel better?"

Pauls' head just dropped and he knew she wanted to snap out of the hurt and pain she was feeling.

He sits on the bed and put his arm around her—pulling her carefully to lean into him.

Looking down at her and holding onto her, kissing her forehead he knows he has to choose his words. He has to make her see he cannot live without her.

"You are worried about not being able to have more children . . . I know you are. You think it will upset me because you can't give me another child. I know you Maggie and I want you to stop right now. Stop worrying about me and let me tell you why."

"I will be forever grateful to you for giving me my son. I don't care that we can't have more children and not because I have a son. If the baby was a girl and the same thing happened—I would be fine with that too. I am so happy you are still alive and know I cannot survive without you and if it came down to you or a child in that delivery room I know it will sound terrible, but I would choose you in a heartbeat.

That is how much you mean to me. I am not disappointed and will never be. You are my angel Maggie and you handled everything I put you through and we both know I put you through enough for one lifetime in just four years. You never complained. You never even yelled at me and I know you should have flipped out on me on many occasions. If it were just the two of us for the rest of our lives—I would still be thanking God for you!"

"Now, I want you to rest and know—I love you Mags. I don't care about having another child. If you want more—we could adopt. Whatever you want to do will be fine with me."

Tears run down her cheeks as she is listening to her husband reassure her he loves her even though she cannot give him another child. It calms her down and he said everything she hoped he would. To say it eased her mind -was how she felt and seemed to relax her immediately.

Just then the baby cried and Paul told her—"just rest Mags. I will get him and bring him here. For some reason I want the 3 of us to be together."

He gets his son, changes him and brings over a happy baby to see his mother. He lays him in between them as they are oohing and cooing to him and he is just smiling away causing them to smile also. This was a special moment! One of many to still happen between them and with their son!

"Paul, let me hold him now." Paul smiled widely at her. She wanted to hold her son when before they almost had to force her.

She took little Paul and talked to him—kissed him over and over again and told him how much she loved him. Then she apologized to him with tears streaming down her face. "I am so sorry I couldn't tell you how much I loved you until now. I promise to always tell you from now on. You are my son and I waited nine months to see you."

Paul was so happy just then, until, she said . . . "too bad, you look just like your father because everyone knows I am prettier . . . !"

Paul's face just dropped when she cracked a joke and then they both burst out laughing. He immediately kisses her and she responded with happy sighs. Then he bent down to kiss his son while holding the two of them in his arms.

The Doctor came in just then and saw the three of them all smiling and it made her smile too.

"I think we are fine now and look forward to going home tomorrow." Paul told her.

Finally, he felt—they were going to be fine and it relaxed him immediately. He called everyone and told them what happened and they were all at the house when he brought her and little Paul home. Everyone couldn't wait to see her and help out. The frig was stocked with food because they all knew as hard as he tried—Paul wasn't good in the kitchen. Joseph and Frank calmed down a lot also when they saw her. She looked a lot better than she did in the hospital.

"Maggie, I want you to go rest now. There are plenty of people here to take care of Paul Jr." He takes her by the hand and he slowly guides her upstairs to bed. She didn't even argue because she was beat and knew she had to take it easy if she wanted to get better quickly.

The florist delivered a massive bouquet of flowers to her and Molly carried it up to her room while she was resting.

"These just came for you!"

"Oh my God they are gorgeous! Where's the card?" as she sits up in bed.

She opened it and wept covering her face with her hands. She handed the card to Molly and just then Judy came in because she saw her go upstairs with them and wanted to see who sent them.

The card said "I promise you—every year on our sons' birthday—I will send you the biggest bouquet to show you how much I love you and always will, *and* to thank you for giving me my son! Paul"

Well, Molly and Judy started crying just then too and when Paul came in to check on her and saw them all, he made a u turn and headed back downstairs until all the crying stopped.

They both came down and told him to go up to see Maggie—she wanted to see him.

"Thank you so much for the flowers and mostly, thank you for the beautiful note on the card. I love you Paul!"

He sits on the bed with her and wrapped her in his arms and they both gave a sigh except right then Paul Jr. interrupted their moment with the biggest wail and they both laughed.

"So—he is coming between us already I see!" laughing as he told Maggie that.

When Paul found out Maggie was giving him a son he called Nicky immediately and told him "It's up to you now Nicky. I have half of the point guards and it is up to you to supply the other half." Nicky would just laugh because he already knew he and Elizabeth were having a boy. He knew Maggie was waiting for him to come home before she would go for her ultrasound too. So when Paul called to say it was a boy . . . Nicky told him they were now complete. He was having a boy too. They were both unbelievably happy about it and planned out both sons lives together. They knew they would be brothers too, just like their fathers.

Nicky and Paul spoke about it later—if one of them was having a girl . . . well . . . she would just have to marry the one that had the boy. They had that figured out too making Elizabeth and Maggie laugh all the times they talked about it. Luckily—they both were getting what they wanted. Sons to carry on the Newman and Tanner basketball tradition.

CHAPTER 62

First Game

All of a sudden Paul Jr. and Nick Jr were 3. Paul and Nicky couldn't wait to finally take them to some games at the University.

Elizabeth and Maggie thought they were too young to go any earlier which disappointed the fathers at the time, but they understood.

Paul and Nicky bought them University gear and they had their names on the back of their jerseys with each of their #'s. Tanner Jr #5 and Newman Jr #11. They couldn't wait to show everyone.

Off they went and the four 'boys' were so thrilled to be going out together. They went for pizza first and once they got to the gym they took off their coats and all walked in holding their fathers hands. Everyone noticed immediately and went wild when they saw them. Not to mention they were spitting images of their fathers. Paul Jr had curly blond hair and Nick Jr had thick black wavy hair and they both had the same hair cut as their fathers too. They all started clapping and yelling—so Nicky and Paul picked up their sons and told them to wave to everyone. "Wave to everyone, they are clapping for you. I will tell you why later but now you have to wave. Ok?"

Paul Jr would smile and wave and again everyone went wild. Then Paul put him down because he saw his Uncle—Coach B and wanted to go see him.

"Nick, there is Uncle B.!" Paul Jr told him.

"Let's go see him Paul. We have to tell him we are here!"

They both squirmed out of their fathers arms and took off onto the floor to see their Uncle. He saw them coming and bent down to pick them both up in his arms and again the crowd went wild which made Coach smile.

"Uncle B—we didn't know you would be here. My father didn't tell us."

"Maybe he wanted to surprise you two. What do you think?" They both are shaking their heads yes—agreeing.

"Do you want to go see Aunt B too? She is here and I think she is saving seats for you."

Again they both nodded their heads yes and they kissed him before he put them down.

In the meantime Nicky and Paul ran after those two but they were too quick for them and got to the floor before they could catch them.

"Coach, we are so sorry. They got away from us."

"Not a problem but they are making me look bad. They made me smile in front of my players and I didn't want that to happen!" Now everyone is laughing as they took their sons and went to find Mrs. B for their seats.

Everyone had a great time and the boys seemed to know what was going on in the game. Paul and Nicky had watched tons of games on TV with them explaining how the game was played and what was happening. It seemed they knew what was going on and the 2 fathers were so thrilled and proud. So was Mrs. B who was so happy to see them and made sure she got enough hugs and kisses from them both. When they got home from the game Maggie was waiting for them with some cookies and milk and they sat at the snack bar telling her all about the game. Paul Jr did all the talking while Paul just smiled being so proud of him and the way the evening turned out.

"Well-being that you had such a good time—I don't see why you can't go to more games. Would you like that?"

"Dad, can we go to more games? Mom said its ok!"

"Yes—that is a good idea but only if you behave for your mother. You have to be a good boy when you are home and at school—Ok?"

"I try daddy but . . . I will try harder now."

Paul and Maggie just shook their heads always amazed at what Paul Jr comes out with. Sometimes they have to walk away as not to laugh right at him and then they come back as soon as they have a straight face. They both loved him immensely and he was such a sweet boy.

When he was two he always met Paul at the door—waiting for him to come home from work. *And* he met him usually naked. For some reason he hated his clothes on.

"I cannot keep clothes on your son. He rips them right off!"

"Maggie, really? He is *your* son and just like his mother who can't get in bed with clothes on."

They both would laugh and Maggie's face would turn all red when he said that. Then there was a time when he came home from day care (School) and told them both during dinner "Dad, you know my friend David?"

"Yes, you told me about him." Looking at his son wondering what he wanted to tell him.

"Well . . . he told me that my penis was a dick!"

Paul just dropped his fork on his plate and Maggie got up and went in the bathroom because she didn't want him to see her laughing.

When she came back out "You left me here with that! How could you? I didn't know what to say to him! I was trying not to laugh and then I couldn't stop. Paul Jr is just looking at me wondering what was so funny. Now, I have to call Nicky to see if Nick told him the same thing and how he handled it!"

They are both laughing now and Paul Jr still can't understand why.

They were hoping he would just forget it.

"If you think that is all that is going to happen, then just wait. This is only the beginning and I think you should be ready and prepare yourself. Especially when it comes time to have 'the talk' with him. *And* you *will* have that conversation with him and he *will* get what you mean! Do *you* understand?"

Paul's eyes got wide and all he could do is nod his head to his wife as he turned pale thinking about that and what he would say to him. Thank God that wouldn't be for a few years yet.

CHAPTER 63

Anniversary

On their 10th anniversary Paul sent Maggie a bouquet that was the same design as he picked out for her bridal bouquet. He wanted to do something special and they were going to dinner while Elizabeth and Nicky babysat Paul Jr. Paul did not know his wife booked a room for the night and that Paul Jr would be spending the whole night with the Newman's. She wanted to surprise him. But once she got that bouquet, it overwhelmed her. The little white flowers with all the pearls and greens were just completely gorgeous. *He remembered* was what she thought when she got it.

She called his Receptionist Vita and asked her to block off noon to one on Paul's calendar for a meeting but not to tell him who the meeting was with. That way he would be free when she got there for that hour. Vita was in her early 50's and worked for Paul and Nicky almost from the beginning. She was the first person they hired and she kept the both of them in line and on time. They knew she was the one when they interviewed her. She was a strong person and they needed someone like her to run the office. On occasion—*they* even feared her.

"Vita, who is my appointment at noon with?"

"I forgot!"

"What do you mean? How could you book an appointment and not get a name?"

"Stop pressuring me! Vita make the coffee, Vita answer the phone. Vita this, Vita that . . . I am only one person here!" She walks out of his office smiling and trying to get away from him asking any more questions. He doesn't know what got into her, so he just left her alone after that outburst and it kind of shocked him.

Maggie walks in looking beautiful that day. She just glowed!

"Go right in Mrs. Tanner. He knows he has an appointment but not with who—so he is waiting for *someone*!" Smirking at Maggie.

She walks down the hall and into Paul's office where he is so surprised to see her. She turns and closes the door and locks it. Then she unwraps her coat and drops it right there.

Paul almost dropped too, when he saw her. She only had on a black lace bra with matching panties and his mouth just hung open. She also had on the pearl bracelet he bought her for a wedding present.

She bent down to pick up her coat right in front of him and strutted over to his coat rack to hang it up. Then she pranced in front of his desk smiling and called him out from behind it only to see him laughing because he had the biggest hard on just then.

"Would you like me to take care of that for you Mr. Tanner?" Smiling at him.

He just nods his head and kisses her deeply and passionately knowing she absolutely *could* take care of that.

She took off the little clothes she had on and laid a blanket down on his couch in his office, and well . . . you know what happened . . . and it was so nice!

Holding her in his arms enjoying her body on his he smiles saying "So . . . *You* were my noon appointment today! We should schedule more meetings like this. It was very productive" and she laughs when he said that.

"Those flowers Paul . . . How did you even remember 10 years ago? They are so beautiful. I cried when I got them. Thank you so much!"

"How about we both play hooky right now. Let's call it a day and get started early." He said as his fingers ran up and down her back so softly. "We already got started early and I have to close the shop today.

So you will have to wait to see me at 5:30. I promise—I will be worth the wait!"

"You are always worth the wait Mags. Even if you only have sweats on. You are always so beautiful to me."

She leans in for a kiss and then just thought *I have to go now or I will never unlock that door*—smiling to herself and gets up and dresses. Then she helps him get back into his clothes . . . buttoning his shirt . . . fixing his collar . . . running her fingers through his hair all the while watching the biggest smile her husband has on his face.

"Well our appointment here is up so I will see you for dinner later. I already can't wait?"

She turns and flashes him a big smile while still seeing the biggest grin on his face too which means she accomplished her goal that afternoon.

Later, as promised, Paul picked her up at the shop at 5:30 and not a minute later. He even had a suit and tie on and couldn't wait to be with her again. They went to dinner and she wore a black dress which showed off her figure and her legs in those heals—well let's just say heads turned when they walked into the hotel lobby to go to the restaurant. He placed his hand on her back to guide her and they just kept smiling at each other.

They had some champagne and dinner and talked like they didn't see each other in days. They pulled their chairs next to each other and leaned in so they could be closer. He had his hand on her arm while speaking to her and she loved feeling him touch her. Conversation was never an issue between them. They were always relaxed and calm when they were together.

"Do you want to have desert and coffee?"

She slips a room key to him "I ordered desert and coffee to be sent to our room in an hour! Will that be acceptable Mr. Tanner?"

Again she stumped him and he lowered his head shaking it back and forth.

"I cannot tell you how much I love you Maggie. Can you tell me how I got so lucky? Why did you marry me and why did you just accept everything that happened to us. All of my *mistakes* as you called them."

Just then he pulls out a box from his suit pocket. It was so beautifully wrapped.

"Can I open this now?"

"Yes—I can't wait for you to see it. I hope you like it. I picked it out myself and thought it was so you."

She is smiling at him while unwrapping the gift and her eyes got wide and tears filled them she was so happy.

"This is so beautiful Paul. I love it so much!"

It was a pearl ring to match the bracelet he gave her 10 years before. It had two rows of tiny pearls on a gold band and was just exquisite. She loved it.

He saw she was pleased just by the look on her face and took the ring out of the box and placed it on her finger on her right hand. It fit perfectly.

"Nicky and Elizabeth are watching Paul Jr tonight. We can pick him up tomorrow. He is thrilled he is staying at Nick's. We can call him when we get up to the room. Can we go now?"

Paul stands and holds out his hand to help her up and kisses her softly. Everyone around them were smiling at them. Mostly everyone knew who they were too.

So up to their room they went holding hands and smiling at each other. Maggie already had their things in the room waiting. They called Paul Jr and he was so happy he was staying at Nicks. "Dad . . . can Nick stay at our house next time?" making his father laugh.

Their son was all set and so were they. They had the best night ever and enjoyed room service for breakfast. "Maggie I'm so hungry this morning. You wore me out last night!" he told her laughing.

"Who wore who out? I will be fighting you for that last piece of bacon on your plate!" both smiling at each other.

"Let's go collect our son. We have never been away from him" she told him and he just nodded he couldn't wait to get him too.

CHAPTER 64

My Son—The Gift

Paul and Paul Jr were inseparable. When there was no school he and Nicky took the boys to work with them. They would sit them in a small conference room and they just played or watched TV or videos. Vita loved when they came for the day—she doted over them both.

Paul and Nicky dressed up for work because they were always meeting with clients so Maggie and Elizabeth dressed Paul Jr and Nick up too and the boys loved it. For some reason the boys always waited to see what color pants and shirts their fathers had on and choose the same for themselves. It always made their parents laugh when they did that.

"No mom" Nick would tell Elizabeth.

"Dad has on a blue shirt today. I need a blue shirt!"

Of course they knew they always went out to lunch too and the boys could never wait. They would walk to a local restaurant and beam when they had their sons with them. One time after lunch Paul told Nicky, "Paul and I have something to do, so we will see you back at the office." Nicky and Nick went one way and they went the opposite way.

"Where are we going dad?"

"We're going to the florist to buy your mother some flowers."

"But it's not her birthday so why are you sending her flowers?"

"Because it's *your* birthday and every year for your birthday—I promised her when you were born, that I would send her the biggest bouquet of flowers."

"If it's my birthday—wait . . . I don't understand."

Paul just smiled at his son and told him why. "Your mother had a difficult time when you were born. She was in a lot of pain which is kind of normal when a woman is having a baby. Are you with me so far?"

Paul Jr just nodded his head.

"Well—I was so happy she gave me a son . . . and went through all of that for me. So as a gift to her for giving me the best gift ever—*you*—I made a promise to her. Every year on your birthday—I would send her the best bouquet of flowers out there to thank her for giving me you!"

"Does that make sense? Do you have any questions?"

"Dad, you think I'm a gift? From mom?"

"Does that upset you?"

"No, I think I like that. I like thinking I was a gift. You know how happy I am when I get gifts so it makes sense. You were so happy because I was a gift? Right?"

"Yes, exactly, but you were the best gift in the whole world Paul and for your mother to go through all of that just for me . . . well . . . . it made me love her even more that I already did! Do you know what I mean?"

"I think I do. Every day you love someone more than the day before. Right?"

"Yes, that's right! Every day your mother and I love you more than the day before. That is exactly the way we feel about you."

Now Paul Jr was so happy with the way the conversation was going and he felt—*I love my mom and dad so much*. He just put his arms around his dad—looking up at him smiling away while they walked down the street to the florist.

When they walked in Paul Jr took right over.

"Hello, what can I help you with? Do you need to send someone flowers? Maybe to someone you love?" Mary from Mary's Flower Shop asked, smiling at Paul while asking Paul Jr. She knew why he was there. She knew it was around the time he sent his wife flowers every year in January.

"Yes—we need to send the biggest bunch of flowers to my mom for giving my father me!" He so proudly announced which made Paul and Mary smile and laugh.

"Ok. Do you want to come back and see what I have and pick some out yourself? She might like it even more if she knew you helped pick out the flowers."

"Dad is that what you do? Do you help because I will help you too? We can both look."

"Yes, I usually do pick them out. I know what your mother likes, so those are the ones I send."

"How do you know what she likes? Does she tell you?"

"No son. I just look at a flower and think—*I think Maggie will like these.* I just guess and every year she loves what I pick out. Do you want to try with me now?"

"Ok. I think I can do it."

They both followed Mary in the back where all the flowers were and Paul Jr goes right to some white roses. "I think she would like these dad." Then he walked around and very seriously looked at all of the flowers.

He turns to Mary and asks "What are these called?"

"They are called Lilli's and they smell real good. Here, smell this one." She hands one to Paul Jr.

Turning to his dad "I love these dad! They smell so good and I think mom would love these too. I see what you mean now. I think I know she will love these. It was so easy. Thanks for telling me how to do that." Paul and Mary were laughing and nodding their heads.

"Ok Mary. I think we have our flowers. The white roses and the pink Lilli's and you can fill in whatever will look good."

"I think you made a very wise choice Paul" Mary said smiling looking at Paul Jr.

"Can you deliver them on the 4th?"

"Yes, not a problem. At the shop or home?"

"Send them home and after 6. Is that OK?"

"Yes, not a problem. Thank you Mr. Tanner. Do you want to sign the card?"

Looking at Paul Jr. "Yes, we will both sign it. Right?" Paul Jr is just nodding his head he wanted to sign it too.

So they left and walked back to the office but young Paul had a questioned look on his face. "What is it son? Do you want to ask me something?"

"Well, you said you would send mom flowers on my birthday but you are sending them the day before. My birthday is on the 5th."

"That's right Paul but that is *your* day and your mother and I talked about it and she asked me not to send them right on your birthday because that was *your* special day. Do you understand now?"

"Oh, I get it now. Ok dad. Thanks for explaining that to me."

Paul Jr couldn't wait to tell Nick where they went and why. Vita just smiled listening to him explain how his father thought he was a gift from his mother when he was born. He was mesmerized by that story. Now he couldn't wait for the florist to bring the flowers and tell his mom he helped pick them out.

Paul Jr was anxious all day on the 4th. He kept watching the clock at dinner and his mom finally asked "Why are you looking at the clock Paul?"

He didn't know what to say—so big Paul just said "We are watching a game tonight and he is probably just looking to make sure we don't miss it. Right?"

He nodded his head and put it down not wanting his mom to ask any more questions. Then right at 6 the doorbell rang.

He flew out of his chair and yelled "I will get it too with you!"

Maggie walked to the door and the florist was there and handed her a massive bouquet of flowers.

"Oh my God! This is huge. Will you help me take the paper off?"

"Yes mom—I want to see!"

The bouquet was simply gorgeous. The pink Lilli's and white roses and all these other little flowers in between and the vase was beautiful too.

"Mom, now I can tell you a secret I had."

"You had a secret you were keeping from me?"

"Yes—well . . . it's more of a surprise than a secret."

"What is it then?"

"I helped dad pick out the flowers for your bouquet!" He proudly told her.

"You did? They are so beautiful. I love them so much and they smell so good. How did you know I would love these?" Asking, while smiling at him and Paul.

"Dad told me how to do it and it was easy mom. He said look at the flowers and just pick out ones that I thought you would like and it worked because you like them all—right?"

"I love them all Paul." She bent down and hugged him so tightly and kissed him many times and told him she loved him so much. Then she looked up at Paul who was smiling away and had tears well up in her eyes as she leaned up to kiss him too. "I'm remembering why you send me flowers every year and can't tell you how much I love you Paul. These are so beautiful—thank you so much."

"I love you too Mags. Paul and I had a discussion on how we love people more and more every day and it's true. Just when you think you can't love someone more than you already do—you find there is more room in your heart for them."

She nods her head and hugged him with Paul Jr watching and smiling at them both.

CHAPTER 65

Time Flies

Just like that, Paul was getting ready to graduate high school. Paul and Maggie talked about where that time went while lying in bed one night.

"It seems like yesterday he just got his driver's license. Then he was going to his junior prom. Now, I just ironed his graduation gown. When he tried his cap on with the gown—I almost lost it Paul."

Paul takes a deep breath and sighs—"I know Mags. I remember Nicky and I taking Nick and Paul to sign up for the midget basketball league. They were only seven at the time. I wish I could slow down time and keep him here longer. He is such a good son. I'm so proud of him. All of the offers he got to play ball too. It just blew me away and I know Nicky too with the offers Nick got. We talk about it all the time. I'm amazed Maggie about how everything turned out. He is so smart too. He barely has to study and he gets good grades. That has to have come from you!" now he kisses her head as she lies in his arms.

"Go ahead and say it! I know you want to!"—She is laughing telling Paul.

Paul just laughs too and continued "Yes—he got my good looks and your brains!"

"Holy geez Paul. Men and their egos!"

"Ego? Well, would you like to check out my biggest ego? It is up and ready for you . . ."

She just giggled away when she felt him poking her and that was the end of that conversation for the rest of the night.

Graduation was so emotional for the whole family. Sarah, Joseph, Molly, Frank and Judy all were there to see their nephew graduate along with Paul's parents. Even Coach and Mrs. B. They were with the Tanner and Newman's always. They attended every birthday party, cook out Paul or Nicky had and were certainly not going to miss the boys graduation.

Paul and Nick partied hardy all during the summer. They went to all of their friends graduation parties and came home very tipsy most nights stumbling through the door . . . trying to sneak up to their room before someone saw them. Paul and Maggie spoke to Nicky and Elizabeth about it and they decided they would let them go because it was only a temporary thing and they didn't drive when they drank. Secretly—Elizabeth and Maggie worried and never slept until they got home and safely.

CHAPTER 66

Deja Vu

It was late summer and Paul Jr was still out all night partying. The graduation parties were all over so Maggie felt Paul had to step in and put a stop to it. He was underage and while they let him go right after graduation—it was time to real him back in. Nicky and Elizabeth were having the save issue with Nick. They knew they had to step in before something happened.

Then all of a sudden Paul's personality started changing. Elizabeth and Nicky felt it too with Nick. They seemed withdrawn and agitated. Their complexion looked almost clammy all the time and they hardly ever were around. They would always say they were going to play ball but it would be after midnight when they got home.

Paul was a mess watching his son behave like that. He recognized those symptoms from his firsthand experience. It happened to him—all of those years ago when he drank and did drugs. He knew that is what was happening now to his son and couldn't believe it. He always felt it would never happen to *his* son. He kept him near all the time and watched to make sure he walked a straight line and now, after hovering over him his whole life—he doesn't know how that happened to him. *How could it happen to him?* He thought he raised him right and with enough love to make him think twice about doing something so wrong. Just then he realized those thoughts were probably the same things his parents thought about him. They raised him right with so much love and he almost threw that away—not giving it a second thought.

Paul, Maggie, Elizabeth and Nicky had to go to dinner one night with clients. They didn't want to go but it was an important account and they had to.

Kristin was working at the Gift Shop now and wasn't home and Paul and Nick did not share their plans with their parents.

Dinner dragged on and everyone was trying to be so polite, when they just wanted to get home. They felt something was going to happen and wanted to be home. Nick and Paul were in bad shape and they didn't know how they could help them.

Paul and Nicky had talk after talk with them and couldn't reach them. Maggie even tried and he would just get defensive and walk out of the house slamming the door in his mother's face. Four hearts were breaking.

Finally—dinner was over and they rushed home. Nicky saw Nick was at Paul's so they parked out front instead of in the back alley. They got out, wanting to get in the house, especially since they saw a car parked out front that they didn't recognize.

When they got in the house—Paul Sr and Nicky almost dropped dead. Paul's dealer from college 20 some years ago was in his house. He caught him handing Paul Jr a baggie and Paul almost killed him, lunging towards him and grabbing him.

"What are you doing in my house?' As he has him by the throat. Paul Jr said "Dad—let him go! What are you doing?"

"What am *I* doing? What are *you* doing?"

"Why is this drug dealer in my house Paul? Do you owe him money? What did he just give you?"

Paul Jr did not know what to say until he saw his mother . . .

Maggie went right to the man who Paul had since released and slapped him right across his face. Paul never told her who he was all of those years ago . . . so that slap was for her husband and now her son.

Mocking and laughing at her he said "Mrs. Tanner. It's *sooooo* nice to finally meet you. You took a lot of business away from me when you married Paul, but I knew sooner or later I would get Paul's back. I just didn't realize it would be with *the little one*. And you too Nicky.

Having Nick Jr as a client makes up for all the times you ignored me back then. Sweet!"

Elizabeth couldn't control herself just then. While Maggie only slapped him, Elizabeth kicked him in his balls with her $500 Louboutin's that she got on sale. He bent over screaming while Nicky and Paul grabbed him by his shirt and dragged him out the door, throwing him on the street in front of his car.

"Don't come near our sons again—ever. I will call the police the next time I see you near them or on our street." Paul screamed and his face was beet red, as was Nicky's.

"Go ahead and call them. I'll tell them all about the famous Paul Tanner the druggy."

"No problem. It will be worth going to jail to *save—my—son*—if I even had to kill you!"

Paul Jr and Nick's eyes went wide just hearing Paul say he would kill him and seeing all that was happening—listening to everything the dealer said about Paul. Then seeing what their mothers did to him. They were trying to keep everything straight because they were coming off of a pill they took earlier in the day.

The dealer crawled in his car and slowly drove off.

Nicky and Paul came back into the house and Nicky just screamed "Nick—get in the car now—we're going home!" He looked at Elizabeth who was crying, so he took her by the arm and helped her in the car. Nick did not even argue, having never heard his father yell like that. He just did as he was told.

As soon as the door closed Maggie looked at her son and then back at Paul. She was white and shaking. She was never so mad in her entire life and she just wanted to scream.

So . . . she did . . . as they both just looked at her!

Paul tries to go to her and she backed away from him. Her head is down and she is trying to regroup but her anger gets the best of her. She keeps saying "no, no no . . . this is not happening!"

Finally, looking at Paul Jr she yells "Do you have anything to say to us?"

He is just looking back at her and not saying anything. She never yelled about anything and he was stunned.

"You brought a drug dealer into *my* home. You introduced him to the whole street, bringing him here. Not to mention the park across the street where hundreds of children, all ages play every day and night. How do you feel knowing you just showed him a whole new territory for him to solicit?"

"How would you feel if it was your fault if one of those kids died from taking that drug he gave you? Could you honestly live with yourself?"

"If you say you could . . . then you are not my son! Not the one I raised!" She is so upset.

"Give me now what he gave you or I will come over there and take it from you!" Screaming at him.

Paul takes out a baggie from his pocket with two pills in it. "How much was this?" She is still yelling.

"$50"

"$50? Where did you get $50? You don't work! You don't work because your father and I granted you that luxury. Your father and I both work hard so we can give you that opportunity!"

"From my graduation gifts!" He says it almost in a whisper with his head down.

Maggie goes to him and rips the baggie from his hand, then sees his phone on the coffee table.

She picks it up and throws it at him yelling as it hits him in the chest "Call your uncles and tell them what you did with their graduation gift. They might have a heart attack when they find out!"

Then out of control now—she slaps him too and it more than stunned him.

All the while Paul Sr is not saying a word. When she looks at him he is just pale and looks like he could fall over. His nightmare was now happening to his son and those thoughts immobilized him!

She was not done yet! She was still flipping out. She hits Paul Jr in the chest with her fists yelling.

"How dare you disrespect your body with this?" Showing him the bag with the pills in it.

"How dare you disrespect your life like this?"

"After I gave you life . . . after I almost *died* giving birth to you and you do this?"

Now she is uncontrollable—looking back at Paul Sr.

"Fix this and fix this nowwwwww . . . !" Crying while yelling. Finally—he tries to go to her and she just backs away again.

Looking at them both she just screams: "I don't want to talk to either one of you until this is all fixed."

"Don't call me . . . Don't come near me!"

She turns and stomps up the steps to her room but neither knew what was going to happen next.

Paul sees his father is now distraught and for many reasons. He just broke both parents' hearts and his mother didn't want to talk to either of them. They pushed her over the edge and she was wild with grief. Paul just sits on the couch trying to grasp what is happening with his son and now his wife.

Not even 10 minutes later she comes back down the steps with a suitcase—walking past both of them and not looking back.

Paul Sr dropped to his knees crying and young Paul couldn't believe he caused all of this.

"Maggie—please, I am begging you not to leave me. Maggie . . . please . . . I am begging you. I can't be without you. Maggie we have never been apart—never for even a night in the past 18 years. Please don't leave me. Please . . . Maggie!"

She could not control the tears streaming down her face. Her heart was breaking leaving Paul because it was true. Ever since he got home from Europe 18 years ago—they have never spent a night away from each other. He promised her he would never leave her again and he kept all of his promises he ever made to her. She never thought she would be the one to leave.

She quietly replied with her back to the both of them "You have never broken any promise you ever made to me and now you will promise me, you will fix this or I won't survive if my son continues on this path."

Desperately—Paul tells her "I promise right now I will fix this. I promise, somehow I will fix this!"

"Good" . . . She whispers with her head down. "Call me when you do." And she continues walking out the back door and to the garage to get her car to leave them both.

Paul is still on the floor and now he collapses lying face down after he watched her leave him. He didn't know how he would survive even a night being away from her, especially after what happened with Paul Jr.

Paul Jr went to his father knowing everything that happened was his fault. He sat next to his dad on the floor and pulled him into his chest—wrapping his arms around him.

"Dad, I'm so sorry! I'm so sorry! Please dad—please tell me you forgive me!" now he is distraught too.

"Maggie please come back" . . . was all he got out of his mouth. Like he didn't even hear what his son said to him. That is all he kept saying over and over . . . "Maggie please come back!"

Paul Jr found his phone on the floor and dialed his mother but he was shaking so much he had a hard time trying to get to her number. He still had his father in his arms who was incoherent.

After many tries he gets her and she answered but didn't say any-thing—so upset he just told her "Please mom, come back! Dad just col-lapsed here. You are the only one that can help him! Please mom! I'm so sorry mom. Please come back and help the both of us."

All of a sudden the door opens and she is standing there. She never made it out of the garage and when her son told her Paul collapsed she rushed back in the house.

She goes right to Paul on the floor and pulls him into her body running her fingers through his hair and kissing his forehead rocking him back and forth.

Neither is saying anything except he is holding onto her so tightly—not wanting to let go.

"I'm here Paul. I could never leave you." She said so softly—still kissing his head.

"I never made it out of the garage. I can't be without you either.

How could I love you that much?"

He continues to lie in his wife's arms trying to calm down.

She looks at Paul Jr and said "Thank you for calling me" with tears still streaming down her face and she sees he is still crying too.

"Mom, I was so scared. I was so scared you would never come back and it would be all my fault and I was so scared seeing dad so upset. I thought I almost killed him with all the stuff I just put you both through. I don't know how this all happened. It just got so out of control. I'm so sorry."

She pulled him over to her and Paul where they both grabbed him and held him so tightly. He returned the embrace while they all just continued with the crying but being relieved, thinking and hoping they were starting to heal now.

After a few minutes laying there she finally told them "let's get to bed now and put this night to rest until we can talk about it some more when we are calmer."

They both moved to get up and she continued. "Paul Jr. I want you to realize—we are not done speaking about this. You have to understand we will be talking this entire night out until we feel we are all fine now."

Paul Jr looked at his mother and leaned into her and she knew he wanted a hug and kiss so she did just that. He melted into her and then felt his dad grabbing onto him too and returned his hug also.

They helped Paul up and he was still shook—both realizing they were the reason he was not himself yet. She helped him upstairs to their room and undressed him like a child. He was spent and so emotionally drained. She knew once they got in bed he would unwind.

She lays him in bed and covers him up and he panicked when she didn't join him until she said "I am going to take off what's left of my makeup and clean up some. I will be right back. Will you give me a few minutes?" Then he relaxed, as Paul Jr knocked on their door.

"Do you want to stay with us tonight?" She knew he would and confirms that thought when he nodded his head yes. He felt he needed to be with them after everything that happened.

Paul opened up the covers so Paul Jr could join them and once he covered his son he wrapped both arms around him hugging him like he was still five. Paul Jr returned the embrace grabbing onto his dad's arms and squeezing as tightly as he could.

Maggie comes out of the bathroom and says—"Paul Jr, close your eyes I have to walk to my closet and you don't want to see you mother in her underwear!" Trying to make them laugh.

Paul immediately put his hand over his son's eyes while they smiled as Maggie ran to her closet to get something to wear to bed.

"Your mother is so beautiful but for my eyes only right now!" making Paul Jr hide his head in his pillow.

Once dressed she climbs next to her husband and stretches her arm over her men. They both held onto it and finally started relaxing. She kissed Paul and Paul Jr lifted up his head for her to reach so she could kiss him too.

"I know you have a lot of questions Paul and your father and I will answer any for you tomorrow. Let's just rest tonight."

Paul Jr nodded his head and they both felt him melting into his parents' bodies. They finally fell asleep all latched onto each other.

CHAPTER 67

I Have To Tell Him

Paul got up early as did Maggie. He went right for his phone to see how Nicky made out with Nick. Nicky's story was just as bad as what happened in the Tanner house the night before too.

He told them he didn't think Elizabeth would ever calm down after what happened. She actually was so furious with Nick, she went after him with her big 6" high heel shoes. Nicky had to take them off of her, fearing she would kill him.

That alone shook Nick so badly—seeing both of his parents so upset and emotional and then when Kristin got home from work—hearing everyone yelling and crying not knowing what was going on—she got just as upset too. When they went to bed she crawled in bed with her brother and was shaking so badly—Nick held her all night because she couldn't calm down either! He couldn't believe he caused all of that.

Nick will never forget his sister trembling in his arms that night, crying and asking why. "Why Nick. Why would you do something like that? Aren't you happy at home? Are you unhappy with me? I tried to be a good sister. It never bothered me how dad dotes on you so much. I just don't understand Nick. I'm sorry if I did anything to push you to do drugs Nick. I'm sorry!"

Nick could not believe Kristin thought it could be her fault somehow and had to keep reassuring her—it was no one's fault but his own. He could only hold her tightly until she calmed down.

Nicky heard Kristin tell Nick she thought it was somehow her fault he started doing drugs. Then his heart broke when he heard her mention how he dotes on Nick so much. In truth—Kristin was the apple of his eye. Nicky always smiled widely every time someone just mentioned her name. He knew he had to speak to her to let her know just how much he loved her. He couldn't let her go on thinking Nick, was more important to him.

The next morning, he got up early knowing Kristin was an early riser just like him and waited for her in the kitchen. He had her coffee ready and it shocked her when she saw him waiting for her. She thought he just wanted to speak to her about Nick. It stunned her when he said he wanted to tell her some things.

He starts, "Kristin, I want to tell you how much I love you. I am so sorry you feel I favor Nick more than you." Kristin turned white because she just realized he heard her talking to Nick last night.

"Dad, I know you love me. I think you just love Nick and me differently."

"No, Kristin. That's not true. When you were a baby—did you know I used to take you to most of my basketball practices? I always felt so proud every time I took you somewhere. You would be running around the gym and everyone just loved you and wanted to babysit you. You were as beautiful as a baby as you are right now. In fact—I think you get more and more beautiful by the day. I see you growing every day Kristin. I notice everything about you. I mean your personality, your spirit, your love of life. You amaze me every day. I want you to know that. I went to every game you cheered at too. Your mother would tell me when your games were and if I had a meeting—I would go afterwards just to see you. I remember when you fell off the top of your pyramid and hurt your ankle. I got so nervous and paced up and down the aisle but your mother said—'don't go down there. She will be embarrassed.' So I had to hold back from flying down those gym steps to get to you and help you. I was a mess."

"Dad, I never knew that. I remember falling and hurting my ankle but didn't know you were there and how upset you were."

"I never missed a game Kristin. I am so proud of you. You are always so happy. You work hard and were a good student when you were in school and then at the University."

Nicky's head is down thinking again about what Kristin said about him doting over Nick.

"Dad, please don't be upset over me. I know you love me."

"No—you don't Kristin. You don't know how much I love you because I didn't show you enough. I'm so sorry and will promise you right now—I'm going to remedy that. You will always know how important you are to me. You will always feel how special you are and you will always feel how much I love you."

Kristin started crying being so happy her father just told her how he felt about her. She waited forever for him to say those words to her. She knew he loved her but never knew how much.

Nicky went to Kristin and wrapped his arms around her hugging her so tightly just saying, "I am so sorry my baby girl. I love you so much. You are my first born and the light of my life. I love you Kristin and will always show you how much."

"We are going to go for lunch or dinner at least once a week. Just you and me so we can talk and just have some alone time together. Would you like to do that?"

Through her tears she squeaked out a yes to her father.

"One more thing." Kristin lifted her head to look at her father now. "Don't bring any boys home because you are not allowed to date or get married."

She started laughing and after trying to keep a straight face—so did Nicky. They had a plan and both were so happy with it.

Elizabeth was listening at the top of the stairs and was crying too, hearing Nicky tell their daughter how important she was to him. She was extremely happy the way things with them at least were working out—better than she ever expected.

Now back to his call with Paul, "Nicky, I have to tell Paul why we were all so upset. I have to tell him all about myself and how I was destroying my life the same way . . . with drugs and drinking. I feel that is the only way he will be able to see what he is doing with his life."

"Paul, do you think you didn't reach him last night?"

"No, I know Maggie and I did. But he has so many questions and I promised him I would answer them all today. I want him to know everything, even if he winds up hating me. I just feel he has to know and will hope for the best, hope I didn't disappoint him and hope he doesn't think less of me."

"I was thinking of telling Nick about Elizabeth and me too. I really want to reach him and I also think telling him the truth will help. I will hope he doesn't think less of me or his mother knowing how we got together."

"Nicky, why don't you and Nick come for a hike with Paul and me? I was going to take him on a hike around the gorge at the park across the street and sit and have a heart to heart with him. Don't tell Nick about how you and Elizabeth got together. I will tell Paul about some girl coming to the gym with a baby to tell me I was the father. We don't have to say it was Elizabeth. Don't do that to Elizabeth. It will break her heart if Nick feels differently about her after he finds out. Just follow my lead and then tell Elizabeth and I will tell Maggie so we are on the same page."

"Why would you do that Paul? He might resent you for that."

"If he does, then he will need you Nicky. So one of us has to be there for him. Let's just do this my way and I will have to suffer the consequences of all of my actions when I was young and so stupid. I cannot believe I am still paying for my mistakes. How could this happen? We were all so happy just a few weeks ago and things change by the hour it seems."

Nicky could hear the defeat in Paul's voice and didn't know how to help him or what to say to him right then.

"What time do you want to go Paul?"

"How about at 11 this morning?"

"Ok, Nick and I will walk down and pick up you and Paul Jr."

"See you then."

Maggie comes in the kitchen just then and knew he was talking to Nicky so she asks "how is everything over there?"

"Elizabeth went after Nick with her high heels and Nicky had to take them off of her thinking she could kill him with them."

His head was down and Maggie replied "Oh! Just as good as here then!" He lifts his head and she knows what he is going to say.

"I know you want to tell him your story. If you feel you can reach him with it—then I will support your decision. But you have to know Paul—he might not feel the same way about you once you tell him. Please leave Elizabeth out of your story too. Please!"

"I am and already told Nicky. He wanted to tell Nick their story too and they are both coming with Paul and me. I am going to take him for a hike and talk to him."

"Well, I have to open the shop this morning so I will try and be home after noon in case you need me. It is going to be another tough day—isn't it?"

He walks over to Maggie and hugs her -laying his head on her shoulder. He seemed weary and he still had a tough job ahead of him. "Paul. I'm so sorry about last night. I could never leave you. We can't be apart for even one night. I was just so upset and didn't know what to do."

Shaking his head he just tells her "No Maggie. No apologies needed. I deserved everything that happened and more. Once again you had to pay for my mistakes. But they were from so many years ago! I thought if I tried to be a good person—my past would just go away and I see all of our pasts are etched in stone and cannot be erased. Once again I pushed you over the edge. I'm so sorry Mags. I don't know what else to say. I love you Maggie! That is what will get me through today. That and how much I love my son."

"I'll go get him up. I made the egg and sausage bake for the both of you for breakfast. Just take it out of the oven when the buzzer goes off. I already know there won't be any leftovers." Smiling at him she gives him a soft kiss and goes to get her son up but not before he pulls her back for another kiss.

"Paul, time to get up. Your father is waiting for you in the kitchen for breakfast and I have to go to work."

"He's not *making* me breakfast—is he?"

"Yes, that is why he is waiting for you."

"Mom, you know how bad he is at cooking! He burns toast!" Now they both are laughing—joking about his cooking.

"I made the sausage bake you like and it is in the oven. It will be ready in 10 minutes so get up and get cleaned up too."

"Oh, thank God mom! I better get down there so we can get it out of the oven on time."

"The timer is on Paul."

"Right, and he will be walking around the house asking 'what is that beeping' when it's done."

They both laugh again as he lifts his head so she could kiss him goodbye and crawled out of bed to get ready.

"See you later son! I love you Paul!"

"I love you too mom!"

"Mom!" he calls before he leaves and walks over to her.

All of a sudden his arms are out and he wraps her in them surprising her.

"Mom . . . I'm so sorry. I don't know what else to say. I can't believe how much pain I caused you and dad."

"He will speak to you today about all of the questions you have. Keep an open mind and try and see how your father is today. It will be so important that you see that."

Not knowing what she is talking about—he nods his head acknowledging he would.

CHAPTER 68

Revelations

Paul, Paul Jr, Nick and Nicky went for a hike at the park down t the street. They had beautiful walking trails and places for picnics and cookouts. Everyone was so quiet that morning while walking and it happened to be a gorgeous day with the sun shining and everything still green. Once they got so far—Paul stopped and told Paul Jr and Nick he wanted to talk to them. They sat down on some logs so they could see what Paul wanted to tell them. Nicky got nervous once it was time for Paul to start telling them about his life before he met Maggie. He knew it was going to be hard for Paul remembering a time they both wish they could forget.

"Paul and Nick, I have a story to tell you both. I hope you don't think too badly of me once I finish. I had a horrible past before I met your mother Paul. I can't begin to tell you how bad it was and *I* made it that way. Poor decisions on my part caused me and your mother so much hurt and pain and I really thought all of that was behind me until I saw that drug dealer in my house yesterday. I realized—your past never leaves you. It follows you throughout your whole life. I tried to be a good person since the very first day I met your mother Paul. I wanted to change and be a good husband for her. She did so much for me. I want you to know that. She gave up everything for me and you'll see what I mean as my story goes on."

"When I met Uncle Nicky—we were assigned a dorm room together. We both had basketball scholarships to the University and they paired us together for that reason. He had just buried his brother David. David, died of a drug overdose and he was you fathers best friend Nick. He loved him more than anything and the fact that he didn't even know David had a drug problem—hit him so hard. Our friendship took off immediately. We clicked together on the court and as friends. I always felt for some reason—I was *supposed* to meet him. I was *supposed* to be his best friend. I was *supposed* to be his brother. I know Nicky feels the same way about it." Nicky is nodding his head yes . . . he always felt that way.

"Dad, you never talk about Uncle David. I know it's because it hurts you so much thinking about him and now I see why. It explains a lot."

"It still hurts every time I think about him Nick. If I knew he was in that kind of trouble—maybe I could have helped him. Maybe I could have saved him. I would never know and it's like a story that keeps going on with no ending—happy or otherwise. It's unfinished.

Like unfinished business."

Paul continues while nodding his head agreeing with Nicky.

Paul spent hours telling Nick and Paul Jr all about his past. They were both shocked and upset at all the things that happened.

They asked questions and cried and hugged many times during the stories.

When he was done both he and Nicky were upset rehashing his life when it was going so badly.

Paul Sr was . . . distraught . . .

Distraught having to tell his son all about his bad habits . . . distraught about remembering everything he put his wife through . . . distraught his son might be following in his footsteps . . . distraught remembering his wife almost leaving him the night before.

Paul Jr goes to his father and the two of them hug each other so tightly.

Nick and Nicky did the same. The four of them were crying.

"Dad, I'm so sorry I put you and mom through all of this! I will never do this again! Never! I never want to see that dealer again and if he comes near me I will call the police. I'm so sorry dad—so sorry!" Collapsing in his fathers' arms.

Nick is doing the same to Nicky. "Dad I'm sorry too. I'm so sorry. I will apologize to mom when we get home. I'm sorry dad. It was me that brought that dealer to Paul's house. I am the one that introduced him to him. I'm sorry. I could have destroyed so many of our lives. Everyone was so upset and it was all my fault!"

Nicky was so shocked just then. He releases Nick from his embrace and just looks at him and backs `away from him.

"No, no don't tell me that Nick! You brought that dealer to Uncle Paul's?"

"I'm so sorry dad. Please forgive me!"

"You turned your brother on to drugs with you?"

"Dad, please . . . I'm so sorry!"

"Nicky—please forgive him!" Paul screamed, still with Paul Jr in his arms.

"He wants to heal now and he knows what a mistake it was."

"Nicky . . . look at him! He needs you to forgive him!"

Nicky looks at Nick and sees how upset he is and how sorry he is and drops his head.

"I'm trying to wrap my head around this Nick! I don't know what to say." Upset being so disappointed.

"Dad, please don't stop loving me. I couldn't take it if you do. I'm sorry dad. Please don't stop loving me. Please!"

After he said that Nicky goes right to him, pulling his son in his arms and just said "I can never stop loving you Nick. You are my child. A parent never stops loving their children. I love you so much Nick!"

Finally, all the healing started!

After a while they all pulled themselves together and were ready to head back home. It was late in the afternoon—and they didn't realize just how long they were gone.

Paul Jr needed to see his mother and couldn't wait.

"Dad, I need to see mom so badly now. Do you know what I mean? I need to see my mother, now!"

Paul Sr nodded his head and put his arm around his son as they walked back down the trail to get home.

CHAPTER 69

Thank You Mom

Paul Jr. flies in the house to find his mother calling out to her. "Mom ! Mom!"

She ran down the steps because she was upstairs when she heard him. He sounded like he was upset and she ran right to him, stopping on a step so she could face him directly.

"Paul! I'm here! What is it? Are you alright?"

Then she sees Paul behind him coming in the house next.

He runs to her and she wrapped her arms around him like he was a little boy and got a cut running in for her to fix it.

"Mom!" He was crying and couldn't speak which made her so emotional too, not even knowing what was wrong, although she could have guessed.

"How can I help you son? What can I say to make you feel better?"

"You want to make *me* feel better? I want to make *you* feel better mom! I will never disappoint you or dad again. He told me everything mom! Everything! All about how you put up with everything that happened to you because of his past. You must have loved him so much to do all of that!"

"Yes—I do Paul, back then and now. More than I could say and I know it might have been hard for you to understand but when you love someone . . . you help them and you trust them. It all comes with the package!" Smiling at her son trying to make him feel better, wiping the tears from his face.

"Dad!" now he is calling for his father and he walks over to the both of them and wraps his arms around his family.

"Dad, I know you were probably worried I would look at you differently after you told me about your life when you were young. I do look at you differently, but in a good way. I see how you wanted to straighten out your life and how much you love mom. It always makes me feel so safe and happy here at home."

Then he just blurts out "I don't want to live at the dorm next year. Maybe when I'm a sophomore but this coming year . . . I want to stay home with you. Can I still live here?"

Both Paul and Maggie's faces dropped just then. They didn't want him to move out but were letting him make his own decision. They were so happy he wanted to stay home.

"Of course you can still live here. This is your home Paul. When you are ready to move out, you can. We won't stop you from staying or leaving. You can live here until you are 50 if you want!" Paul told him.

The three of them looked at each other with the biggest smiles on their faces. Paul Jr continued.

"Mom, dad told me how you almost died when I was born. I will never disrespect my life again. Never Mom! Is that why dad sends you flowers every year on my birthday? To thank you for not dying?"

"No Paul. He sends them to remind me how lucky we are to have *you*. He said when you were little that you were a gift and you are. We will always feel that way. Lucky to have you and I guess lucky I was still alive."

"But, am I the reason I don't have any more brothers or sisters?"

"No, it wasn't your fault. The Doctor told us sometimes things like what happened to me just happen for no reason. You were not the reason! How happy we were to even have you. Please believe us Paul! The sun rises and sets with you. You are our first thought when we get up in the morning and last thought when we close our eyes every evening and will always be." She is wiping the tears rolling down his cheeks and tenderly pushes his hair out of his eyes.

"I'm sorry for what I did the past few weeks. It will never happen again. Never!"

"We believe you! You are a Tanner and we never go back on our word. Never!" Paul Sr. told him.

Still in his parents embrace he felt so good. He loved them just as much as they loved him and would never forget what happened. How he almost lost them both. Knowing too—his father kept all of his promises to his mother and now he was going to keep his promise to them too. He will never go down the same path his father pulled himself out of—ever . . . again!

CHAPTER 70

Nat and Gio

Freshman and sophomore year came and went and Paul and Nick both decided they still wanted to live at home that 2nd year also. By the time they were juniors—they felt it was time to try living on their own. Of course the University was only four miles away but they had their scholarships and it provided for housing for them both. The University also paired them together and they were roommates just like their fathers before them.

They still came home a lot and it was like they were still living at home they were there so much. Maggie and Paul never minded and neither did Nicky and Elizabeth.

For weeks Paul kept mentioning someone named Nat. They just thought he had a new friend because he always said "Nick and I are going over to the park to play ball with Nat and Gio". So both sets of parents thought—they must be new on the team that year.

Everything was Nat and Gio. They went for pizza with Nat and Gio, they were going to the movies with Nat and Gio, they were at the gym with Nat and Gio. No one thought twice about it until it was Maggie's birthday and Paul was taking her to dinner along with Nicky and Elizabeth.

Paul said "Mom, we are going to meet you here after your dinner. Nat is making you a birthday cake. We will have coffee ready and you can all come back here after your dinner. Kristen will be here too".

Maggie and Paul just looked at each other. Paul's friend Nat . . . was making a cake! Paul Sr was beside himself. He called Nicky immediately and told him what Paul said.

"Nicky, have you ever met Gio?"

"No—all I know is that they are always playing ball at the park or down at the gym on campus."

"Nicky, do you think they are gay?"

Nicky turned white and both Elizabeth and Maggie were listening to the conversation and laughing at them.

"Do you think because Nat can bake—it makes him gay?" Nicky asked.

"How the hell do I know! I really don't know what to think right now." Paul is pacing back and forth.

"Well brother—we will have to wait for desert tonight to find out. We should prepare ourselves if they are and support them fully. I'm a little surprised though. If they were gay—I really thought it would be with each other."

Paul doesn't know how to respond to what Nicky just said and thought he was taking it well which is something he wasn't doing. Finally Maggie grabbed him and said "let's go or we'll miss our reservation. We can all talk over dinner."

"Maggie, I don't want to spoil your birthday dinner but I don't know if I could eat right now. I don't really know how I'm feeling. I really thought Paul JR would get married and have lots of kids to make up for him being an only child. I know you would love to have as many grandchildren running around the house and back yard as possible. I always felt—it would make up for us not being able to have more children. I hoped for it—for you Mags, more than for myself."

Maggie went right to Paul and touched his face—looking directly into his beautiful blue eyes and responded with "Paul, thank you for thinking about me like this. Yes, I would love tons of grandchildren running around this house. We could still have them even if he has a partner. So we shouldn't even worry about that. Now—I want to put this conversation away until at least we meet both Nat and Gio. Can we do that for tonight? And you *will* be gracious when you meet them later. Understand?"

Paul lowered his head and Maggie kissed his forehead—giving him a big smile to try and calm him down. Off the four of them went to Maggie's birthday dinner celebration.

While driving home—Paul was almost hyperventilating. He wanted to get home and then he didn't want to get home. He wanted to meet Nat but didn't want to meet him. He was trying to stay calm and when Maggie and Elizabeth looked at Nicky—they saw the same expressions on his face as well. Finally they parked the car in the garage and headed into the house. Maggie whispered to them both—"please be nice . . . please!"

When they got in the door they found the table was beautifully set with Maggie's good china from her mother and candles lite everywhere. The coffee was made and the smell was throughout the house and it did smell heavenly. They saw the cake on the island and it was so beautiful—decorated with so many colorful flowers on top. No one was in the kitchen just then but once Paul Jr heard everyone coming in the door he and Nat, Kristin, Nick and Gio all came out to see them. They all said happy birthday together and just then Maggie flashed the biggest smile at her son and his friend Nat.

She let him take over the introductions. "Mom /Dad, this is my girlfriend Natalia."

Maggie turned to Paul Sr and just stared at him with a big smirk on her face as if to say—*I told you to wait until you meet Nat before you form an impression.*

Paul Sr was just beaming and you could see he calmed right down. Maggie went right to Natalia and hugged her telling her "I'm so happy to meet you. Paul mentioned all the time he was going places with you and we wondered who you were. Now I know and am so happy he has you in his life. I could tell he has been so happy lately and now know why."

Then all eyes went to Gio and waited for Nick to introduce *her* to everyone.

"Mom/Dad, this is my girlfriend Giovanna."

Elizabeth then went right over to her and hugged her too telling her "It's such a pleasure to meet you. Nick has been talking about you as well and I can honestly say he also has been a lot happier since he met you."

Elizabeth just glared at Nicky with the same look Maggie gave Paul and they were trying not to laugh at their husbands.

"Natalia, did you really make this cake because it is just beautiful."

"Yes Mrs. Tanner. Paul told me you love white cake with lots of buttercream icing, so that is what I made. I love to bake and was only too happy to do it."

"When I first talked to Paul's parents over 20 years ago—I called them Mr. and Mrs. Tanner. His mom immediately told me to call her Lois and Paul's dad Mike or if I felt comfortable enough—just to call them mom and dad. What a lesson that was and I didn't even know, until just now." Now she is looking at Paul Sr remembering and smiling at him.

Paul takes right over. "Natalia, you can call us Maggie and Paul and when you feel comfortable enough—mom and dad would sound very good to us. OK?"

Paul Jr is so happy and is beaming at both parents and then looked at Natalia and gave her the biggest smile going over to her and planting a soft kiss on her lips—right in front of everyone. They all knew they were the real deal. They were a couple and could tell they loved each other. The same thing happened with Giovanna and Nick. Nicky and Elizabeth told them the same thing and Nick was also so pleased with how things were turning out as well as Kristen. She immediately took to Giovanna and Natalia and knew she now had two new sisters.

So, Natalia took the cake and put some candles on it, but not too many and invited everyone to the table to sing happy birthday. She handed Maggie the knife and said "mom, you have to make the first slice and then I can cut pieces for everyone."

Having her call her mom, almost made Maggie cry she was so happy. She looked at Paul Sr who knew how she was feeling and he came right over to her and kissed her—leaning his head on hers because he was so happy too and told her "happy birthday Mags". He also knew the drama was over for the night and they could all now enjoy desert and being with family.

"Mom, Natalia is going to stay over tonight. Is that ok?"

"Of course, as long as her parents know where she is."

"She lives with her grandmother and she told her she was going to stay here. Her grandmother said she used to go see dad play at the U when he was on the team."

"What a small world" she said looking at Paul Sr.

It also turned out that Natalia and Giovanna played on the women's basketball team at the U. That is why they were always at the gym on campus or playing at the courts in the park down the street and told their parents that is how they met.

Elizabeth said, "Give us your schedule when your season starts. Maggie and I will come to see you play!" Both girls were so happy they wanted to come see them.

"Mom, my grandmother can't come see me play and Gio's family lives so far away so it would be nice to have someone there to support us. Thank you!"

Nick said "Thanks mom. Most of the times we have practice or are at our own games and it is hard for us to get to see Gio and Nat play, so it makes me feel better if you could go for me." Elizabeth was all smiles when Nick thanked her. Kristen also said she would get to as many as she could also.

After everyone left—her and Natalia cleaned up and then Maggie said goodnight—kissing them both, pulling her husband up the steps to bed.

"Natalia is staying here with your son in his room. You gave him *the talk* right?"

Paul Sr just turned red and said—"No—I kept putting it off and now see it could have been a big mistake Mags."

"Did I not tell you—time after time—that you had to have that discussion with him?" She is kind of glaring at him.

He just bursts out laughing because he and his son had multiple conversations about sex—without Maggie knowing.

"Mags, we had the talk and many more after the initial one. He was always wondering about things and some of our conversations were so embarrassing and painful. My face would be beet red and I would start sweating and stuttering but I felt I was so happy he was asking me. So we are all set in that regard. Do you feel better now?"

She lets out a big sigh and then starts laughing about it. Paul comes over to her and unzips her dress to help her get naked and tells her "I am going to show you what your son and I talked about. He wanted to know how to show someone he loved them. Are you up for a demonstration?"

All she could do is smile and pull him to bed. "Well . . . basketball . . . wasn't the only field you excelled in."

The whole University and town for that matter were buzzing with excitement. Coach B recruited the top 2 point guards in the state for the basketball team that year along with a big 7'2" center. Everyone couldn't wait for the season to start.

Tickets for that first game sold out in 20 minutes. Everyone was stunned about what was happening.

On the night of the game the gym was packed to the rafters. The excitement and electricity throughout the building was amazing to everyone sitting there. Then the announcer came over the loud speaker, thanking everyone for coming to the game, went over the good sportsmanship rules and introduced the visiting team first. Everyone clapped for those 5 players and sat, almost holding their collective breaths just waiting to meet the new recruits.

The lights lowered and you could hear the excitement in the announcers' voice as he one by one introduced our players starting with the two shooting guards. Next he introduced the big 7'2" center and the crowd went wild when they saw him. Then—came the reason the game sold out in 20 minutes. The anticipation in the stands was unreal.

Finally the announcer, almost in a singing loud voice said:

"At point guard. . . 6'2" freshman . . . wearing #5 . . . Paaauuul . . . Tannnnner . . . Juniorrrrrrr!"

The place was complete bedlam. It was an amazing site to be a part of. People were jumping up and down and clapping and screaming. The announcer gave everyone a minute to settle back down and they did because they were waiting for the next player to be introduced.

"At Point guard. . . 6'1" freshman . . . wearing #11 . . . Nickkkkk . . . New wmannnn . . . Juniorrrrrrrrrr!" He dragged out every syllable of both their names and once again the crowd was wild.

The buzzer sounded. . . everyone was standing. No one could sit down. The starting 5 walked out on the floor and Nick and Paul had arms around each other talking about something and then they nodded to the big center who acknowledged something they might have said to him.

The ref threw the ball up . . . Paul took off for the basket and our center tipped it to Nick who threw the ball down half the court . . . off center of the basket, where Paul Jr caught it . . . feet off the ground . . . in the air and dunked it . . . !

The place went wild. It was crazy and it was just the first play!

Paul quickly ran back to play defense with Nick where they slapped each other's hands and did something that made half of the people in that gym who had seen their father's play before them almost weep!

Running backwards to get into position they both put their hand over their hearts and pointed to where Nicky and Paul Sr were sitting. That play was their fathers' signature play and they did it in tribute to them. Even Coach B couldn't hide how pleased he was with his two point guards and tried to hide the smile on his face but was losing.

In the stands Nicky and Paul hugged each other and lowered their heads in amazement. Maggie, Elizabeth and Kristin were crying along with Mrs. B, the Tanner and Newman grandparents, Joseph, Molly, Judy and Frank. Everyone knew what a year it was going to be.

Coach turned for a moment and looked at Mrs. B giving her a small smirk. She knew then, what he was thinking.

Coach. . . *Had a feeling . . . .*

A NOTE FROM THE EDITOR

I love College Basketball for a few reasons. One being—it gets me through the tough winter months here in the Northeast and second being—I love sports. I find College Basketball to be exciting and entertaining. I watch multiple teams so I could recognize the players' names once the tournaments begin. My brother Frank and I even take trips to Madison Square Garden once the Regional Playoffs begin to see some games. It became something we do together every year.

Back in the late 70's and 80's my husband and I used to go to the University of Scranton basketball games. They were just crazy! Sometimes you couldn't even get tickets. I would run up on my lunch hour as soon as the box office opened to get two for us. In 1980 the announcer interrupted the game to tell us the US Hockey Team beat Russia in the Olympics. The place went wild with screaming and chanting USA... USA... USA. I was so happy to be a part of that.

After I was done writing my first series of books 'The Band 4 Trilogy'—I thought I was done with my writing. Then one night looking at the March playoff schedule—I said to my husband "Remember how crazy the U games used to be"? That is what triggered this story. The fans were crazy, the games were so exciting and my mind became flooded with ideas for a story line.

Please keep in mind though, that this story is totally **FICTITIOUS**!

Nothing that happened in the book actually happened in real life.

I hope you like it. It was so much fun thinking about those times and conjuring up this story.

Marguerite

OTHER BOOKS BY INDIE AUTHOR

Marguerite Nardone Gruen

THE BAND 4 TRILOGY

Book 1

The Band 4—The Air We Breathe

Book 2

Ed—For Love and Hope

Book 3

Mam and Chase—Forgotten Stories